a kis
in the
dark

Cat Clarke was born in Zambia and brought up in Scotland and Yorkshire, which has given her an accent that tends to confuse people. Cat has written non-fiction books about exciting things like cowboys, sharks and pirates, and now writes YA novels, usually about teenagers being mean to each other. Her first novel *Entangled*, won the Redbridge Teenage Book Award and was long-listed for the Branford Boase Award.

Also by Cat Clarke

ENTANGLED

TORN

UNDONE

a kiss
in the
dark

CAT CLARKE

Quercus

First published in Great Britain in 2014 by
Quercus Editions Ltd

55 Baker Street
7th Floor, South Block
London
W1U 8EW

A CIP catalogue reference for this book is available
from the British Library

ISBN 978 1 78087 047 2

1 3 5 7 9 10 8 6 4 2

Printed and bound in Great Britain by Clays Ltd, St Ives plc.

For Caro

before

chapter one

I saw her before she saw me. It was better that way. I watched her looking for me, craning her neck to see over the crowd. Trying to match the faces in front of her against my profile picture. That was all she had to go on. No bigger than a passport photo and you couldn't even see my face properly. Half-turned away from the camera, fringe flopping down over my eyes. It was one of the only photos of me I didn't hate. She must have liked it too, I guess.

Jonni and Fitz had abandoned me in favour of the mosh-pit with vague promises to catch up with me later. I was glad to be rid of them; I didn't want them embarrassing me in front of her. Jonni especially had the tendency to say exactly the wrong thing at exactly the wrong time. He didn't mean to – his brain just worked differently from the rest of us.

I put down my drink and rubbed my palms on the

back of my jeans but they were sweaty again a couple of seconds later. I could feel sweat trickling down my back too. It was way too hot to be wearing my hoodie, but I wasn't going to tie it round my waist like Dad does with his golf jumper. Plus I'd been wearing it in my profile picture, so I thought it might help her recognize me.

I lost sight of her for a little while and for a second there I thought I'd screwed up and she'd left because she couldn't find me. But she appeared again a minute later – right in front of me. It reminded me of when Jamie used to dive under the sea and then pop up underneath me or grab my leg, pretending to be some kind of sea monster. This was scarier though.

'Hi! Alex?' Her voice was bright and clear, exactly how I imagined it would sound. Hers was more of an Edinburgh accent than mine.

She was waiting for me to say something. To confirm that I was actually Alex. She cocked her head to the side like an inquisitive bird in a gesture I've seen her do a hundred times since that night.

Somehow I managed to unglue my tongue from the roof of my mouth. 'Yeah, hi.' I cleared my throat because my voice sounded strange. She smiled and I'd never been on the receiving end of a smile like that in my entire life. No one had *ever* looked that happy to see me. There was no sign that I was anything other than exactly what she was expecting. I had no idea how to feel about that.

Sometimes I close my eyes and picture her at that exact moment. *Before*.

Her hair was long and blonde and shiny, just like in her profile picture. I'd spent so long looking at the picture I'd have recognized her anywhere. Her eyes were blue – cornflower blue if I was going to try being all poetic about it – and they were fixed on me in a way that made me even more nervous.

She was wearing grey skinny jeans and a band T-shirt that you could tell was brand new. Bright white Converse on her feet, contrasting nicely with my scruffy old black ones. In her profile picture she was wearing some kind of flowery top that looked a bit like something my mum would wear. It made me wonder if she'd bought a whole new outfit just for tonight. It made me wonder if she wanted to impress me. And it made me wonder if I wanted that to be true.

She didn't seem to be wearing any make-up, but maybe she was wearing the kind of make-up girls wear when they want to look like they're not wearing any. Her cheeks were flushed red, which could have just been down to the fact that the place was a total sweatbox. But it also could have been something to do with me. I knew she was shy; she'd told me in one of our very first messages. I'd said I was shy too.

'I can't believe it's you! In real life! I wasn't sure you'd show up. My friends think I'm completely crazy, by the way – coming here by myself to meet some random . . . not that you're random or anything! Oh God, I'm babbling, aren't I? Sorry! I'm so nervous. I don't . . . *do* this sort of thing . . . please tell me to shut up before I embarrass myself even more.'

She talked so fast it was hard to follow, and the support act had just come onstage so there was even more for my ears to contend with. 'Shut up, Kate.'

Her eyes widened before she caught on and laughed. 'I'm not normally like this. Honestly. I'm usually much more . . . normal.'

'Don't worry about it – seriously. What's so good about normal anyway?' My voice had this new lazy, hazy sort of quality. Like everything was under control and I wasn't sweating profusely and my heart wasn't hammering in my chest. I sounded like someone else. Then it hit me: I sounded like Jamie.

'You're right. It's about time I was . . . *ab*normal. Hmm. That doesn't sound so good, does it?' She paused and I wasn't sure what she was going to do or say next. I certainly wasn't expecting her to hug me, but that's exactly what she did. I've never been much of a hugger; I'm a big fan of personal space. I didn't seem to have much choice in the matter though. Before I knew what was happening, she had her arms around me. I kept some distance between our bodies without even thinking about it. An automatic reflex.

It wasn't a date. We just happened to be going to the same gig so we'd arranged to meet up. That was all. But the way Kate looked at me that night, the way she laughed at my crap jokes and touched my arm, there was no mistaking it. I kept trying to convince myself otherwise but all the signs were there. She liked me.

I got her a Coke and we stood near the back and talked through the rest of the support act. Kate relaxed pretty fast and before long we were chatting about all sorts of stuff. It was just like it had been online, except she was standing right in front of me. It seemed entirely normal and entirely not normal at the same time.

I kept an eye out for Jonni and Fitz, pretty confident that they wouldn't come looking for me anytime soon. I spotted an empty space on the balcony and ushered Kate upstairs. We squeezed into the space, which was only really big enough for one

7

person, earning a glare from the guy next to us. He didn't glare at Kate though, and I was glad.

The band came on and Kate grabbed my arm and squeezed. She was surprisingly strong for a girl. 'I can't believe this is happening!' It was the first gig she'd ever been to and to look at her you'd think she'd never been allowed out of the house before. She started singing along to the first song and then abruptly stopped when she noticed me staring at her. 'Sorry, I really love this song . . .' She looked sheepish.

She'd misinterpreted the look on my face. The truth is, I was in awe of her. I wondered what it was like to be the kind of person who'd happily sing in front of a stranger (or in front of anyone, for that matter). I thought it might be nice to be someone like that. But Kate didn't sing again – not that night anyway.

It was the second time I'd seen Saving Serenity this year and the set-list had barely changed. I was more interested in the girl standing next to me than what was happening onstage. I kept looking at her hands out of the corner of my eye. Her fingernails were nicely manicured, without nail varnish. The only jewellery she wore was a slim silver band on the ring finger of her right hand. They were nice-looking hands.

A couple of times Kate looked over and our eyes met. Neither of us said anything. We didn't have to, I

suppose. Meeting in person had just confirmed things.
She liked me and I liked her. It was simple.

It was anything but simple.

chapter two

I only really knew the score the day before we met. It had all been fine at first. Kate had posted on the Saving Serenity forum a couple of weeks before, asking if anyone was going to the gig. I'd never seen her on the forum before. I usually just lurked on there, watching other people's conversations and not bothering to join in, but for some reason I replied to her. I suppose I felt sorry for her – no one had replied to her post after a couple of days and I *was* going to the gig, so I thought I might as well say so. What harm could it do?

Kate replied with a private message and things went on from there. I kept on expecting the conversation to come to a natural stopping point, but it never did. She looked nice in her profile picture – friendly and normal and definitely not a crazy person. She told me she liked my profile picture and put one of those little blushing face emoticons. I thought that was a bit weird but I shrugged it off.

After a couple of days talking on the forum we exchanged phone numbers (her idea). Kate told me a lot about herself – more than I would have told some random I'd met on the internet. She asked me a lot of questions and I answered them. I only told one lie – when she asked what school I went to – and I'm not even sure why I did that. Maybe it just didn't seem all that sensible to give out personal information to someone I'd never even met. I said I went to the same school as Jonni – it was the first one that came to mind. It felt like a harmless sort of lie. Maybe not a white lie, but definitely grey at least.

We talked a lot about our favourite Saving Serenity songs and music in general. I introduced her to some other bands I thought she might like and she downloaded the music and listened to it straightaway. She was massively into music, but she confessed (with another red-face emoticon) that she'd only really listened to chart stuff and classical stuff until recently. She played the piano – *only* grade 7, she said.

From the sounds of it, Kate's mum was pretty full-on – way too involved in her life. Kate had lied about the gig, saying she was going to Astrid's house and she'd be home by eleven. Astrid was one of her two 'best' friends; I didn't like the sound of her.

We messaged each other non-stop as soon as we got home from school. It was amazing to me how quickly that connection developed. Because that's what it was – a genuine connection between two people who had never met before. Mum's always going on about the dangers of the internet and 'weirdos whose only friends are on their computer screens', but she just doesn't get it. It's entirely possible to get to know someone without actually seeing them in person. In fact, it's better like that because none of the superficial stuff gets in the way. You really get to know a person. And it's easier to express yourself when you're writing things down. At least it is for me. I like to order my thoughts, and delete them if they don't make any sense. You can't do that in real life.

A few days before the gig, Kate asked if I wanted to meet her there. My heart did a little jump. I didn't want to think about what it meant, my body reacting like that. Things were confusing enough already.

I told her I was going with Jonni and Fitz, but I'd be up for meeting her. She was really happy about that. Then I sat back and tried to picture what it would be like, meeting her in person. Talking to her. Looking at a real person instead of a tiny profile picture. I could kind of get my head around me looking at her, but as soon as I started thinking about her looking at *me*, well . . . that's when it all got a little hazy. Would she be disappointed? Had she built up some false idea of me based on what I'd told her?

We texted each other constantly after I got back from running the night before the gig. We always texted, never called. The thought of a phone call was terrifying to me. I never even called Jonni and he was sort of my best mate (not to say that I was necessarily *his* best mate). Anyway, I was just about to say I was off to bed when Kate texted something that confirmed the suspicion that had been lurking at the back of my brain. I stared at my phone and tried to work out if there was any other way to interpret her words, but I was kidding myself.

I went to reply, to set her straight, but none of the words were right. I kept on typing and deleting them, trying to find a way to say it – a way that would make her still want to see me at the gig. But I couldn't do it. There was no way out. In the end I turned off my phone without replying.

I couldn't sleep that night. All I could think about was Kate's message and what the hell I was going to do about the gig. It was the kind of text Jamie probably gets at least once a week from his various conquests.

You're really different from other boys.

In a parallel universe, a different version of me was thrilled to bits.

In this universe, I was mostly devastated. Kate was right: I was different from other boys.

I was a girl. I *am* a girl.

chapter three

The most embarrassing moment of my entire life was when Mum came up to my room a couple of years ago, acting all suspicious. I was sitting at my desk doing some homework and she hovered next to me. Then she asked me if my bin needed emptying, before perching on the edge of the bed.

'Yes? Can I help you with something?' I was busy colouring in a chart for my geography assignment. Any subject that involves colouring in instead of thinking is OK by me.

Mum didn't reply so I had to turn to look at her. She was fiddling with her wedding ring, a nervous habit of hers. Not that she's a particularly nervous sort of person. She flashed a smile and asked how I was getting on with my homework.

I narrowed my eyes. 'Fine . . . *why*?!'

She sighed and tucked a stray bit of hair behind

her ears. 'OK, fine. You got me. I'm not here to ask about your homework. Not that it looks particularly arduous!' I gave her a look which she obviously interpreted correctly because she went on, 'OK, OK! I'll say what I've got to say and leave you to it.' More fiddling with the wedding ring – twisting it round and round her finger. 'There's something I've wanted to say to you for a while now, but it never seems like the right time and I know what a private person you are . . . but I'm still your mother. And it's my job to be grown-up about this stuff, I suppose. So I'm just going to say it and we'll go from there, OK?'

I knew, I think. At least, I suspected. There weren't many subjects that would cause this level of awkwardness in my normally calm, level-headed mother. I said, 'OK,' but I didn't mean it.

A big deep breath and then she launched into it. 'Alex, you know how much we love you and how proud we are of you, yes? Well . . . we'll love you and accept you no matter what. It's really important that you never forget that. I'm not going to ask you or embarrass you so please stop looking at me like that, but if you're confused about your sexuality–' We both winced when she said that word, '–or if you're worried or want to talk about anything at all, I'm here. And your dad is too. Even though he's not here right now. Obviously. So. To sum up, we don't care if you like boys or girls or both or neither or . . . anyway. You understand what I'm trying to say, don't you?'

I was horrified. 'Muuuum! I'm not . . . why would you think I was . . . ? Can you just leave me to get on with my work? *Please*?' I wanted her gone. I wanted to forget we'd ever had this conversation, if you could even call it a conversation.

She held up her hands. 'Fine! I knew it wouldn't be easy, but I had to say it. I'm sure you can understand that.'

I'd already turned back to my homework and was furiously scribbling with a black pencil in a column that was supposed to be red. 'Yeah, whatever.'

I could hear her stand and move towards the door. There was a few seconds of silence and then, 'I love you, Alex.'

'Yeah.'

The door shut quietly and my head met the desk. I felt like she'd broken some sort of unwritten pact we had – Mum and I didn't talk about that kind of stuff. We just *didn't*. We talked about TV and took the piss out of Dad. This was . . . wrong.

I struggled to sleep that night, thinking about my reaction and wondering what Mum made of it. Did she believe my denial, even though I hadn't said the actual word I was supposed to be denying? Or did it just confirm what she clearly thought was the case?

I was angry. Mum and Dad had clearly been talking about me behind my back, thinking there was something wrong with me just because I wasn't the female equivalent of Jamie. He brought girls home all the time. Two years older than me and the kind of good-looking that's impossible to ignore, Dad's always saying Jamie's a chip off the old block (and Mum's always saying, 'You *wish*'). Clearly they thought *he* was doing his teenage years properly. Sowing his wild oats or some such bollocks. But it was hard to believe Dad would have been cool with me bringing random boys home. That's how it works – one rule for boys, another rule for girls. So maybe they just wanted me to have a boyfriend – a boring, responsible one who wore shiny shoes and had a neat parting. Whatever it was they wanted, they obviously thought there was something wrong with me. Never getting in trouble at school, never drinking or taking drugs or missing my curfew . . . that wasn't good enough. That wasn't *normal* enough for them. And according to them, there was only one explanation: I was gay.

How dare they? How fucking *dare* they? I could just picture the two of them sitting at the kitchen table, drinking tea and listening to Radio 4. They did it every night – Mum called it 'us time', which was kind of sickening. They weren't supposed to be talking about me though. I'd done everything I could do be the best possible daughter but they still weren't satisfied.

Gay. I rolled the word around in my head, testing it. It was a ridiculous idea, plain and simple. I'd had pictures of boybands and actors on my wall a few years ago. I thought the drummer in Saving Serenity was pretty hot. Anyway, Jonni and Fitz were boys, weren't they? And they'd been round to our flat at least twice. So what the hell was the problem?

There had been a time last year (about two weeks, to be precise) when I'd wondered if I fancied Jonni. There was nothing really wrong with his face, he looked nice when he smiled, and he had reasonably interesting things to say, which was more than could be said for Fitz. Still, I couldn't muster up much enthusiasm for the idea and the thought of kissing Jonni kind of turned my stomach. But that wasn't because he was a *boy*, it was because he was my mate. You don't go round randomly kissing your mates.

The thing is, there was no way on earth Jonni would have ever kissed me. It couldn't have been more obvious that he didn't think about me like that. Sometimes I think he even forgot that I was a girl at all. He'd be talking about some girl or other (usually the pathetic groupie-types who hung around Bristo Square hoping to bag a skater boyfriend) and he'd say something unbelievably crude and me and Fitz would both laugh but then Jonni would look at me funny and say sorry. As if I cared.

If I'm being brutally honest with myself, I knew that Jonni and Fitz weren't that keen on me hanging out with them all the time. They didn't mind at first, when I first turned up at Bristo Square. I was a bit of a novelty, I guess – a girl who could actually skate. And we were into the same kind of music so we had a fair bit in common. But when I started turning up every day after school (and started showing them up in front of the girls), they didn't seem so happy. I didn't realize anything was up at first – only when Jonni texted that they weren't going to be at the Square after school one Friday and I went anyway and found them there, just like always. Jonni tried to cover it up, saying he'd changed his mind at the last minute, but I knew the score. I was hurt but I was never going to let him see that; I just shrugged and said 'whatever'.

After a couple more incidents like that I knew Jonni was trying to phase me out. The novelty had well and truly worn off for him. This was only a couple of months before I met Kate and I was pretty down about the whole thing. Maybe not *depressed*, but definitely not happy. I'd thought that meeting Jonni and Fitz might be the start of something good for me – a new life away from school. Skating at Bristo Square was my escape. I felt like I was finally fitting in, like I'd found my place in the world.

Getting the tickets for the Saving Serenity gig was pretty much a last-ditch effort to impress the boys. I said I'd won them in some competition I saw online, but the truth is I used most of my birthday money. Jonni hadn't seemed all that impressed and wouldn't even commit to turning up. But then Fitz texted the day before the gig to say they'd meet me outside. Like I should have been honoured by their presence or something. It was a pretty desperate move, I suppose, buying those tickets. And if you look at it in a certain light it might seem like I was trying to buy friends. That wouldn't be quite fair though. Loads of things can look bad if you look at them in a certain light.

chapter four

I had no idea if the boys tried to find me at the end of the gig; I didn't stick around long enough to find out. If I'd told them I was meeting a girl they'd have come to find me for sure. Kate had asked where my friends were and I'd pointed vaguely at the seething mass of bodies in front of the stage. Maybe she wanted to meet them to check they were real, but I was desperate for them not to meet. And not just because Jonni might take the piss out of me. That was when it really began, I suppose. If I had to pinpoint a single moment, that would be it. That pure blast of panic that shot through me at the thought of Kate meeting the boys. Because one of them would say something and she would find out the truth.

I guess I thought she'd realize as soon as we met and she might be a bit embarrassed, but she'd get over it and we would laugh about it. It's not like I purposefully dressed up as a boy to deceive her. I was just wearing my normal clothes, like I wear every day as soon as I can get out of that godawful school uniform. That skirt was the bane of my life. None of the other girls seemed to care. When I tried to get a petition going to allow us to wear trousers, at least in winter, there were a grand total of seven signatures (including three fakes). That was the first and last time I ever tried to participate in the school system. When Marcy Davies set up a petition to get them to serve tropical fruit in the cafeteria, almost every girl in our year signed it. Democracy favours the pretty, I suppose. And those who are really into mango and pineapple.

So I really hadn't gone out of my way to trick Kate. Jeans, Converse and a hoodie. And I hadn't done anything special with my hair. It was shorter than it is now, but not *really* short. I didn't have anything against long hair – it just wasn't for me. Too much maintenance and a baffling array of haircare products. Anyway, it's not like I was totally masculine or anything: most of my clothes came from the women's section of the shop (even if they did look kind of unisex). I didn't really like wearing skirts or tight tops and I never bothered with make-up because I didn't know how to apply it and no one ever bothered to show me. Plus I'm not exactly blessed in the chest department. Girls at school used to moan about their boobs all the time, saying that they couldn't *wait* to get boob jobs and inane things like that. But having small boobs never bothered me – it was better for running, for one thing. I just never got why girls cared about shit like that. Seems to me there are a lot more important things to worry about in the world.

So, Kate and I met up at the gig and it was obvious she still didn't realize I was a girl. What the hell was I supposed to do? Slip the information into the conversation somehow? There's just no easy way to do that. She would have been *mortified* if I'd told her the truth. She probably would have run off and never spoken to me again. After twenty minutes or so in her company I knew that I didn't want that to happen. It felt good and easy being with her and I wasn't about to let that slip through my fingers.

There was one potentially tricky moment during Saving Serenity's only boring song, when I said I was going to the toilet and she said she'd go too. I had to think fast, telling her we'd lose our spot on the balcony if we both went at the same time. Thankfully you couldn't see the ladies' toilets from the balcony, so Kate didn't see me go in there. The toilets were a mess: loo roll clogging up three out of four sinks, water flooding on to the floor from the cubicle at the end. When I was washing my hands I caught a glimpse of myself in the mirror. I didn't think I looked like a boy. And no one ever batted an eyelid when I went into the ladies' changing rooms or toilets. So why did Kate see me differently? Was it all down to that profile picture on the forum? Was that all it was? Plus me not saying anything to make her think any different. We were both to blame, a little bit, maybe.

Kate grabbed my arm again when the band came back on for the encore, asking if I reckoned they'd play her favourite song (everyone's favourite song, really). I just smiled and she jumped up and down saying 'Tellllll meeeeeee!' and at that exact moment the drums kicked in. Kate's face lit up, and it was this perfect moment. She didn't sing along this time, she just took my hand and held it in hers and we stood and just listened.

It didn't feel strange to be holding hands with a girl. It felt like something I'd been waiting for.

As soon as the band left the stage for the second and final time, we headed for the doors. Kate had to rush to catch the bus if she wasn't going to get busted for lying to her mum. It suited me just fine because I knew Jonni and Fitz would be hanging around after the gig, trying to impress random girls with how sweaty they were.

Kate was buzzing on the short walk to the bus stop. 'That was incredible. *In*credible. I mean, I knew it was going to be good, because how could it *not* be good, you know? But that was SO good!'

'I'm really glad you had fun.' We weren't holding hands anymore so I jammed my hands in the pocket of my hoodie. I'd put the hood up too; it was bloody freezing. I worried that Kate would get cold waiting for the bus but she didn't seem to notice the chill in the air.

'It was . . . Honestly? It was one of the best nights of my life.' She said this quietly, almost shyly.

I wasn't sure how to react to this. I wasn't sure whether it made me feel sad or happy that this night had meant so much to her. But when I really gave it some thought, I realized I felt the same way. I didn't tell her though; I should have told her.

The 26 pulled up just as we arrived at the bus stop and there were only a couple of other people getting on it, so Kate couldn't hang around. She gave me a quick hug, said 'I'll text you' and before I knew it I was standing alone on the pavement. Wondering what might have happened if the bus had been delayed by a few minutes.

My phone buzzed in my jeans pocket maybe thirty seconds after the bus pulled away. A text from Kate:

Sorry we didn't get to say a proper goodbye. Next time, OK? x

I grinned at my phone. *Next time.* There was going to be a next time. With a 'proper' goodbye, whatever that might mean. Neither of us had ever put an 'x' at the end of our texts before. This new development made me feel nauseous in the best possible way.

chapter five

It's hard to remember what it was like, back then. I mean, I can remember everything that happened clearly enough. But it's hard to remember *exactly* how it felt. I suppose that at any given moment there were a whole bunch of feelings, all mixed up in varying quantities. There was guilt, obviously, for not telling Kate the truth when I had the chance (even though I maintain I never really had the chance). There was excitement that something good was finally happening to me. This excitement was tinged with a healthy dose of disbelief. Then there was the anxiety. It was always there, lodged somewhere around the middle of my chest. A heavy, hard lump I was never able to get rid of. But that first night? Walking home that first night, there was one feeling eclipsing all the others. I had my headphones on, listening at full blast to the last song Saving Serenity played and I was walking down Princes

Street past the shops, all closed and shuttered. Actually, I wasn't so much walking as strutting, you know that way you do when you feel like you're in a music video? I must have looked so stupid, but I didn't care. Because I was happy.

I bounded up to the front door and unlocked it. Mum and Dad had a couple of friends over for dinner and they were being raucous as anything. Four empty wine bottles on the kitchen table went some way to explaining the noise. Mum's laugh is ridiculous at the best of times, but when she's wasted ('tipsy', she calls it), it's something else entirely.

'Alex! My little girl's home at last! How was the gig?' Mum's face was flushed in the candlelight. She said the word 'gig' like it was something exotic to her. She wasn't the gig-going type when she was my age if the embarrassing old pictures are anything to go by.

I shrugged and headed over to the fridge to grab a smoothie, then scarpered along the hall to my room before Mum could say anything else. Before I closed my bedroom door, I heard her say, 'What is it with teenagers these days, eh?' She probably didn't even realize she sounded exactly like my grandmother.

I lay down on my bed and took out my phone. I

must have spent at least ten minutes trying to work out what to say before ending up with: *No worries. I like the sound of next time.* x

The 'x' was a hard call to make, but I added it in at the last minute. It's raising the stakes, isn't it? That tiny little letter. As soon as someone brings it to the table, you sort of have to respond in the same way, otherwise it's a bit rude. I thought Kate might be disappointed if there was no 'x', and disappointing her was the last thing I wanted to do. But I didn't want to go over the top and seem too keen, so I left the rest of the message fairly low key.

I stared at my phone until I got a reply: *Tomorrow?* x

I hadn't even considered that she might want to see me again so soon. This time I didn't hang around: *Tomorrow sounds good.* x

I was supposed to be going through to Glasgow with Mum and Dad, but there was no question of me saying no to Kate.

We texted a bit more before I went to bed – nothing major, just stuff about the gig and arrangements for meeting up the next day. She suggested a walk down by the Water of Leith so we arranged to meet in Stockbridge. It was a little too close to my flat for my liking, but I just had to hope we wouldn't bump into anyone I knew.

Kate sent the last text, a little after midnight: *Sweet dreams. x*

The feeling I had inside was something like marshmallows, only a bit less sickly.

My dreams were definitely sweet. I woke up early and stayed in bed listening to my iPod, the same song on repeat. When I went through for breakfast Mum was frying up some bacon, which she only ever did when she was massively hungover. She didn't kick up much of a fuss when I said I had too much coursework on to go to Glasgow – she was always weirdly agreeable the morning after the night before as if arguing was just too much of an effort for her fragile brain. Dad didn't seem bothered at all, probably because he gets annoyed by the music blaring from my headphones in the back of the car. He thinks we should all listen to the same thing or have an intellectual discussion or something.

By ten o'clock I had the flat to myself. I jumped in the shower and let the hot water pound against my head. I reached for the shower gel and hesitated. Mine was some kind of fruit concoction – some overly sweet one that Mum had got from the Body Shop. Standing next to it was a tube of Hugo Boss shower gel. It was nearly empty, which must have been why Jamie left it behind when he went off to uni. I flipped open the lid and gave it a sniff. The smell was pure Jamie; it made me miss him even though I'd only seen him last week. I was sure he wouldn't mind me using a tiny blob of his shower gel. Maybe he'd even approve.

After my shower I wrapped a towel round myself and headed into Jamie's room. I was pretty sure he had some Hugo Boss deodorant too – some girl had given him a gift set for his eighteenth birthday. It made sense to use the Hugo deodorant rather than mine, because what was the point in using the fancy shower gel if you go and cover up the smell with Impulse deodorant? I sprayed myself a little bit too liberally but I was sure the smell would dissipate as soon as I got outside. It was a bit weird, me smelling like Jamie, but I sort of liked it too.

I spent longer deciding what to wear than I'd like to admit – way longer than the previous night. It seemed different somehow. Before the gig I'd been fully expecting Kate to realize I was a girl. And now I was really, really hoping she wouldn't.

I don't know what I was thinking. It's not like I thought she was never going to find out. I was trying not to think about it, I suppose. But of course I *had* to think about it: I'd got myself into something and instead of trying to get out of it, I was digging myself in deeper and deeper. It didn't matter that I was a girl – that wasn't the point. Kate liked me for being me. That was the important thing. I would tell her when the time was right – which was definitely not today.

I eventually put on one of my favourite T-shirts. But when I stood in front of the mirror I winced. I'd never really noticed before because I'd never given it any thought, but you could definitely see my boobs. There was no mistaking the fact that I was a girl. I tore off the T-shirt and chucked it in the bin. I was shaking a little – almost panicky. I checked my watch – I was supposed to be meeting Kate in half an hour so I needed to get a move on. Then I had a brainwave. And this is where things start to look not so good for me. This is where it looks like it was all premeditated but it wasn't like that. It really wasn't.

I rummaged around in the bathroom cabinet until I found what I was looking for. The first-aid kit was right on the top shelf, almost out of reach. I took the green box back to my room and dumped the contents on to my bed. Sure enough, there was a roll of bandages. It was that adhesive sort of bandage that sticks to itself so you don't need to use a safety pin.

I took off my bra and started winding the bandage

around my chest as tight as it would go. It took a few tries to get it right, overlapping it enough to make it stick. There was just enough bandage to do the job. It was itchy and constricted my breathing a little, but it was bearable. I jumped up and down a few times and waved my arms over my head to check it was totally secure. I stood in front of the mirror, then turned sideways. It had worked: my boobs were gone, flattened into nothingness.

I grabbed my T-shirt out of the bin, brushed off some stray pencil shavings and pulled it over my head. Stepped back and looked in the mirror again. Better. Much better. I smoothed down the T-shirt, checking to see if I could feel the bandages beneath. Took off the T-shirt and put a vest on underneath it, just to be on the safe side. Another look in the mirror to check I looked OK, then I concentrated on sorting out my hair.

I went for the same Converse and hoodie I'd worn to the gig. I didn't want to look like I was making too much of an effort – it was a balancing act. By the time I was finally looking presentable it was nearly time to meet Kate. I didn't want to be late and have her think I couldn't be bothered making any effort at all. One last glance in the mirror and I was good to go.

I grabbed my keys, wallet and skateboard and headed out. I didn't realize it then, but I can remember clear as anything now: all that looking in the mirror and not once was I able to look myself in the eyes.

chapter six

We'd arranged to meet outside Pizza Express at eleven, which left me five minutes to get there. I jumped on my board and skated along St Stephen Street. I never normally skate on the pavement when it's busy, but I was desperate not to be late. I nearly knocked down an old lady shuffling along with a tartan trolley and I got shouted at by a woman getting out of a Saab. I had to keep shouting 'Sorry' and 'Excuse me' and hope that no one came chasing after me.

I probably should have left the board at home, but I'd have had to run to get there on time. I didn't want to risk dislodging the bandages, for one thing. But I'd be lying if I said that was the only reason; if the girls up at Bristo Square were anything to go by, there was a good chance Kate would be impressed that I was into skating.

I saw her before she saw me. Again. She was leaning

over the wall of the bridge next to the restaurant. The Water of Leith was flowing fast below. It had been raining a lot recently, but that day was clear and sunny.

Kate was wearing jeans and a black V-neck jumper. She had a red raincoat slung over her arm. She was wearing the same Converse as last night too. That made me smile. Her hair was tied back and I decided I really liked being able to see more of her face. She turned when she heard me approach and I stopped dead right in front of her, kicked the board up and tucked it under my arm. She smiled. 'I see you've brought wheels . . . I don't suppose there's room on there for two?'

I grinned. 'Sadly not, but you can have a go if you want. It's not as hard as it looks, you know.'

'I know. I had one when I was little.' She smiled mischievously and it put me right in my place.

'So you think skateboarding is for little kids?' Trying to sound like I didn't care one way or the other.

'That's not exactly what I said now, is it?' She was still smiling. 'So are you going to give me a hug or what?'

I obliged and this time I didn't need to worry about our bodies touching. It was only half a hug anyway – Kate's coat and my skateboard saw to that. I was almost tempted to chuck my board in the river;

my lame attempt to impress her had well and truly failed and now it was just getting in my way.

When she stepped away from the hug, Kate coughed awkwardly and looked away and I fiddled with the wheels on my board. There was a weird tension between us and I wasn't even sure where it came from. Maybe we were both remembering last night's text messages. Or maybe Kate really was turned off by the skateboard. I mean, what kind of idiot brings a skateboard to a date? Because there was no doubt in my mind now. The awkwardness had just confirmed it: this was definitely a date. My first ever date and it was with a girl. A girl who thought I was a boy.

We walked down to the water and headed upstream. It was busier than I'd have liked – joggers and couples and families. I wanted them all to disappear and leave Kate and me to wander in peace. It was distracting, passing all those people, scanning their faces to see if I knew them. I tried to do it surreptitiously but I think Kate noticed. She didn't say anything though.

The awkwardness between us dissipated after we'd been chatting for a while. It was easier when we were walking side-by-side rather than face-to-face. It was less intense that way. There were other things to focus on, like putting one foot in front of the other and trying not to slip on the soggy leaves underfoot.

Kate was quizzing me about my family, my friends, anything she could think of. I tried to answer as honestly as I could. It felt like she was filling in the gaps of her knowledge about me, maybe trying to reassure herself that she wasn't making some huge mistake. I told her a couple of stories about Jamie to make her laugh; she said she'd really like to meet him one day. I tried to imagine that actually happening. Maybe I could tell her the truth and she'd be cool with it and she'd understand why I hadn't been honest from the start. If things went to plan and I kept liking Kate and she kept liking me (that was the tricky part of the equation), then there was a chance everything would be alright in the end. Because that was how life was supposed to work, wasn't it? True love will prevail or whatever. Not that I was in love with her or anything. Not then, anyway.

We stopped on a bridge when we got to Dean Village. It was one of my favourite spots in the city. You could look around and almost imagine you were in a different century – as long as you ignored the blocks of flats on the south side.

Kate leaned against the railing and raised her face

towards the sun. She closed her eyes and sighed. 'This is perfect.'

She stayed like that and I wasn't sure whether I was supposed to say something. I didn't want to ruin the moment, and I didn't want her to open her eyes. I was enjoying watching her. Not like some creepy stalker or anything. It's just easier to look at someone when they're not looking at you. You get to notice things you haven't noticed before – the little details that make a person's face pleasing to your eye. I noticed that Kate's eyelashes were longer than mine, that her eyebrows were a shade or two paler than her blonde hair, that her nose was impossibly straight, that she had a tiny scar on her forehead. I wanted to keep looking, drinking in every last detail until I'd memorized that face. Just in case this all went wrong, whatever 'this' was, I'd always have the memory of her standing on that bridge.

Kate opened her eyes and caught me staring. She smiled and I wondered if she'd done it on purpose – closing her eyes to let me look at her. That seemed too calculated for her though. 'It's actually pretty warm when you concentrate, you know. The sun's making a real effort but you have to stop and pay attention otherwise you'll just think it's cold because it's October and it *should* be cold . . .' She trailed off when she saw my baffled expression, then she rolled her eyes and shook her head. 'Sorry, that doesn't make much sense, does it?'

'Um . . . I think I know what you're getting at . . .' I didn't though – not really. I didn't really understand her, back then. I knew I liked her and that was enough for me. I knew that I *wanted* to understand her.

Kate laughed and gave me a gentle shove on the shoulder. 'You don't have to pretend, you know. You can tell me to shut up when I'm talking rubbish – I can take it!' She paused and her face transformed into something serious. 'I want you to be honest with me, Alex.'

My mouth went dry and I was suddenly sure that she knew. That she'd just been humouring me and all along she'd been waiting for me to say something, to come clean and admit that I lied to her. But then the way she was looking at me convinced me otherwise. There was a sparkle in her eyes, a warmth that surely wouldn't be there if she knew the truth. I had to say something now. Something special and deep and meaningful. 'OK.' *I fail.*

But Kate smiled as if it was exactly what she wanted to hear. 'Good.' A mischievous glint appeared in her eye. 'Now . . . race you back to Pizza Express? I'll even let you use your skateboard.'

I was just about to ask if she was serious when she turned on her heels and ran. An old couple who were crossing the bridge turned and looked at me — the woman was frowning as if I'd done something to make Kate run off like that. I stood there looking like an idiot, watching Kate run away from me. She was pretty fast. She looked back over her shoulder and narrowly avoided colliding with a kid on a scooter. I sighed; I was going to have to chase her, wasn't I?

I started to run. I quickly realized Kate had an advantage: people were way more likely to get out of the way for a pretty teenage girl who looked like she might be late for something important. They weren't so accommodating for a teenage boy disrupting their Saturday stroll and generally making a nuisance of himself. I could have sworn some people deliberately got in my way.

That was the first time that other people thought I was a boy. At least I think it was. You don't exactly go round stopping people on the street, asking them to guess your gender. But as I dodged past people in pursuit of Kate there was no doubt in my mind that people saw a *boy*. Maybe it was just because they expected to see a boy or maybe it was because *I* wanted them to see a boy. Whatever the reason, I was glad.

For the record, I've never actually wanted to *be*

a boy. People seem to think I had some kind of evil master plan, like I woke up one day thinking, *Hey, you know what would be really fun? Pretending to be a boy.* As if.

Mum always had this idea that I wished I was a boy because I always looked up to Jamie so much when I was little – copying everything he did and following him and his mates around. And I usually liked his Christmas presents more than mine. I never understood why everything I got seemed to be pink or fluffy or both and everything he got was just . . . *better.* I would have liked a remote-controlled car or a Transformer or Lego or whatever. Teddy bears and dolls were not my cup of tea, no matter how much Mum wanted them to be. She only stopped buying me dolls when I decapitated Barbie in the name of science. Then she moved on to mostly buying me art stuff, which was fine because I've always liked drawing.

I grew up thinking Jamie was the coolest person on the planet and I think he enjoyed the hero worship. He used to get me to run around after him, fetching chocolate digestives from the kitchen and running down to the shop to buy him sweets. Mum didn't like that – she'd always tell him off if she caught me doing stuff for him, saying I wasn't his slave. But Jamie would just laugh it off and say that I *liked* helping him. He was right. But I didn't want to *be* him. It was more that I wanted to be able to do the things he did. Life just seemed a lot more fun for boys sometimes. Less complicated somehow.

I got stuck behind a bunch of French tourists stopping to take photos of leaves or something, so by the time I caught up to Kate she was nearly back where we'd started the walk. She was standing with her hands planted on her hips and she did this fake yawn as if she'd been there for ages (when she was blatantly still out of breath).

'I let you win. Just so you know.' I shrugged. 'I'm pretty charitable like that.'

She rolled her eyes and shook her head. 'Yeah, yeah, whatever you say. I thought you were supposed to be good at running? I think you might need to train a little harder. Let me know if you need any tips, OK?'

'Thanks. That's really kind of you . . . But we're not quite at the finish line yet, are we? So *technically*, the race isn't over yet . . .' I bolted, laughing my head off as Kate chased me down the path and across the road.

She was laughing too, in between shouting out things like 'CHEAT!' and 'NOT FAIR!' She didn't care that people were stopping to look at us. I loved that about her – she wasn't self-conscious. This time people saw a teenage girl chasing a teenage boy and they smiled indulgently because *that* was cute, apparently. I slowed down and let her catch up, so she slapped her hand on the wall of Pizza Express a split-second before I did.

Kate turned to me, panting. 'You really did let me win that time, didn't you?'

'Maybe. Maybe not . . . you'll never know for sure, will you?' I gave her what I hoped was a charming grin.

She narrowed her eyes. 'I don't need you to *let* me win. I'm perfectly capable of winning on my own, thank you very much.'

I couldn't tell if she was being serious. I put my hand on my heart. 'I'm sorry. I solemnly swear to never ever let you win, at anything, ever. I will win at ALL the things.'

'Oh shut up, you.' She elbowed me in the side and for the first time in a while I was aware of the bandages itching against my skin. 'I'm buying the pizza, OK? I don't want to hear any arguments from you.'

I promised that I wouldn't put up a fight to pay for the pizza, even though I felt awkward about Kate paying for stuff. I know Jamie usually pays for drinks when he goes on dates, but there's no reason why guys should have to pay for everything. It's like those girls at school always going on about finding a rich boyfriend (preferably a footballer) to buy them loads of presents and take them to 'all the best places'. I'd rather buy my own stuff and pay my own way, and I had less than zero interest in 'all the best places'. Kate clearly had similar feelings so it was weird that I suddenly felt uncomfortable about her buying me lunch. It was almost like I was starting to slip away from myself.

chapter seven

We shared a pizza after a long discussion about our favourite pizza toppings. It turned out we mostly liked the same things (pepperoni, jalapenos) so we didn't have to get one of those half-and-half pizzas. We pretty much devoured the whole pizza – and the side of garlic dough balls she'd insisted on ordering. Clearly she wasn't planning on doing any kissing today. I was relieved, because the thought of kissing her made me feel a bit sick. I'd thought a lot about kissing her. Of course I had. And I wanted to. Of course I did. But that didn't make me feel any less nervous about the prospect. Anyway, maybe she didn't want to kiss me. Maybe she was coming to the conclusion that we'd be better off as friends. And then I'd be able to tell her the truth and everything would be OK.

Towards the end of the meal Kate looked at

me shyly. 'Can I tell you something? As long as you promise not to laugh . . .'

'You can tell me anything.' I meant it. There was nothing she could say that I wouldn't want to hear.

'I've never been on a proper date before.' She scrunched up her napkin and started tearing off little pieces.

I laughed and Kate frowned. 'You said you wouldn't laugh! Oh God, this is so embarrassing. I knew I shouldn't have told you. Forget I said anything. I've been on lots of dates . . . LOADS. At least three every week. In fact, it leaves me very little time for anything else. So there.' She stuck out her bottom lip in the perfect pout and it was unbelievably adorable.

'I'm sorry! I wasn't laughing *at* you . . . honestly. It's just . . .' I hesitated. Could I be as brave as her? About this, at least. I had to. 'I've never been on a date before either.'

She didn't believe me. I could tell that before she even opened her mouth. 'You're just saying that to make me feeling better.'

'I'm not.' We looked into each other's eyes for a second or two and then she sat back in her chair and smiled.

'So we're both newbies then? For some reason I thought you were really experienced or . . . I don't know. You seem so . . . cool with everything. Like nothing fazes you.' She couldn't have been more wrong. 'So this is really your very first date?' I nodded, pretending to be as cool as she thought I was. She narrowed her eyes. 'So this is definitely a real, proper date?' I nodded again.

Kate considered that for a moment or two. 'That makes me happy.'

I considered for a moment or two longer. 'Me too.'

We sat there grinning at each other. It was the kind of thing that's a bit sickening if you're not actually involved in it. But I *was* involved in it and it was brilliant.

It was nearly three o'clock by the time we'd finished eating. I went to get my wallet out but one stern look from Kate stopped me in my tracks. I held up my hands in surrender and she looked smug. 'You can pay next time . . .'

Another next time. Another chance. I wondered if she kept saying 'next time' deliberately, like she sensed I needed reassurance. Or maybe *she* was looking for reassurance.

We left the restaurant and wandered back up the hill towards town. I didn't say anything when we passed the end of my road. Princes Street was rammed with people who have nothing better to do on a Saturday afternoon than shop for crap they don't need. I waited with Kate at the bus stop. There were loads of people waiting – old ladies and women with buggies mostly. The bus came and we stepped back to let everyone else on first. Kate took my hand and squeezed it. She whispered in my ear and her breath tickled a bit. 'I really want to kiss you but I have terrible garlic breath and I'd rather not do it in front of all these people. Can we go somewhere more private next time? Assuming you . . . um . . . want to kiss me too?'

'I . . . yes. I really do.'

I had never wanted anything more.

It was a good first date. As good as a first date can be when there's a secret that huge hanging over you, threatening to flatten you the minute you slip up and say or do the wrong thing. There was only one thing missing, but I was happy to wait. It was excruciating, of course – the anticipation of what it would be like when her lips met mine.

I took off the bandages as soon as I got home and breathed the biggest sigh of relief. Now that I knew for sure that Kate wanted to kiss me, I was on top of the world – nothing could touch me. When Mum and Dad got back from Glasgow and Mum was in a foul mood because there was nothing in the fridge for dinner so we'd have to get takeaway again, I just smiled and fanned out the menus in front of her like a magician. Said I'd even go and collect it. She looked at me suspiciously; I never volunteered to get the takeaway.

Mum knew something was up, but she couldn't figure out what it was. It must have been the smiling. I wasn't one for pointless smiling. Anyway, she didn't push the matter and we actually had a pretty decent evening, stuffing ourselves and taking the piss out of people on some TV talent show. Kate texted a couple of times and asked what I was up to. I said I was listening to music in my room. Weirdly enough, this tiny lie made me feel guilty. Probably because there was no good reason for it, other than the fact that I didn't want Kate to think I was the sort of loser who watched Saturday night telly with their parents. I decided that one day soon I'd come clean about it. Strange how you can focus on the little things when there's a massive black cloud looming over you.

On Monday the real world was waiting for me. I showered quickly and got dressed. I zipped up my skirt and stared at myself in the mirror. My shirt was at least three sizes too big. Most of the girls wore theirs tight, desperate to show off their boobs. Which you could just about understand in a co-ed school, but in a girls' school it was just bizarre. Everyone else usually rolled up the tops of their skirts to make them as short as possible. I never bothered. There was no way to make it look good so what was the point of trying? I hated the tights too. I went bare-legged for as long as possible every year, waiting for the day Mum insisted I wear tights. By that time it was usually so cold that my legs went mottled and blue-ish.

I looked like crap in my uniform, there was no question about that. It just looked *wrong* somehow. Like I was wearing a costume, dressing up like someone playing a schoolgirl in a play. The first day of secondary school when I came down for breakfast decked out in my new clothes, Mum clapped her hands together and said, 'Look at my baby girl, all grown up and off to big school!' Dad smiled indulgently. Jamie laughed for five minutes straight. I didn't even mind; I laughed right along with him.

There was a strict no-phones policy at school, so I didn't even have texts from Kate to get me through the horrors of Monday. I tried to convince myself that none of this mattered – the teachers droning on, the girls ignoring me, the boredom. This wasn't my *real* life. My real life was skating and music and . . . Kate?

I spent most of the morning thinking about Saturday, trying not to cringe at the moments I'd made a right twat of myself. There weren't too many, but that didn't stop me going over them in my head, again and again, trying to work out just how lame Kate thought I was. When I'd had enough of beating myself up about things I focused on the good stuff. The way she laughed when I was trying to be funny, the way she looked at me all intense when we were talking about something serious, her shy smile when she thought she'd said something outrageous. These thoughts were enough to get me through double Maths before lunch.

I always brought a packed lunch with me. Mum used to make it for me but she gave up a couple of years ago. She usually made fancy stuff like quinoa salad and Moroccan wraps but I was happy with ham sandwiches (white bread, a tiny bit of mustard), an apple and a banana. The way I saw it, there was no point having anything better. School was a depressing place to be and I hated the thought of it tainting any nice food Mum made for me. Ham sandwiches were inherently disappointing (to me at least), so they were the perfect lunch for schooldays. I never tried to explain all this to Mum because she wouldn't have understood.

I usually ate my lunch on some steps near the staff room. No one else hung around there, obviously. It was getting way too cold to sit out there though; my hands were numb by the time I'd finished my sandwich. I was just getting started on my apple (I always had the banana last – always) when I heard voices. They were getting closer and I was pissed off that someone had dared to invade my space. Two girls came round the corner, leaning against each other to hold themselves up, laughing and screeching. Anyone else and it would have been OK. Anyone else in a school of eight hundred pupils. But no. It had to be *her*. Heather Harris.

Heather Harris with her stupid messy dyed red hair and her eyeliner and her pierced nose (totally against school rules but no one ever challenged her on it).

Heather Harris, who somehow managed to make the school uniform look halfway decent. Like it had been custom-made to fit her just right.

Heather Harris, who'd tried to kiss me last week. And succeeded.

chapter eight

Heather Harris was this year's New Girl. She'd arrived after the start of term and was specially introduced by the headmistress in assembly. Mrs Goldberg made Heather stand up in front of everyone. I would have died of embarrassment but Heather stood there like she didn't give a toss that the entire school was staring at her. She looked like she was waiting for a bus and so not impressed that it was late. Whenever I saw her in the corridor after that, she usually had that same expression on her face. I couldn't blame her: school was unimpressive in every way.

For the first week or so Heather was by herself every time I saw her. It even crossed my mind that maybe I should talk to her. She looked different from the rest of them – she didn't seem to be another clone of Marcy Davies for one thing. She looked like she might have something interesting to say for herself.

Of course, I didn't end up approaching her, because that's not the kind of thing I would ever do.

A few weeks before I met Kate, Heather Harris and I talked for the first time. She'd joined the running squad even though she was crap at running. I always waited until the changing room was empty before taking a shower. Undressing in front of people has always been a bit of a phobia of mine. The one and only time I've ever been invited to a sleepover I didn't even have to fake a stomach ache to get Mum to call Priya's mother to say I couldn't go – I threw up three times from nerves. I could tell Mum was disappointed that I couldn't go to Priya's – she probably thought that me being invited was the start of something for me. She wasn't to know that Priya's parents had forced her to invite every girl in our class.

That day after training I was sitting on a wooden bench in the furthest corner of the changing room, waiting. I knew someone was still there, but I didn't know who. I wouldn't allow myself to look up in case I had to engage in conversation. I unlaced my trainers painfully slowly, like I was defusing a bomb. The mystery person *still* hadn't left by the time my Asics were off. I was going to have to get a move on otherwise I'd be late for English. I'd just have to be really quick about it and hope that whoever it was would leave as soon as possible. I took a deep breath and went to pull my T-shirt over my head. The fabric was right over my face when I heard a voice in front of me.

There was a cough. 'Hi. I was just wondering where you got your trainers from.'

I quickly pulled my T-shirt back down, hoping my face wasn't too red. It was Heather. Barefoot, wearing running shorts and a sports bra and nothing else. 'Um . . . that shop on Lothian Road?' As if I wasn't entirely sure.

'I don't know it.' Of course she didn't. She'd just moved here.

Heather was staring at me, waiting. I was clearly going to have to elaborate. 'It's pretty decent. They video you on a running machine so they can work out which trainers you need. It's not cheap – my mum doesn't understand why I can't just get a pair from the supermarket or whatever.'

'Oh God, tell me about it. My mum's the same.'

This seemed like a natural point to end the conversation, but Heather showed no sign of moving. I wasn't sure what to do with myself – there was no way I was getting changed right in front of her. She didn't seem in the least bit self-conscious about standing there in her bra. Her arms were crossed in front of her chest. Mum always says that means someone's being defensive, but I didn't think that was the case here. In fact, I was pretty sure Heather was standing like that to push her boobs up and make them look bigger than they were.

I glanced at my watch and saw that the bell was about to go. I was going to be late. Heather took my hand and turned my wrist round so she could see the time. 'Shit!' She rushed over to the other side of the changing rooms and whipped off her bra. She carried on talking as she changed back into her uniform. 'Oh God, I'm going to stink this afternoon. Reckon I'll be giving Mr Perkins a run for his money.' She paused to spray copious amounts of deodorant over every inch of her body. I was watching her even though I didn't mean to. She glanced over. 'Aren't you going to be late?'

'Nah, I've got a free period next. I thought I'd take my time . . . maybe wash my hair.'

Heather stopped for a second and looked at me. She knew I was lying – I was sure of it – but she just nodded slowly. 'So I was wondering if you need a training partner? Maybe we could run together on weekends or something?' She was buttoning up her shirt really slowly as she said this.

'Yeah, that would be cool.' There was no way in hell she'd be able to keep up with me, but I wasn't bothered. For some reason this new girl seemed to want to be friends with me. Maybe she *was* different from the others. It would be kind of nice to have a friend at school.

'Cool.' Heather smiled and held my eye for a moment or two – slightly longer than was comfortable, if I'm being entirely honest. 'I'll leave you to it then. Enjoy your shower.' There was something about the way she said 'shower', something sarcastic. Like she wanted me to know she knew I was lying. Not in a mean way though – almost as if it was our little secret. It made me feel uneasy all the same.

In the end I was ten minutes late for English, but I just told Mrs Enthoven I'd been helping one of the PE teachers with something. She believed me. Teachers always believed me, because I always handed in my work on time and got good grades. My thoughts kept drifting back towards Heather all afternoon. There had been something strange going on between us – a weird kind of tension in the air. But I couldn't work out where it came from or even whether I liked it or not.

Heather and I weren't left alone together for another couple of weeks. She hadn't asked again about us running together, and I wasn't about to talk to her first. I'd noticed her watching me a couple of times during training. I thought she might be trying to pick up a few tips – she certainly needed them.

A week before I met Kate at the gig, Heather and I were the last ones in the changing room again. I'd dawdled around outside, taking extra time over my warm down exercises. Some of the girls were already coming out of the changing rooms by the time I went in. I sat in my little corner and waited. When silence finally descended I looked up and saw her looking at me. I wondered how long she'd been watching.

'Hi.' Sounding as uncomfortable as I felt.

'Hi.' Heather didn't sound at all uncomfortable.

There was a long silence, which I had to break with an insightful 'Um . . .'

Heather smiled and rolled her eyes, as if my awkwardness was endearing. She glanced towards the door then walked over and sat down next to me. 'You really don't like getting changed in front of people, do you?'

'What? I don't—'

'It's OK, you don't have to explain yourself.'

So I said nothing. Just waited to see what happened next.

'You're not big on talking, are you?'

I shrugged and Heather laughed. She shifted closer

to me on the bench. Our legs were nearly touching. My mouth was dry all of a sudden.

'I'm not going to bite, you know.' Her voice was a whisper now. Her hand was on my thigh. I could not believe what was happening.

'What are you doing?' I turned to face her. I had no other option, really.

Her face was really close to mine. Close enough for me to see the spot brewing just under her nose. 'You know full well what I'm doing. I've seen you watching me.' I had no idea what she was talking about. I didn't watch her more than I watched anyone else — and it was kind of hard to avoid watching people, due to the whole 'having eyes' thing.

'Um . . . sorry. But I really don't think . . .'

And that's when she did it. Closed her eyes and tilted her head and put her lips on mine. All the signs had been there (a hand on my leg, for Christ's sake) but I still hadn't seen it coming.

I froze. Her tongue was prodding at my closed lips, trying to find a way in. I jerked my head back, hitting it against the metal bar behind me. Heather looked surprised but then she leaned in again. I jumped up from the bench. 'I'm sorry . . . I . . .' My words trailed off when I saw the look on Heather's face.

'What the fuck is wrong with you?' She stood up and stalked back over to her side of the room.

I didn't know what to do with myself. Should I say something? Go over to her? Say sorry again? I couldn't decide so I did nothing.

Heather gathered up her things, stuffing her uniform into her bag. All her movements were sharp and forceful. She was furious.

When she was done she shouldered her bag and stomped over to the mirror. She smoothed down her hair and swept her fingers across her eyes. I could see the tears glinting from where I was standing. I had to say something before she left. 'I'm sorry.' I'm not sure exactly what I was apologizing for – I hadn't done anything wrong, but it's never good to make someone cry.

Heather swiped away another tear and took a deep breath before turning to look at me. 'Don't you *dare* tell anyone about this . . . If you breathe a word I swear I'll . . .' She didn't finish the sentence so I never found out exactly what she planned to do if I told someone. Besides, I had no intention of telling anyone – ever. It was way too embarrassing.

One last look in the mirror then Heather stormed out. The bell went. I was twelve minutes late for English this time.

chapter nine

I didn't tell anyone about what had happened. I don't think Heather did either because a couple of days after that I saw her hanging out with Marcy Davies. She didn't come back to training. As far as Heather Harris was concerned I did not exist. And that suited me just fine.

I kept myself to myself even more than usual after that, wrapping myself up in thoughts of Kate. But then Heather had to go and stumble round that corner with Marcy, shattering my peace and quiet.

Heather noticed me first. And I was sure she was going to stick to her new policy of ignoring me. But she made this big show of stepping away from me and dragging Marcy back with her. 'I didn't realize this was the designated dyke corner. They should put a sign up or something – warn the rest of us to steer clear.'

Marcy laughed in that way you do when you're

not supposed to be laughing. 'Heather! That's *terrible!*' But she was smiling; it was obvious she didn't really think it was terrible at all. And there was something about the way Marcy was laughing that made it clear that this was not the first time my sexuality had been questioned. People must have been talking about me behind my back and I'd been too stupid to even realize.

I put my half-eaten apple back in my lunch box, then gathered the rest of my stuff together and stood up. I skulked away without saying anything. Their laughter followed me round the corner. It briefly occurred to me that Kate would never let these two girls get away with acting like this. She would say something. She would stand up for what she believed in. I was the worst kind of coward.

I didn't talk to Heather again but I couldn't help thinking about her, trying to work out what the hell had happened in the changing rooms that day. Had I done anything to encourage her? Had I led her on in some way? I was pretty sure I hadn't. Not that I was in any way experienced with this stuff, but all I'd done was talk to the girl. I hadn't said anything that would make her think that it was OK to kiss me. Maybe it had been a moment of madness on her part – a mistake that she'd instantly regretted as soon as she'd seen my reaction. Or maybe she'd pounced on an unsuspecting girl before and things had worked out just fine. I'd never know the truth unless I asked her and there was no way that was ever going to happen.

I played the kiss over and over in my mind. It hadn't felt *bad*, exactly. But it hadn't felt right either. It wasn't how I'd pictured my first kiss, that was for sure. I'd always thought it would be with someone I really liked. I'd always thought it would be with a boy. But the more I thought about it the more I wondered if I'd only ever thought about boys because that was the way I'd been conditioned to think. Way back when I was little, Barbie went with *Ken*. That was how things were supposed to be.

I couldn't help wondering if Heather had recognized something in me. Something I'd never even realized myself. Had she *known*, somehow?

When I thought about Heather kissing me I'd try my hardest to imagine it was Kate instead. By the time my second date with Kate came along, I'd done so much imagining that sometimes it felt like the kiss had already happened. Of course, when it actually did happen, it was nothing at all like I'd imagined.

chapter ten

It was up to me to decide what we were doing for our second date. I reckon Kate was testing me, seeing whether I'd come up with something decent. I put a lot of thought into it – all the places I usually hung out suddenly seemed inadequate somehow. I wanted it to be special.

It was Jamie who gave me the idea in the end, not that he knew it. I was rummaging around in his room after school because I'd run out of hair gel. I was finding all sorts of interesting things in his desk drawer – condoms and Rizlas and porn. I wasn't surprised that he hadn't cleared out his drawers before he'd gone off to uni. Jamie wasn't the sort of boy to care if his mum knew what he was up to – he knew his status as Number One Son and Golden Child was safe, no matter what. I eventually found a crusty-looking tube of hair gel, but I kept on looking out of pure nosiness.

I found it right at the bottom of the drawer. It was one of those cheesy pictures you get at tourist attractions. I had one in my room somewhere from a family trip to York Dungeons years ago. In that one, a twelve-year-old Jamie is swinging a fake axe at ten-year-old me's head with a look of pure glee on his face. This photo was a lot more recent. It was in some dark underground place and Jamie had his arms around a girl. I recognized her but I couldn't remember her name. She looked very happy to be in my brother's arms.

The photo had been taken in Mary King's Close. I didn't know much about it other than the fact that it was a bunch of old streets and houses running under the Royal Mile. I vaguely remembered something about the plague, but history has never been my strong suit. It was supposed to be haunted, which was what made me think it would be the perfect place to take Kate. I didn't know for sure that she hadn't been there before, but it was worth a shot. She'd told me that she loved scary films even though she couldn't help screaming whenever the killer jumped out from behind a bush or whatever. I got on the internet and booked the tickets (expensive, but worth it, hopefully), then texted Kate to tell her where to meet on Friday. She was desperate to know where we were going, but I was keeping quiet – I wanted to surprise her.

I was always in a good mood on Fridays because we got to go home at lunchtime. I was the first one out of the school gates and I ran all the way home. I'd arranged to meet Kate at two so we could spend as much time together as possible before she had to go to another bloody piano lesson.

I bandaged myself up and put on a black and red checked shirt, black jeans and my Converse. Looked in the mirror and decided something was missing, then added a grey beanie. I actually sort of liked the reflection looking back at me, although I'd never admit it to anyone in a million years. I went into the bathroom and started brushing my teeth. I've always been a bit obsessive about brushing my teeth – when I was little I used to do it after every meal and snack until Mum told me it would wear down my gums and my teeth would fall out.

Toothbrush in mouth, I wandered down the hall to Jamie's room and opened up his wardrobe. There was a jacket of his I'd always liked and I was pretty sure he'd left it behind. I started rifling through the clothes on the rail, picking out a couple of old shirts that could work for me. Then a sleepy voice behind me said, 'And what the heck do you think you're doing, missy?' I jumped a mile and spluttered on the toothpaste, spraying white gunk on to the shirts I was holding.

Jamie was sitting up in his bed, hair all over the place, yawning wide like a walrus. I scarpered back to the bathroom to rinse the foam out of my mouth and try to clean up the shirts.

'Nice one, sis.' Jamie stuck his head round the bathroom door. He was wearing an old faded T-shirt that was way too small for him and a pair of board shorts. He had a creased red mark on his face from the pillow.

'Jesus Christ, Jamie! Are you trying to kill me?'

He smirked as he elbowed me out of the way to get to the mirror. Jamie's always been a big fan of mirrors. 'What kind of a welcome home is that?'

'Sorry. Um . . . welcome home.' I remembered I had the bandages on. What would Jamie say if he realized my boobs had magically disappeared? The shirt was fairly baggy, at least. And Jamie wasn't exactly renowned for his powers of observation. It had taken him two weeks to notice that Dad had shaved off the moustache he'd had for seven years. I just had to make sure I kept Jamie talking to distract him – and get out of there as quickly as possible. 'Do Mum and Dad know you're here?'

'Nah, I thought I'd surprise them. It was a bit of a last minute thing – a mate was driving down this morning, so I thought I might as well get a free ride.

Get some decent food, get some washing done, spend some time with my favourite sister.'

'*Only* sister.'

He swiped the beanie off my head and ruffled my hair. 'And that's what makes you so *special* . . . So, are you going to explain what you were doing rummaging through my wardrobe? Missing me so much that you wanted to find a jumper to keep under your pillow?'

'Yeah, that's *exactly* what I was doing.' I grabbed my beanie off him and put it back in place, making sure my fringe was just right. 'Actually, I was looking for that jacket of yours? The black one?'

'Jeez, I've only been gone a few weeks and already you're scavenging my stuff! You're out of luck with the jacket though. I gave it to Camilla – a little something to remember me by.' He grinned. 'Now . . . are you going to make me a cup of tea or what?'

'You'll have to get your own tea, you lazy waster. And while you're at it, you could do your own washing too. This is the 21st century, *remember*?'

Jamie slung his arm around me and we walked through to the kitchen. 'Ah, sis, you have so much to learn. Mum *likes* doing my washing. It makes her feel like she's the mum off the gravy advert or some-thing. Like she's being a *proper* mother. So it's really very kind of me to allow her to do it for me . . . you see?'

I burst out laughing. 'You are so full of shit!' He didn't really believe that stuff; he just liked winding me up.

He smiled like he'd achieved something. 'Pleeeeaase make me a cup of tea, Alex? You have no idea how much I've missed your tea-making skills! No one at uni makes a decent cuppa.'

'I thought uni was supposed to be all beer and cocktails and shots that can put you in a coma?' I checked my watch – just enough time to stick the kettle on for Jamie then I'd have to motor.

Jamie hopped up on to the kitchen island. It was *his* spot. He grabbed an apple from the fruit bowl and started munching away. 'Yeah, well, that's true . . . but you've got to have tea and toast *after* that – to soak up all that booze. Tea prevents comas, don't you know?'

I rolled my eyes as I put just the right amount of milk in his favourite mug and chucked in a tea bag. 'Right, I'm sure you can manage pouring the water . . . just remember to wait till the kettle's boiled, yes? I've got to get going.'

'But I was hoping for a bit of quality brother-sister time before the parentals get back! You're not going to leave me here all alone, are you?' He pouted and you could see how he used to get away with murder when we were little.

'Don't blame me! You should have texted to say you were coming! I've got plans . . . and if I don't get a move on I'm going to be late.'

'Can't you wait ten minutes and let me tag along? I've got no one to hang out with – everyone's away! God, look what I've been reduced to . . . begging my baby sister to let me spend time with her. How the mighty have fallen!' His words were garbled as he talked around a mouthful of apple.

'No can do, brother dear. Let's do something tomorrow though, yeah? A walk up Arthur's Seat or something?'

Jamie sighed. 'Don't want me cramping your style, is that it?' He looked at me slyly. '*Or* . . . do you have a hot date?' My face must have reddened immediately because he leaped off the counter and wagged his finger at me. 'That's *it*, isn't it! I *knew* it! I can read you like a book, sister dear, so there's no point in lying to me. Come on, spill. I want details.'

There was no point in denying it. Despite being spectacularly unobservant, Jamie really does know people. He can almost always tell what I'm thinking, and one of my favourite things about him is that he's always been able to cheer me up when I'm down. He just needs to crack a joke or do his Blue Steel Zoolander face.

'I'm saying nothing. But you'd better not tell Mum and Dad, OK?'

He mimed locking his lips and throwing the key over his shoulder. 'My lips are sealed. This secret will go with me to my grave. Or at least back to Aberdeen.' He smiled. 'I'm happy for you, sis. Really. And if you ever do want to talk about it, you know where I am.'

'Hundreds of miles away?'

'Smart arse. You know what I mean.'

The kettle had boiled so I poured the water myself. 'Thanks, J.'

Jamie took the teaspoon from my hand and gave me a gentle shove. 'Now off you go. But make sure you're not early. You never want to be the first one there otherwise you look desperate. Have fun, OK? Don't do anything I wouldn't do.'

There wasn't much Jamie wouldn't do. But I'm pretty sure pretending to be a member of the opposite sex fell into that category.

On the way into town I mulled over the fact that Jamie hadn't pushed to know more. He hadn't asked who the 'lucky' boy was. I would have bet money on him asking that. It made me wonder if there was a reason – other than him respecting my privacy. Maybe Jamie didn't want to back me into a corner. Maybe he would have wanted to ask about the lucky *girl*.

I briefly wondered if I could talk to him about Kate before dismissing the idea immediately. Even if he was OK with the idea of me dating a girl, there was no way he would understand what I was doing. He'd insist I come clean, tell the truth. He might even tell Mum and Dad. No. Jamie had to stay firmly in the dark along with everyone else.

chapter eleven

Kate was there before me again, but I didn't think it made her look desperate at all. She was staring down at the ground, at the spot we'd arranged to meet. She looked up when I was a couple of paces away and smiled. 'The Heart of Midlothian?'

A heart shape embedded in the cobblestones. It was supposed to be the exact centre of the county. And it was a *heart*; I thought it would be romantic. I'd forgotten that it was supposed to be good luck to spit on it. So essentially I'd arranged to meet Kate at a place with a whole lot of phlegm. I shrugged and looked sheepish.

I hadn't realized how much I'd missed her. I felt like I was able to breathe again now that she was next to me. I felt more balanced somehow.

She had no idea where we were going. I took her hand and led her across the street to the entrance to Mary King's Close. Kate clapped her hands. 'I've always wanted to go here! How did you know?!'

'Just a hunch, I guess.' It was hard not to look smug.

We went into the gift shop and joined the queue for our tour. A couple in their twenties were in the queue in front of us; they didn't talk to each other at all. She gazed at the TV screen in the corner, twiddling her hair between her fingers, while he stared at his phone as if it held the key to the universe. I couldn't stop looking at them, wondering if they'd just had an argument or if they were always like that.

I felt Kate lean in close to me. Lips brushing against my cheek. 'Thank you for this,' she whispered.

'No worries.'

'It feels like you *know* me.'

She couldn't have said anything more perfect.

There were ten of us booked on the tour, including the most annoying kid in the world. A weaselly little boy who wouldn't shut up when the tour guide was talking and kept on saying how boring it was and asking where the ghosts were. I was worried he was ruining it for Kate, but she just smiled at the kid indulgently and that made me feel bad for wishing he'd trip and smash his head open on a flagstone.

The tour guide was dressed up in character as some girl from the seventeenth century, but the American accent and the braces on her teeth kind of ruined the effect. Still, she knew her stuff. It was hard to concentrate on what she was saying when Kate slipped her hand into mine, our fingers locking together as if they'd always meant to be that way.

I kept on turning to look at Kate, to check that she really was enjoying herself. Every time I looked she was either listening carefully to the tour guide or smiling back at me. There weren't any ghosts jumping out at us, which may have disappointed the annoying kid but not me. I don't like surprises. It was still pretty creepy down there though. I didn't like the waxwork models of plague victims; I kept on expecting them to move when I wasn't looking.

One room was supposed to be haunted by a little girl whose family left her behind when she got the plague. Apparently some Japanese psychic had talked to her spirit or whatever. Total bullshit but there was something unsettling about the huge pile of toys people had brought down there and left for the ghost girl. Kate squeezed my hand and whispered, 'It's so sad.' I was going to take the piss but thought better of it.

Right at the end of the tour we finally reached Mary King's Close itself. We posed for the obligatory cheesy picture (Kate insisted). We lingered behind the rest of the group as they made their way up to the top of the close towards the exit.

'Just imagine what it must have been like, living down here!' said Kate, and I just *knew* that she was actually imagining it, picturing what it would have been like centuries ago.

'Just imagine the *smell*.'

Kate smiled and rolled her eyes. 'Oh *you*.'

I shrugged. 'Sorry.'

'No need to apologize . . . it's not your fault you have *no* imagination.'

I pulled a little frowny face that she must have found endearing because she said, 'Come here, you,' and that's when it happened.

She kissed me.

Her lips were warm and soft on mine. It was better than I could have ever imagined. All memories of what had happened with Heather were blown away. This was how it was supposed to be. *This* was how you were supposed to feel when you were kissing someone you wanted to be kissing.

Kate pulled away first and looked at me shyly. I must have had the goofiest smile on my face because she took one look at me and laughed. 'Was that . . . um . . . OK?'

I took a breath to try to calm my hammering heart. 'That was definitely very OK.'

'Maybe we should do it again sometime soon then.'

'I think that would be acceptable.'

We held each other's gaze for a few seconds before bursting out laughing.

After the tour we wandered along George IV Bridge towards the Elephant House. We walked in silence, occasionally meeting each other's eyes and grinning. The kind of sight that would have made me want to puke a couple of months before.

Kate bought us both hot chocolates and we shared a slice of carrot cake. We sat snuggled up on the sofa by the fire and I tried to pretend we weren't surrounded by tourists and rabid Harry Potter fans. I put my arm around Kate and she rested her head on my shoulder.

'This is perfect, isn't it?' Her breath tickled my neck.

I mumbled my agreement; the hot chocolate was making me sleepy.

'It makes me nervous, you know. It's almost as if it's too perfect and I'm just waiting for something bad to happen.'

I winced, but Kate didn't see. 'That's not very

optimistic, is it? I thought you were all about the rainbows and pandas and happy things?'

'I'm serious!' A gentle elbow to my chest, grazing the bandages under my shirt.

'I'm sorry. I'm listening . . . honestly.' In actual fact I wanted to divert this conversation away from where it was heading. But Kate clearly wanted to say something. Most girls are like that – always wanting to talk about their feelings. I've always preferred to keep my feelings to myself, well away from public view. It's safer that way.

Kate sighed. 'I suppose what I'm trying to say is that I like how things are going with us. I mean, I know it's early days. *Really* early days. But this feels like something . . . real.'

I closed my eyes. *Real*. It did feel like something real, and it *was* something real.

I nearly told her right then. And I think maybe I would have if we hadn't been in the middle of a jam-packed coffee house. It seemed like she was waiting for me to say something – almost like she knew and was giving me a chance to tell her the truth. But she *didn't* know; she was waiting for me to say something else – something reassuring.

'It *is* real.'

'Promise?' Her voice was small and vulnerable.

'Promise.' I didn't feel good saying that word, but it was what Kate needed to hear.

She sat up and sort of shook herself like a dog in the rain. 'Sorry, I didn't mean to get all intense. I suppose I can be a little . . . um . . . thinky sometimes. That's OK, isn't it?'

'A little thinky is just fine with me.'

'So you don't think I'm a total weirdo?'

I paused and furrowed my brow. 'Not a *total* weirdo, no.'

She gave me a fake withering look. 'Thanks for that.'

I knew I needed to say something serious then. Something meaningful. It was all very well teasing her and trying to act too cool for school, but Kate deserved more. I took her hand in mine. Her fingers were longer than mine. I traced my finger around the silver band on her ring finger. 'I like you, Kate.' That wasn't very meaningful so I tried again. 'I've never met anyone like you before. I'm . . . I'm really glad you're in my life.' That wasn't particularly great either but it was the best she was going to get.

Kate's eyes widened and her face lit up and I knew that by some miracle I'd said the right thing. That was definitely one way that being a boy was easier than being a girl. You don't have to make big poetic declarations about your feelings. Pretty much anything you do say is a bonus, since the most people expect you to do is grunt and turn your attention back to Call of Duty or Halo or whatever. When expectations are so low, anything more than that is a bonus.

Kate kissed me on the lips. 'I like you too, Alex.'

The happiness was almost too much to bear.

chapter twelve

I didn't see Kate for a whole week after that. It was half term and she went away on holiday with her mum. We weren't even able to text that much – it was too expensive. I usually love half term – a temporary reprieve from school – but I felt lost without Kate to talk to. Not that we ever actually *talked* when we were apart. I hate talking on the phone – it's a bit of a phobia of mine. For one thing, I hate my voice. It doesn't sound anything like I'd expect me to sound like. Plus I always get tongue-tied, no matter who I'm talking to. There's something about a phone call that seems like a trap to me – as if whoever's on the end of the phone is waiting to catch me out in some way. I think maybe Kate felt the same way, because she never tried to call me. Or maybe it was something to do with the fact that our relationship started that way, so it seemed like the best way for it to continue.

Normally I'd be up at Bristo Square, but I hadn't heard from Jonni or Fitz for a couple of weeks, and I wasn't going to be the first one to get in touch. I had *some* pride, at least. I'd bought them the gig tickets – the least they could do was say thank you. I hadn't skated since my first date with Kate. Suddenly it didn't seem like something I wanted to spend my time doing. I wasn't running nearly as much as I used to, either. I didn't really want to spend my time doing anything apart from thinking about, seeing or talking to Kate. A lot of the time I ended up lying on my bed listening to the mortifyingly cheesy playlist I'd created the day after our first date.

Jamie eventually managed to drag me out of the house to go for a walk the day before he headed back to Aberdeen. Said it was time I stopped moping around being all emo. I think he thought my date had gone horribly wrong so he felt sorry for me. He wasn't to know I was spending all my time daydreaming. Remembering that kiss. Imagining future kisses. It would never occur to him that I would be that lame. Mind you, it would never have occurred to me either. I was learning new things about myself every day and quite a few were things I would never want another human being to know about.

I tried to pay attention to Jamie's stories about

university life and how *amazing* it was as he huffed and puffed his way up Arthur's Seat. He'd have been able to run up that hill a couple of months before – he clearly wasn't getting much exercise. As usual, he was juggling a couple of different girls, but reckoned one of them was a keeper – 'the kind of girl I could bring home for a weekend'. Of course that got me thinking about Kate. She was the kind of girl I could bring home for a weekend. Except she lived in Edinburgh, so it would be a bit weird to bring her home for a weekend. And she was a girl, so I'd probably have some explaining to do to my parents first. And *I* was a girl so I'd have some explaining to do to Kate as well.

We didn't hang around at the top of the hill; the wind was like having ice-cold daggers plunged into your ears. Jamie took a picture of us with his phone, both of us with our hats pulled down as far as they'd go. He posted it straight on Facebook: 'Bonding with little sis up a big fucking hill'. Jamie likes to document his whole life online. It must make it harder to juggle all those different girls without them finding out about each other.

All the way home I kept thinking about that photo being on Facebook. Not worrying, exactly. But it made me uneasy. Jamie had a *lot* of friends. And what if one of them was friends with someone who knew Kate? And what if she happened to be with them when they went on Facebook and saw a picture of me? *Little sis.*

By the time we got home the thinking had morphed into full-on paranoia. I asked Jamie to delete the picture, saying I looked crap, but he said no and pulled my beanie down over my eyes. Then I practically begged him to delete it and he told me to stop being so vain because it didn't suit me, and besides we both looked good in the picture (good genes, he said). I stormed off to my room and slammed the door and I could hear him laughing and telling Mum.

It would be fine. I was almost sure of it. Edinburgh's not *that* small. I'd have to be extremely unlucky for Kate to somehow miraculously see that picture. I'd just have to cross my fingers and hope that it didn't happen. And be more careful in future. There was too much at stake.

I saw Kate the day she got back. Neither of us wanted to wait a minute longer than we had to. I arrived at the cafe ten minutes early. We only had an hour before she had to head home for her piano lesson. I thought it was a bit much that she had to have a lesson the day she got back.

When she walked in the door I literally breathed

a sigh of relief. The longest week of my life was over. Finally. It was incredible to see her face light up as if she felt exactly the same way. She rushed towards me and the strap of her bag caught on the handle of a pushchair at the next table. She got all flustered trying to disentangle herself while apologizing to the woman whose baby she'd just woken up. It was a scene straight out of a romantic comedy.

Kate was finally in front of me, blushing and out of breath. She dropped her bag and flung her arms around me and it seemed like we stayed like that for the longest time. It felt . . . right. That's the only way I can explain it. Profoundly *right*.

When we sat down, Kate scooted her chair across so she was sitting next to me and we could hold hands. When the waitress came over to take Kate's order she smiled as if maybe she remembered what it was like to be our age and in love. Because I think that's what it was, even then. I was in love with Kate. I wasn't sure when I'd started loving her, or exactly what it meant, but that didn't stop me knowing it. And it made me feel good to know it, even though I had no intention of putting it into words. I didn't want to freak her out.

Kate didn't have a tan – she was so fair she had to stay out of the sun – but a tiny sprinkling of freckles had appeared across her nose. 'Nice freckles,' I said.

Kate shielded her face with her hand and half-turned away. 'I hate them!'

I grabbed her hand and held it tightly in mine. 'Well I happen to think they're seriously cute.'

'*Really?*' She was always saying that. Usually whenever I said something nice or paid her a compliment. As if she found it hard to believe that there was anything worthwhile about her.

'Yes, really.' I kissed her nose and she laughed as she tried to squirm out of my embrace.

She was serious all sudden. She held my face in her hands and looked at me as if she was trying to memorize my features. She was looking so hard it made me wonder how she wasn't able to see me for who I really was. Maybe she didn't *want* to see the real me. 'God, I missed you.'

I smiled. 'I missed you too.'

'*Really?*' This time I just rolled my eyes. I wasn't about to admit that I'd spent the whole week thinking about her. But Kate said as much – that the only thing that had made a whole week with her mum bearable was knowing I was waiting for her when she got home. Then she kissed me and there was something a bit forceful about it – almost desperate. I pulled away after a second or two because I was worried about people looking at us, but when I looked around no one was paying any attention.

Kate had bought me a present. She acted all shy about it, like she wasn't quite sure if we were at the present-buying stage yet. It was a necklace, except I'm not sure it's called a necklace if it's for a boy. Still, it was a leather string with a cool black stone on it. I put it on straightaway and told her I loved it. I really *did* love it – it was just like one Jamie used to wear. I liked the fact that something Kate had given me would be close to my heart. I probably should have told her that.

I'd got her something too. I'd bought it a couple of days ago when I was at the newsagents. Kate laughed when I pulled it out of my bag, slightly dented. 'Oh my God, you remembered?!'

I shrugged, not wanting to show that I was pleased with myself. She'd mentioned she used to be obsessed with Kinder Surprise even though she hated the chocolate. It was all about the tiny little toy inside. Kate tore into the wrapper and broke the chocolate eggshell in half. She held a shard of chocolate between her fingers and gestured for me to take it. I ate it while she opened up the yellow plastic capsule. It was a little panda; Kate loves pandas. I couldn't have planned it any better. I'd spent less than a quid and Kate was acting like I'd bought her diamonds.

Kate thought it was really cool that we'd bought each other a present at the same time. I thought it was pretty lucky I'd been stuck behind the old lady who insisted on paying for her cigarettes with pennies, meaning I had time to notice the Kinder eggs in the first place. It was luck, pure and simple.

An hour with Kate was not enough. I kept on looking at my phone to check the time. Five minutes before she had to go, she turned to look at me and it was obvious that she had something she needed to say but wasn't all that keen on saying it. I looked at her expectantly.

Kate coughed a cough that wasn't really a cough. 'So.'

'So what?'

'My mum wants to meet you.' She scrunched up the Kinder wrapper.

I very nearly spat out my tea. 'Um . . . what?'

'She wants you to come round for dinner. This week.'

Meeting was bad enough but *dinner*? That was just . . . no. There were so many things I wanted to say – different variations of 'no' – but I kept my mouth shut.

'Alex? Say something . . . please?' She squeezed my hand then entwined her fingers in mine.

'What do you want me to say?' That came out a little harsher than I meant it to.

'I just want to know what you're thinking.' She often wanted to know what I was thinking; I never asked her what she was thinking. Thoughts are private.

I sighed. 'So your mum knows about me?'

Kate looked puzzled. 'Er . . . yes? Of course she does! Why? Do your parents not know about *me*?' She withdrew her hand from mine. That had to be a bad sign.

'It's none of their business.'

She was quiet then. I waited her out. I find that most people will talk if you let the silence go on for long enough. 'Are you . . .? You're not ashamed of me, are you?' Her voice was small.

'No! I just don't really talk to my folks about stuff like that. It's nothing to do with you, Kate. Honestly.'

She didn't look entirely convinced but she didn't push it. 'I had to tell Mum – she knew something was up anyway. Apparently I've been wandering around with my head in the clouds or something. She even asked if it was a boy.'

I should have probably seen this coming. Meeting the parents was a normal thing to do in a relationship – I *knew* that. Jamie had done it enough times – dressing up in his least scruffy clothes and heading off to some girl's house, coming back with stories that had Mum laughing so hard she got hiccups (especially the time when he blocked the toilet).

I was in a *relationship* now. I should have thought ahead, but I'd been too wrapped up in the bubble of me and Kate to see anything outside of it.

'Alex? Are you OK?'

I shook myself. 'Yeah, fine.' I reclaimed her hand and immediately felt better. Whenever I was touching her I felt more settled.

'So you'll come round for dinner then?'

I kissed her on the cheek. 'Of course I will.' There was no other option, was there?

'Thank you. It'll just make things a lot easier, you know? Once she's met you and seen how amazing you are.' That made me smile. 'I'll tell her to be on her best behaviour. It'll be fine.'

'If you say so . . .'

'I *do* say so. And I'm pretty much always right. So there. And I was thinking . . . maybe I could meet your . . .' Kate looked at her watch. 'SHIT! I'm going to be late!' She kissed me quickly on the lips and said she'd text later to let me know what day for dinner.

I stayed in the cafe after she left, trying not to think about the ordeal ahead. I'd have to be very, very careful to make sure Kate's mum didn't suspect anything. And after it was over, I'd have to come up with some reason why Kate couldn't meet my parents or come to my house – ever. It was exhausting, always having to think and worry and plan ahead. But it was worth it. *She* was worth it.

chapter thirteen

I knocked on the front door. It was pale green, newly painted by the look of it. The house was a bungalow, semi-detached. Pretty nice if you didn't mind living so far out of town. The bus had taken forever to get there, but forever wasn't long enough for me that day. I pictured the bus crashing. Not a bad crash – just serious enough that I'd have a good excuse to go straight home instead of going to Kate's house. But the bus driver clearly had other plans. She drove steadily and carefully and even managed to drop me off on Portobello High Street a bit early.

The last time I'd been to Portobello was a few years before with Mum, Dad and Jamie. Mum was on one of her 'doing things as a family' kicks and every Sunday we went somewhere different. That day was typically Edinburgh – windy and cold, with some driving rain added in for good measure – but

Dad insisted on a walk on the beach before lunch in the pub. We had the beach to ourselves, apart from a few mad dog-walkers. Jamie chased me along the sand and we hurdled over the wooden barriers that led down to the sea. Mum ran too – laughing as the wind whipped her hair around her head. It was a good day.

I'd spent even longer than usual getting ready. Double and triple checking the binding round my breasts. I was wearing a pair of jeans I'd found in Jamie's room and a shirt of his that I'd nicked a couple of years back. I wanted to look decent and respectable, so Mrs McAllister wouldn't be appalled at the thought of her daughter spending time with me. But I also wanted to look like a teenage boy. I wasn't about to turn up wearing a jacket and tie or something. I'd zipped up my jacket before leaving my room so that Mum wouldn't notice that my boobs had disappeared. I told her I was going to the cinema with Jonni and Fitz and she seemed pleased about that.

Kate answered the door after I knocked for the third time. 'Sorry! Sorry! Have you been there long? We were in the kitchen with the music on. You brought me flowers!' I'd bought them from M&S before getting on the bus. Mum always taught us never to go to someone's house empty-handed. She'd have been proud – if I could have told her.

'Um . . . they're for your mum. Sorry.' I shuffled past Kate into the hallway beyond. It was cosy-looking – soft lighting, a multi-coloured stripey rug, lots of pictures on the walls. Classical music was blaring from the back of the house.

'Oh. That'll get you definite brownie points. Good idea.' She closed the door and leaned against it. She was wearing jeans too. A slouchy wide-necked red jumper. Bare feet. She looked more beautiful than ever.

I took a deep, long breath. I felt like I was about to go onstage in front of hundreds of people and I'd forgotten my lines. Which is exactly what happened in primary school when we were all forced to be in a production of Oliver! I'd been desperate to be in Fagin's gang of pickpockets – all grubby faces, caps, boots and torn trousers. But instead I had to play a housemaid, wearing a dress, an apron and a stupid hat like a shower cap. I was gutted.

'Don't I get a kiss?' Kate pouted.

The girl had clearly lost her mind. '*Here?*'

Kate rolled her eyes and shook her head. She moved closer, wrapped her arms around me and whispered, 'Mum's busy in the kitchen. She won't leave that risotto for a second, I promise.'

Risotto. Great. Food the same texture of vomit wasn't exactly high on my list of favourite things to eat. I kissed Kate briefly. No matter what she said I didn't want to risk her mum catching us. I *had* to make a good first impression.

Kate didn't look pleased at the poor excuse for a kiss, but she knew how nervous I was so she let me get away with it. She took my jacket and hoodie and hung them up on a peg near the front door. I noticed the neat line of shoes underneath the hooks just as Kate asked if I wouldn't mind taking my shoes off. That's when I remembered. *Fuck. Socks.* Why hadn't I thought about socks? I'd been washing my own clothes recently. I told Mum it was about time I started doing more stuff for myself, to give her a bit of a break. The real reason was that I didn't want her snooping around my room, asking questions about the clothes I was wearing. So I'd run out of the plain black socks I normally wore and instead of raiding Jamie's room for an old pair of his, I found a pair in the back of my sock drawer. They were purple – and covered in tiny pink hearts. With bows on.

'Um . . . do I have to?'

'It's kind of a house rule since we got the new carpets last year.'

My mind had gone blank. I had no idea how to

explain away the very unmanly socks. This whole thing was going to unravel because of a pair of bloody socks that my grandmother had given to me four years ago.

'Um . . .'

Kate crossed her arms and looked unimpressed. 'You've got holes in your socks, haven't you?'

Yes. *Yes.* That was exactly the sort of reason a boy would be reluctant to take his shoes off before meeting his girlfriend's mother for the first time.

'Well just make sure you wipe your feet really well on the mat. That'll have to do, I suppose. But if you think I'm sewing your socks for you you've got no chance, OK? I'll teach you how to do it sometime but that's it.' She smiled. Her lecturing voice was pretty adorable.

'I'd never dream of asking you to do that! What do you think I am? Some kind of caveman or something?'

'You boys are all the same.' She elbowed me in the side as she passed by.

I grabbed her round the waist and kissed her neck. She squealed and escaped from my clutches. 'Don't! You'll squish the flowers!'

I was giddy with relief. Somehow the socks thing had worked out in my favour. Someone up there must be looking down on me, helping me out. Either that or I was way luckier than I deserved to be.

Kate took my hand and squeezed it encouragingly as she led me into the kitchen. The smells wafting through the half-open door weren't particularly vomity, so I could at least stop stressing about the possibility of spewing everywhere.

The kitchen was cosy too. Smaller than ours, but nicer, somehow. There was a round table, set for three. The floral napkins had been folded into fans – I guessed that was Kate's handiwork. There were flowers already on the table, and they were way nicer than the ones I'd brought. I cursed myself for not spending that extra fiver.

A woman stood in front of the stove, stirring the pot in front of her. Kate nipped over to the iPod dock and turned the music down, which made the woman turn around.

So this was Kate's mum. Her hair was really short and greying, but it suited her. She wore a long burgundy skirt and a black blouse. Ornate silver earrings dangled from her ears. The whole look was smart and elegant . . . until you looked down at her feet. She was wearing a huge pair of furry pink slippers – the kind Mum used to buy me when I was a kid. I figured someone who wore slippers like that couldn't be *that* scary.

Mrs McAllister smiled when she saw us – a quick,

nervous sort of smile. 'So this is the famous Alex! It's lovely to meet you. I've heard *a lot* about you.'

We shook hands and I tried to go for a proper man's handshake, squeezing harder than I normally would. 'It's lovely to meet you too, Mrs McAllister.'

'Please, call me Belinda.' She was wincing slightly so I must have been squeezing too hard. I dropped her hand and coughed to cover the awkwardness. She looked down at my shoes and I thought she was about to say something, but Kate intervened with 'Look, Mum! Alex brought you flowers. I told you he was a gentleman, didn't I?'

I held out the flowers, obstructing Mrs McAllister's view of my not entirely spotless Vans.

'Oh, you shouldn't have! Gosh, it's been *years* since a man bought me flowers! Thank you, Alex. They're beautiful.' She took the flowers and sniffed them, because that seems to be what you're supposed to do when you get flowers.

'Mum, don't you think you'd better get back to stirring that risotto. Remember the Great Risotto Disaster of 2012?'

Mrs McAllister's eyes widened and she rushed back to the stove and started stirring frantically, flowers in one hand, spoon in the other. 'Don't you even think about sticking to the bottom of the pan.

Don't you *dare.*' Yup, she was talking to the rice. It was easy to see where Kate got some of her more eccentric qualities from. As for the rest, I had no idea. She hardly ever talked about her dad.

Kate took my hand and said, 'I'm just going to show Alex my room, if that's OK?'

I thought Mrs McAllister might have something to say about that – there might be a 'no boys in the bedroom' rule – but she just waved us on our way, too busy glaring at the rice.

Kate led the way along the hall and into her room. It was small and very, very feminine. The walls were pink and the bed was covered with more cushions than there were in my entire flat. There was a white dressing table with a white stool in front of it. There were a few cuddly pandas dotted around the place, the largest of which had pride of place in the middle of the bed.

'It's a bit babyish, isn't it?' Kate sat on the edge of the bed.

'Not at all. It's . . . nice.' It really was. There was something very Kate about it.

'Really? I was going to tidy all those things away – get rid of the pandas, at least, but I decided not to. I . . . I think I wanted you to see it like this. I didn't want to pretend to be something I'm not, you know? I do enough of that at school.' I sat down next to her and took her hand in mine. 'I don't have to pretend with you, Alex.'

'You really don't.'

We kissed and I tried to focus on the kissing, pushing the guilt down as far as it would go. It was getting harder and harder to ignore. Whenever she said something like that, I was torn between wanting to punch the air in joy and wanting to drop down to my knees and confess everything. Nothing was simple anymore; every morsel of happiness was slightly tarnished. But even tarnished happiness is better than no happiness at all.

Kate obviously sensed that I wasn't feeling it, and she pulled away and looked at me questioningly.

'Your mum seems really nice.'

'Wow. You're thinking about my mum when I'm kissing you? I'm clearly going to have to work on my technique.'

I gave her a withering look. 'Your technique's just fine and you know it! I could kiss you forever and never get tired of it.' Saying something soppy often seemed like the best way to distract her.

'You do realize that you're about as smooth as sandpaper, don't you?' She kissed my nose. 'But I appreciate the sentiment.'

'I appreciate your appreciating.'

'I appreciate your appreciating my appreciating . . . Now this is just getting silly.' She looked towards the door like she was using X-ray vision to check her mum wasn't earwigging on the other side. 'Right, here's the lowdown: there's nothing Mum likes more than good manners, so try not to talk with your mouth full or put your elbows on the table . . . not that you would – I'm just saying! Try not to talk about religion if you don't want her to go off on one and quiz you about what you do and don't believe. Um . . . other things to avoid . . . let me see . . . probably best to steer clear of politics. And she's a total feminist, just so you know.'

'You're babbling again.' I stroked the back of her hand with my thumb. 'You told me to tell you when you babbled.'

'Sorry. I know. I'm just . . . I was feeling fine about this – looking forward to it, even – but now that you're here I just really, really want it to go well. I want you two to get along.'

I pulled her into my embrace and held her tight. 'There's nothing to worry about, OK? Everything's going to be fine.' I said this as much to reassure myself as to reassure Kate.

'DINNER!' Mrs McAllister's yell was loud enough to summon diners within a five-mile radius.

I tried to remember my words as we headed into the kitchen. *There's nothing to worry about. Everything's going to be fine.*

chapter fourteen

It *was* fine, mostly. I negotiated my way round the risotto, telling Mrs McAllister that it was the tastiest risotto I'd ever had. This wasn't even a lie, although technically it wasn't the *whole* truth either. We drank organic elderflower cordial from wine glasses. Mrs McAllister drank the same as us – my mum would have been caning the wine, for sure.

I left most of the talking to Kate and her mum. They had this big debate about the merits of vegetarianism, which seemed pointless because neither of them were vegetarians. When Mrs McAllister eventually asked for my opinion I came out with 'Um . . . I can see both sides . . . but I like bacon,' which made her roll her eyes and say 'Men!' with an exaggerated sigh. Kate grinned at me and I had to take a sip of cordial to mask my smile.

Kate clearly seemed to think things were going OK.

Occasionally her bare foot would brush against my leg, like a reminder that we were in this together. It was comforting. Mrs McAllister asked me a few questions. Nothing too tricky – what subjects I liked at school, what I got up to in my spare time. I answered each question honestly, which made me feel better about the whole situation. A couple of times I caught her looking at me weirdly – eyes slightly narrowed as if something wasn't quite right but she couldn't put her finger on it. But maybe that was just me being paranoid.

When Mrs McAllister went rummaging into the freezer for sorbet for pudding, Kate scooted over in her seat and kissed me, slipping her tongue into my mouth. I pulled away so fast my elbow knocked my empty glass off the table; it smashed on the floor and Kate's mum yelped in shock. *Great. Those glasses are probably family heirlooms – handed down over generations, priceless.*

Mrs McAllister hurried over. 'Oh my word! You nearly gave me a heart attack!'

My face was red and hot. 'I'm sorry, I . . .'

Kate interrupted me. 'I'm such a klutz! Sorry, I was just trying to help with the clearing up.'

'Not to worry. I was due a trip to IKEA soon anyway. Just be careful of the broken glass.' So it wasn't a family heirloom after all.

Mrs McAllister got out the dustpan and brush and started sweeping up the glass. I mouthed 'thank you' to Kate over the top of her head and Kate smiled sweetly. I didn't feel bad about her taking the blame – it was her fault in the first place.

We sat and ate our sorbet; it made my teeth hurt. Whenever her mum wasn't looking Kate kept licking the spoon in a very non-PG sort of way. She was just joking around rather than trying to do a genuine porn-star thing . . . I think.

After dinner we went through to the sitting room. The piano was definitely the focus of the room – the sofa was angled towards it instead of facing the TV like in a normal house. There were loads of pictures of Kate – one of them was a photo of the fattest, smiliest baby I'd ever seen. I made a mental note to tease her about that later.

Kate sat next to me on the sofa. We were holding hands even though I really didn't feel comfortable doing that in front of her mum. We'd been chatting for maybe two minutes when Mrs McAllister said, 'Kate, why don't you play something for us?'

I could feel Kate tense up immediately; her hand gripped mine even tighter. 'Oh Alex isn't really into classical music, Mum.'

I resented the implication that I was some kind of heathen. 'That's not true. I'd love to hear you play.' The look on Mrs McAllister's face told me that I'd earned a gold star. The look on Kate's face told me I'd earned a black mark. So they pretty much cancelled each other out.

'I don't really feel like it. Alex, why don't you tell Mum about that tour we did? She reckons she'd be too scared but I told her it'd be fine, wouldn't it?' Kate looked at me intently. There was definitely something weird going on.

'Yes, yes, you can tell me all about that in a minute. Why don't you play the Chopin you've been working on? I really do think you've mastered it now.'

'I *said* I didn't want to play.'

'It's fine, Mrs McAllister. Really. Kate's right – I don't know the first thing about classical music . . . but yeah, you should definitely do the tour of Mary King's Close – it's really interesting and–'

'Why are you being so stubborn about this, Katherine?' All the softness had disappeared from Mrs McAllister's voice.

Kate let go of my hand. 'I'm not being stubborn! I just don't feel like playing, that's all. I'm not some performing seal, you know!'

'You're going to need to get over this phobia of

yours if you're going to be a professional pianist. It's really getting beyond a joke now, don't you think?'

'How many times do I have to tell you that I don't want to be a bloody pianist?! You NEVER listen to me! I can't believe you're doing this in front of Alex – you ruin *everything*!' She stood up and stormed out of the room. There was no door slamming, at least.

My first instinct was to go after her, but I didn't know if that would be rude or disrespectful to Mrs McAllister. I didn't know the rules.

Kate's mum was sipping her coffee as if nothing had happened. Clearly this was a regular occurrence in the McAllister household.

'Um . . . I should go and see if she's . . .' It felt like I needed her permission to leave the room.

'She loves the piano, you know. She wants to play professionally more than anything. And she could do it – her teacher said she's got real potential. She just lacks . . . focus. *That's* what makes the difference. I know it's hard for a girl her age – I really do understand that. But it's so important to think about the future and not get distracted.'

Mrs McAllister's eyes bored holes into my brain when she said 'distracted'. There was no doubt what she was getting at, I just wondered whether she was going to come right out and say it. Was she actually about to launch into the whole stay-away-from-my-daughter thing? I stayed quiet, resisting the urge to apologize or reassure her or say whatever it was that she wanted me to say.

'You seem like an intelligent boy, Alex.' I shrugged – she was half right. 'I'm sure you care about what's best for Kate.'

I nodded. Of course I cared; I just wasn't sure exactly *what* was best for her. I didn't want to think about it too much in case it turned out that what was best for Kate didn't include me. I *thought* I made her happy – Kate *said* I made her happy. But what if her mum was right? What if spending time with me was jeopardizing her future? What if . . . I shook myself. It wasn't going to work. If Mrs McAllister wanted me to stay away from Kate she was going to have to say so, or lock Kate in her room or something. And for some reason I reckoned she wouldn't do either of those things.

I stood and hitched up my jeans. 'Thank you for a lovely dinner, Mrs McAllister. I'm sure my mum would love the recipe for that risotto . . . I'm just going to check on Kate and then I'd better be getting home. Mum really doesn't like me staying out late on a school night.' I smiled my most genuine parent-pleasing smile and left the room before she had a chance to say anything else.

Kate was lying face down on the bed, crying. I sat on the edge of the bed and put my hand on the small of her back. 'Maybe I should have told your mum I think a woman's place is in the home . . . Might have taken some of the heat off you, eh?'

'Alex, would you mind leaving?' Her voice was thick with tears and muffled by the pillow. 'I don't want you to see me like this.'

'Hey, it's OK. It's nothing to stress about. We *all* argue with our parents.'

'I can't believe she did that in front of you. I'm sorry.'

'No sorries, OK?'

'She just . . . I hate her sometimes. I really do.' She turned her head to look at me; her face was blotchy and her eyes were red. 'How bad do I look?'

'Blotchy and red?' I grinned and Kate swatted at me, but there was a tiny smile on her face at least.

'Oh God, you probably hate me, don't you?'

I shook my head and rolled my eyes. 'I could never hate you, Kate. Never. Listen, I'd better be heading home, but I don't want you to worry about anything. I mean it. I think you should talk to your mum, explain how you feel. I'm sure she'll understand.' I had no idea what I was talking about, but the words sounded sensible enough.

'You don't know what it's like. I'm really sorry I put you through this – no wonder you were so freaked out at the thought of meeting her! It's better when it's just the two of us, isn't it? Everyone else can just go and . . .'

'Jump off a bridge?'

'Yes. The whole lot of them. And we'll have the whole city to ourselves and do what we like, when we like, and sit on the front seat on the top of the bus every single time, and we'll just have this perfect life.' Kate was properly smiling now.

'But who's gonna drive the bus if everyone's jumped off a bridge?'

Kate's brow wrinkled in thought. 'You! You can drive the bus and it won't matter if you're not very good at it because there won't be anyone else on the road. I'll sit upstairs and shout where I want to go. You can be my chauffeur.'

We talked for a few more minutes, Kate getting more and more into the idea of everyone else disappearing off the face of the planet. I was quite taken by the idea too. If no one else existed, I'd be able to tell Kate my secret. She wouldn't have to worry about what anyone else thought or said. It would just be the two us, together. Like we were meant to be.

chapter fifteen

From then on we agreed to keep our parents out of it. It was Kate's idea, and she had no idea how relieved I was that I didn't need to come up with reasons why she couldn't come to my house. One less thing to worry about.

We met up at least a couple of evenings a week and usually spent either Saturday or Sunday together. As far as Mum was concerned I was still hanging out with Jonni and Fitz. Kate's mum stayed off her back as long as Kate kept up with her piano practice, which meant that she was practising harder than ever to make sure she was allowed to see me. There were a couple of awkward moments, like when Kate didn't understand why we could never meet each other straight after school. She said she wanted to spend every possible minute with me but I told her I had to train. The truth was I was skipping training sessions whenever they got in the way of me seeing Kate, but I still needed the time to go home and get ready.

Things were good. We got into a little routine, had our favourite places to go. Kate thought it was brilliant that I was always happy to get the bus to see her rather than for her to come to me. Apparently I was the best boyfriend *ever*. She said so when we were walking along the promenade one Sunday afternoon. That was the first time either of us had put a name to what this was. Kate blushed fiercely as soon as the words were out. 'I didn't mean to say that . . . Can we just pretend it never happened? I wouldn't want to presume that—' I put my finger up to her lips to silence her. 'How about we *don't* pretend it never happened? How about I'm completely fine with you presuming?' My finger on her lips stopped her from asking 'Really?' but I beat her to it and said '*Really*'. It was one of those perfect moments that seem so far removed from everyday life.

It was like a dream, those few weeks. A crazy, exciting, amazing dream. But it differed from most of my dreams in one fundamental way: I *knew* I'd have to wake up eventually. And as time went on, that 'eventually' was getting closer and closer to becoming 'soon'. I wasn't entirely stupid – I knew, deep down, that things couldn't carry on like this. The guilt got worse every single day.

I felt like I was running out of time and I was desperate to make the most of it — to wring out every last drop of happiness before my world imploded. Kate wasn't helping — with the physical side of things at least. She'd made it abundantly clear that she wanted to go further than kissing. A lot further. Lucky for me we did most of our kissing in public places.

It surprised me that she was so keen to take things further. I guess I'd thought she was all sweet and innocent. But I think the fact that she was sweet and innocent was part of the problem. Kate didn't want to be like that anymore. She was desperate to break away from that image of herself in any way she could. And sex was another way for her to do that. At least that's how I read the situation. Or maybe she just wanted to be closer to me.

I hadn't thought about sex. Or rather, whenever my mind had strayed in that direction I'd given myself a mental slap and rerouted my thoughts. It wasn't just the obvious fact that I couldn't do anything with Kate without her knowing I was a girl. That was a part of it, of course. There was also her age to think about — she was six months younger than me and wouldn't turn sixteen until 4th February. I knew loads of girls at school had been having sex for years, but

Kate wasn't like them. *I* wasn't like them.

I loved kissing Kate. As far as I was concerned there was nothing better in the whole world. All the guilt and worry slipped away and all there was to think about were her lips on mine.

I honestly didn't want to do more than kissing, not back then. It didn't seem *necessary*. Things were good as they were. All I wanted was the chance to do some kissing somewhere that wasn't freezing cold or surrounded by strangers staring at us. A sofa would have done the job. A bed would be too dangerous.

It was obvious that Kate wanted more from our relationship. Sometimes we'd be kissing and she'd say something like 'You can touch me . . . if you want to . . .' I'd usually just keep kissing her or mutter something about how much I liked kissing her. She thought I was being gentlemanly. It was fine for a couple of weeks but it was happening more and more, and the kissing was getting hotter and heavier no matter how much I tried to keep things soft and gentle. We got kicked out of a cafe in Leith, much to Kate's delight. The owner had said we were putting people off their food so we went down an alleyway and carried on kissing. Kate was pressing up against me in a way that she hadn't done before, as if she wanted every part of our bodies to be touching. And I swear on my life that this was the first time I thought about *it*. 'It' being a penis. Or lack thereof.

The issue hadn't come up before, but now I suddenly realized two things: 1) Kate would expect me to have a penis, and 2) She would probably expect me to be a little bit . . . um . . . excited with her all pressed up against me. It was all too disgusting to think about but as soon as her hand brushed my thigh and started snaking its way upward, I didn't have a choice. I was going to have to do something about it. I grabbed her hand and held it in mine, hoping she'd get the hint rather than giving it a go with the other hand. In between kisses, Kate whispered, 'Don't you want me to . . . ?'

'Not here.' I kissed her harder so she wouldn't think I was anything less than enthusiastic about the idea.

Kate pulled away, breathing heavily. '*Where* then? Mum's hardly ever out of the house, and from the sound of things your parents are the same. It would be so much easier if our parents actually had lives . . . Maybe we should rent a hotel room or something?'

I laughed; I couldn't help it. 'A hotel room?! Even if we could afford it – and we can't – I'm pretty sure you need to be 18 to book a room.' I had no idea if this was the case – I was just hoping Kate wouldn't know any different.

Kate sighed and leaned against the wall. 'I just . . . really want to be alone with you and it feels like the world is conspiring against us!' Classic dramatic Kate.

I leaned next to her. 'It'll happen. There's no rush though, is there?'

'Don't you want to be close to me?'

'Of course I do! You *know* that. But I don't want to pressure you into anything.'

'*You* pressure *me*? That's hardly the way things are going, is it?! If Mum knew what you were like, I swear she wouldn't have a problem with us two being alone in the house. She reckons all boys are the same – "only after one thing . . . blah blah blah". She has no idea about *anything*.'

I was going to have to get Kate's mood back on track if I wanted to avoid the day being completely ruined. 'You know what you need?'

Kate shook her head, still frowning.

'Cake. A big slice of triple chocolate cake and a cup of tea.'

She was wearing her unimpressed face with glee. 'Cake? You honestly think chocolate cake is going to make me feel better right now? That's such a bloody cliché! Not all girls like chocolate cake, you know!'

I waited, trying my best not to smile. It took five — maybe six — seconds. 'OK, OK! You *know* I like cake. Especially with tea. But *I'm* buying. So there.' I kissed her nose. 'But that doesn't mean I'm forgetting about this. We need to be alone. Soon.'

That 'soon' made it impossible for me to enjoy the rest of the afternoon. That and wondering what the hell I was going to do about my non-existent penis.

chapter sixteen

I tried to approach it like a logic problem, instead of thinking about what it *actually* meant. I tried out all the options while wearing a pair of Jamie's pants. (I gave them a sniff first to make sure they were clean.) The two main things to consider were size and hardness. I didn't want it to be noticeable, exactly, but I didn't want Kate realizing it wasn't there. It would be a bit weird to go from nothing at all to a massive bulge in my trousers. Hardness was a trickier problem to deal with. I didn't want Kate thinking I had a permanent erection, but then again the times when she would be close enough to feel it would be the exact same times she might expect me to have one.

I stood in front of the mirror each time, trying to stand like Jamie. Sort of slouchy, legs apart. I stuck out my crotch and examined it from all angles.

It would have been funny if it wasn't so disgusting. Nothing seemed to be working . . . I just looked *wrong*, no matter what I stuffed down there. Then I had a brainwave. I found what I needed in the kitchen, in the drawer under the kettle.

It seemed OK when I looked in the mirror this time, and more importantly it *felt* right. It looked like I was touching myself up in front of the mirror like some kind of pervert, but I had to make the necessary adjustments. I've never actually touched a penis in real life; the thought of it is enough to make me gag. I figured Kate wouldn't have touched one either, so she'd have no point of reference.

It was hard enough but not *too* hard. Not exactly comfortable but I'd just have to get used to it. I'd have to hand-wash Jamie's pants and dry them at the back of my wardrobe. And I'd have to be extra careful not to let Mum or Dad see me or I'd have a lot of explaining to do.

I changed back into my pants and buckled up my jeans, then I grabbed a few more pairs of Jamie's pants before heading back to my room. My 'penis' was safely wrapped up in the bundle of pants.

The penis was made up of a tube of Mum's favourite extra-strong mints, snugly wrapped up in two of Jamie's white gym socks. I just had to hope that Kate wouldn't get close enough to sniff my minty-fresh crotch.

It didn't take long for me to get used to stuffing a packet of mints down my pants – just like the bandages round my boobs. I wore it in my room when Mum and Dad were out, just to practise walking around and sitting. It made me walk differently, which was a good thing in terms of passing as a boy, but I didn't want Kate to suddenly notice I was walking funny.

The penis got its first official outing one Saturday in early December. Kate wanted to do some Christmas shopping and go to the German Christmas market in Princes Street Gardens. I'd already done most of my shopping online – why battle through hordes of people when you can lie on your bed with your laptop? I hadn't got Kate's present though – I was drawing a serious blank where that was concerned.

Kate gave me major puppy-dog eyes when we walked past the ice rink, so I relented and bought two tickets. The skates they gave her were white; mine were black and a bit too big for me. No worries with the socks this time – I'd learned my lesson.

Kate had been ice-skating a couple of times before and while she wasn't exactly pirouetting or whatever, she was a hell of a lot more graceful than me. I was like a baby giraffe, all wobbly, legs going in different directions. I stayed close to the edge so I could hold on to the barrier. Kate held my other hand and tried not to laugh. She thought it was adorable that I was so rubbish, given that I'm not too shabby on a skateboard. She laughed hysterically when I protested that ice was a very different medium to pavement.

I tried to ignore the humiliation of little kids zooming past me at high speed. And I managed not to swear when I fell on my arse right in front of a gang of giggling girls. After fifteen minutes or so Kate took pity on me. 'Come on, I think you've had enough for now. We should probably get you off the ice before you do some real damage.'

When we were changing back into our shoes, Kate said, 'Thank you for that.' Something in her tone made me look up.

'Thanks for what? Making a total fool of myself in front of hundreds of people? You're very welcome.'

She dismissed my joke with a shake of her head. 'I'm serious. It means a lot that you did that even though you obviously didn't want to.'

I shrugged. 'It's no big deal.'

'It *is* though. You always go out of your way to do things that make me happy.' Her eyes were shining and I was worried she was going to burst into tears in front of all these people.

I shrugged again. 'That's kind of my job, isn't it?'

'Well you're really very good at it. I just wanted you to know that I appreciate you. I do know how lucky I am, you know.' She leaned over and gave me a quick kiss on the lips. 'You're the best boyfriend in the entire history of the world.'

The humiliation and bruises had been worth it.

We wandered round the Christmas market, Kate babbling away about whether she should buy one of those creepy nutcracker dolls to give to someone for Christmas.

'Maybe for someone you hate?' I was very helpful when it came to shopping.

'Haven't you seen the ballet? With the mice and the soldier and Clara and oh it's so beautiful!' She started singing the music from The Nutcracker, which I sort of recognized. Then she started doing some ballet moves, right in the middle of the market with people everywhere. She really didn't give a toss what anyone thought. Usually I'd be looking round to see who was watching and getting all embarrassed, but that day I just stood back and laughed. She looked so happy, all wrapped up in her winter coat and woolly scarf, bobble hat bobbing as she danced.

Kate stopped dead right in front of a girl about the same age as us. She was wearing pink ear muffs and a puffy white jacket. She looked like a marshmallow, and not in a good way. A short, stocky boy with a popped collar was lurking behind her.

'Astrid! Hi! This is . . . I didn't see you there!' Kate normally sounded happy and enthusiastic, but I could tell her reaction was forced – she was overdoing it by at least 20 per cent.

The girl raised one eyebrow and you could tell she thought she was the bee's fucking knees. I disliked her already. 'Clearly. If I'd heard you were doing a street show down here I'd have called Stella – she'd hate to miss this.'

Kate didn't tell her to piss off, which was a bit disappointing. 'So . . . what are you doing here? And this must be Justin! I've heard so much about you, it's so great to finally meet you. Kate smiled warmly at the boy and he smiled back a bit blankly. It was obvious he hadn't heard anything about *her*.

Astrid grabbed hold of Justin's arm and pulled him close to her. 'Justin and I have been Christmas shopping, and he *insists* on spoiling me when we should be looking for presents for his family. He just bought me these ear muffs!' Astrid turned this way and that so we could get the full effect of the ear muffs. 'Aren't they the cutest thing?'

Kate smiled. 'The absolute cutest.' If she was being sarcastic, she hid it well.

'I know, right? And that's not even my Christmas present. He's buying me a watch!'

Then there was this silence in which Astrid looked at me pointedly. Kate turned to see what she was looking at and seemed almost surprised to see me standing next to her. 'Oh . . . yes . . . this is Alex. Alex, this is Astrid and her boyfriend Justin.'

'Hi.' The tone I was going for was mild enthusiasm with a dash of nonchalance.

Justin reached over to shake my hand and I mentally prepared for bone-crunching, but his hand shake was surprisingly limp for a boy who was almost as wide as he was tall. 'Alright, mate?' he said. I had him pegged straightaway. English. Rugby player. Wanker.

Kate hadn't been spending much time with Astrid recently, I knew that much. She'd told me that Astrid had a new boyfriend, and that they met at around the same time Kate and I did. I'm sure Kate had told me his name, but I had a tendency to tune out whenever Kate talked about her so-called friends. They sounded awful. I had no idea why Kate would spend any time with them at all, let alone care about their love lives.

I told Astrid it was nice to meet her and she smirked. It was definitely a smirk rather than a smile. Then there was an awkward silence as the four of us played chicken over who was going to speak next. There was no way in hell it was going to be me. I didn't know these people – it wasn't my responsibility to keep up the small talk. In the end, Kate and Astrid relented at the same time.

Kate said, 'Well, we'd better be getting . . .' and Astrid said, 'Why don't you two join us for a cup of tea? Justin was just telling me about this place up on the Mound that does, like, totally amazing cakes.'

Justin nodded and said 'yeah' but it sounded much closer to 'yah'. 'Mum raves about the place. I've been meaning to take A there for ages.' I was surprised he didn't say 'Mummy' but that was probably just me being uncharitable. The fact that he called Astrid 'A' annoyed me too, but I couldn't quite work out why. It was almost like he was too lazy to use her whole name. Or maybe he went out with a lot of girls whose name began with that letter and this way he avoided saying the wrong name by accident.

Kate looked at me to see what I wanted to do but my face was deliberately, unhelpfully blank. It was her call. 'Um . . .' She was clearly hoping I'd step in, maybe with some carefully crafted lie that we'd love to but we had other plans and maybe next time. And I wanted to step in – I really did – but more than that I wanted Kate to stand up for herself in front of this girl.

Astrid took Kate by the arm. 'Oh come on, it'll be fun! Our first ever double date!' Astrid didn't wait for Kate to agree; she practically dragged her away from the market stalls, heading towards the steps to the top of the Mound. Kate turned around and mouthed 'sorry' when Justin wasn't looking. I shrugged as if it was no big deal.

The truth is, I was scared.

Pretending to be a boy around Kate was one thing.

Pretending to be a boy around an *actual* boy was a whole different ball game. No pun intended.

chapter seventeen

The cafe was busy but Astrid insisted on waiting instead of finding somewhere quieter. Kate and I stood by the door with Astrid and Justin in front of us. Astrid kept kissing Justin and you could tell it made him uncomfortable. She was doing it purely for show, that much was obvious. Kate just smiled like she didn't even notice, although her grip on my hand was firmer than normal. Thankfully she didn't try to compete with Astrid by sticking her tongue down my throat or anything.

The girls ordered a pot of tea to share and Justin had a latte. I said I wasn't thirsty, which was a lie. I just knew I'd need the loo if I drank anything; I couldn't risk it. I always drank less than Kate whenever we were out. I don't think she ever noticed.

Astrid and Kate were sitting next to each other, chatting away. Well Astrid was doing most of the talking and Kate was doing a lot of nodding. I'd never seen her like this before – quiet, deferential almost. I didn't like it.

'So . . . are you watching the match later?' Justin was sitting back in his chair, legs spread apart, taking up a lot of my space. I checked myself – I needed to remember to sit like a boy. I sat back and mimicked his position but then our knees touched and we both shrank back.

'What match?' I asked, before I realized that this was probably the sort of thing a boy would know. *Jamie* would know for sure. Then I noticed Justin's rugby shirt. An *England* rugby shirt, all pristine white. My first impression had been dead-on. 'Oh right, yeah . . . sorry mate, I was miles away there. Nah, I'm not really into team sports. More into skating . . . that kind of thing.' That seemed like a safer option than trying to bullshit about rugby, a sport that seemed to be entirely based on big guys grappling with each other for no discernible reason.

Justin looked baffled but tried to hide it. Clearly all of his 'mates' were into guy-grappling too; I was *different* somehow. Which was fine, as long as he didn't have any idea exactly how different I was.

I could see Astrid staring at me out of the corner of my eye. It made me more than a little uncomfortable.

I had no idea why Kate would be friends with someone like her. She couldn't have been more different to Kate – exactly the sort of girl I went out of my way to avoid at school. I was trying to concentrate on what Justin was saying about rugby, but I could feel her eyes burning into me and I knew it was only a matter of time before she– 'So, Alex . . . Kate tells me you go to Fettes? Justin's at Stewart's Melville. They're, like, really close to each other, aren't they?'

I should have known this would come back to bite me. Edinburgh may be a city but it's a small one. Nice if you want to walk around without having to take a bus everywhere, not so great if you want to lie and keep secrets. 'Oh, yeah. They are.'

Justin slapped me on the back, harder than was strictly necessary. Maybe he was trying to make up for the lame handshake. 'Shame you're not into rugby – I've flattened a lot of Fettes players over the past couple of years.'

'That *is* a shame.' I didn't even have a drink to sip to cover my awkwardness.

'Did you see the black eye Gavin Drysdale had last week? All my own work.'

Justin looked smug at the thought of having bruised a fellow human being, but I guess it was supposed to be acceptable because it happened playing sport.

Astrid rolled her eyes affectionately and called him an animal, which made him look even prouder. Kate didn't look too impressed.

I had to tread carefully here. 'Gavin? Yeah, I think I've seen him around.' That seemed like a safe kind of non-answer.

Justin looked a bit puzzled. 'He's head boy, isn't he?'

Shit. 'Yeah, that's right. I know who you mean now . . . I don't really get involved in school politics. Not really my scene.' *Shit.*

There was silence at the table. Astrid was staring at me again; she knew something was up. You didn't exactly have to be a genius to know something was up. I chanced a look over at Kate. She wasn't glaring at me – if anything, she just looked curious.

Justin stepped in to smash the silence. 'Ha! The way Gav tells it he's some big man on campus . . .'

This was getting worse. And I was desperate for the loo all of a sudden. 'He is, I guess. We don't exactly move in the same circles though. Anyway, listen . . . I'd better be getting–'

'Yes, we've got to go. We're having dinner with Alex's parents.' Kate started wrapping her scarf around her neck. I put a fiver on the table to cover Kate's share of the bill; I just wanted to get out of there as quickly as possible. Kate didn't argue about me paying – she wanted to escape as much as I did.

We said our goodbyes and were out of there in a couple of minutes. I glanced back before shutting the door behind us; Astrid was watching me. Kate and I walked down to the bottom of the Mound in silence; we weren't holding hands. Darkness had fallen while we'd been in the cafe and Princes Street was looking all sparkly and Christmassy. It had started to rain.

I caved. 'Why did you lie like that?'

Kate shrugged. 'I didn't like the way she was looking at you. She can be so judgemental sometimes. Her heart's in the right place though . . . at least I think it is.' I wasn't so sure.

I stopped walking. 'I . . .'

'It's OK, Alex. You don't have to explain. And you don't have to be ashamed about not being in with the so-called 'cool' crowd or the rugby players or whoever. I like you just the way you are.'

I could hardly believe it. She thought I was such a loser, such a social recluse, that I barely knew the head boy of my own school. Did she honestly believe that was possible? Did *I* believe that was possible? It was as if she thought I could do no wrong. As far as Kate was concerned, there was a viable explanation for every odd little thing that came up. It felt nice, having her believe in me like that. It also felt terrible.

I hugged her and said thank you. I didn't try to convince her that I wasn't a loser. I said it had been nice to meet Astrid; Kate raised an eyebrow at that. She said that maybe double dates weren't the best idea in the world, and that Justin wasn't as tall as Astrid had made him out to be. She said she thought rugby was a stupid sport.

I walked her across Princes Street and thank God there was a bus just coming. She hopped on it and I legged it into M&S. I took my beanie off, ruffled my hair a bit and chanced my luck going into the ladies' toilets.

I really needed to find a better solution to the toilet problem.

chapter eighteen

I felt unsettled for a few days; I had a weird feeling about Astrid. She may have given the impression that she was vapid as hell, but I couldn't help thinking there was something sly about her. I definitely didn't want to risk spending any more time with her.

The weekend after meeting up with Astrid and Justin, Kate and I had arranged to go to the Modern Art gallery. She thought we needed more culture in our lives or something. A text from Kate woke me up an hour before my alarm was due to go off. Two words, all caps: *IT'S SNOWING!!!!!*

I looked out the window. It wasn't just snowing – it was a blizzard. A pure white blanket covered the garden. The little bird box near my bedroom window had a thick layer on its roof and the blackbird perched on top did not look impressed.

I texted Kate: *IT'S EARLY!!!!!*

Kate suggested shelving our plans and going for a walk in the snow instead. I jumped at the idea. It would give me a chance to do a bit of research so I could say some semi-intelligent things when we eventually went to the gallery rather than staring dumbly and pretending to understand the 'art'.

It had stopped snowing by the time I bundled up in my warmest clothes and set off. There weren't many people around and the snow made everything eerie and quiet. I loved it.

Kate was waiting for me at the bus stop, woolly hat pulled right down to her eyebrows. 'Isn't it beautiful?!' She kissed me and her lips were warm and welcoming as ever.

'*You're* beautiful.' It was a cheesy line, but Kate never minded cheesy.

'Oh *you!*' She slipped her arm through mine and we started walking up the hill. There were only a few sets of footprints in the snow ahead of us. I wished there were none, but you have to get up pretty early to beat the tourists in this town.

The sun was peeking out from behind the clouds by the time we reached the top of Calton Hill. The view was spectacular. We huddled together to take a photo of ourselves with the castle behind us. Kate insisted on taking the photo again and again until she was happy with the result. It's one of my favourite photos of us. Our faces are ruddy and our eyes are shining and we look *alive*. I never thought I looked like a boy in that picture though – there was something soft about me.

Kate decided she wanted to build a snowman so I started rolling a big snowball to make the body. Then she got bored of waiting and decided it should be a snowbaby, but I told her that was creepy so we made a snowpig instead. Half an hour later the snowpig was looking almost like a pig. Except it had no legs. And no tail. Kate named the pig Tallulah and insisted on taking a picture of me kneeling next to it. She made me do a double thumbs-up to make sure the pig knew how much I loved her. I shook my head. 'You are completely insane . . . you do know that, don't you?'

'Shhh! Don't let Tallulah hear you talk that way! I don't want her worrying about her parents splitting up.' Kate covered Tallulah's ears with her mittened hands.

'So let me get this straight. Tallulah the snowpig is our . . . *baby*? How exactly does that work? Actually, now you mention it . . . she *does* look a little like you. There's a definite similarity in the nose area . . .'

Kate grabbed a handful of snow and started packing it into a ball between her hands so I did the same. 'Say that one more time and I guarantee this snowball is headed right for your face. Also, Tallulah's adopted, but I really didn't want her to find out this way. Look, she's crying little icy tears. How could you do this to our baby?!'

I threw my snowball first. Not very hard and I made sure not to aim for her face. It hit her shoulder and she looked outraged. She threw hers and it missed by a mile. Her next shot hit me right in the face though. She'd packed the snow pretty hard so it hurt a bit. I decided to make the most of the situation and fell over as if I'd been shot. I pretended to gasp for air. 'Tell . . . tell Tallulah I'm sorry and I love her . . . I . . . I could never have asked for a better snowpig. I . . .' Then I closed my eyes and let my head loll to the side.

Kate fell to her knees next to me. 'Noooooooo!' I sneaked a look out of one eye to see her shaking her fist at the sky. 'Why, God, whyyyyy? How could you do this to me?! How could you leave me all alone to raise our little pig?! I'll never forget you, Alex! And I'll make sure Tallulah grows up knowing exactly the kind of man you were. Rest in peace, my darling.' She kissed my lips and I grabbed her and kissed her back, hard. We rolled around in the snow, laughing and kissing. I didn't even care that there were people around; I was so wrapped up in the magic of us.

Kate started trying to tickle my armpits, which wasn't that easy when she was wearing gloves and I was wrapped up in about a million layers. I tried to grab her hands but somehow she managed to pin me down – she was stronger than she looked, that girl.

So there we were, lying in the snow on top of Calton Hill, cold wetness starting to seep into my jeans. And Kate suddenly stopped laughing so I stopped laughing too. Then she said the exact words that had been about to come tumbling out of my mouth. 'I love you.' Kate looked almost surprised by her own words, but then she nodded, as if to confirm that she meant them.

I looked up at her. Her face was framed by the perfectly blue winter sky, her nose was red as Rudolph's and her hat was almost falling off her head. I wondered if I blinked really hard whether I could take a mental picture and store it in my brain to bring out whenever life was bleak.

'I love you too.' There was no hint of uncertainty in my voice.

I've never seen a smile more beautiful in my life. Her eyes were sparkling, practically fizzing with happiness. Then she got this mischievous look in her eyes and said, 'Really?'

And I said, 'No, not really. I actually find you kind of repulsive.'

Kate grabbed a fistful of snow and shoved it in my face.

I was in love with a girl and she was in love with me. *This* was what people talked about, what songs were written about, what made the world go round, apparently. Now I could understand what all the fuss was about. I wanted to stop random people in the street and tell them I was in love. But I didn't, because that would have been weird. I couldn't tell *anyone*. I've never been much of a talker, but I suddenly wished I did have someone to talk to – someone other than Kate. I had no one. Jonni and Fitz hadn't been in touch for weeks and there were no likely candidates at school.

I wished I had a best friend to confide in, someone I could bore senseless with how amazing Kate was. It was strange – being in love somehow made me feel more like a girl. I wanted to gossip over steaming mugs of hot chocolate and laugh about how lame I was and maybe have someone to help me choose a Christmas present for Kate. But then I remembered that Kate's 'best' friend was Astrid, and sometimes no one is infinitely preferable to the wrong someone.

Kate told me that Astrid had been really nice

recently, which made me wonder why you'd be friends with someone whose niceness was so rare that it was worth commenting on. Stella was out of favour, apparently. Astrid reckoned she was jealous that Kate and her both had boyfriends now. Kate didn't think that was the case, but she'd always been closer to Astrid than to Stella so she wasn't all that bothered.

It was hard to work out how Kate felt about Astrid. When she told me some of the ridiculous things Astrid said, you could tell she *knew* they were ridiculous. But I think being friends with Astrid was so ingrained in her that she thought she had to put up with her forever. I guess that's what happens when you choose your best friend the first day of primary school (or in Kate's case, your best friend chooses you).

Astrid asked a lot of questions about me, apparently. She hadn't been all that interested before we met – too wrapped up in Justin – but that all changed. Suddenly she was keen to know where Kate and I met and exactly how we got together. Kate thought that her best friend had suddenly realized how a best friend should act and was trying to make up for her previous lack of interest. I wasn't so sure. I was 99% sure that she hadn't suspected the truth, because if she had she'd have said something to Kate, surely? Still, there was that nagging nugget of doubt I couldn't quite shift. I had a bad feeling about that girl.

chapter nineteen

I managed to see Kate a lot at the start of the Christmas holidays — I told my parents I was spending loads of time at the library and by some miracle they believed me. Lying was second nature now.

The snow had turned to slush within a couple of days and now there were only a few patches of dirty grey ice here and there. No chance of a white Christmas if the weather forecast was to be believed. Dad always kept me up to date on the weather forecast — his favourite thing in the world was moaning when they got it wrong (which according to him was almost all the time). I've never really understood old people's obsession with the weather. Who cares if it's raining or windy or cold? Put a coat on and stop whining.

Kate and I had arranged to exchange presents on Christmas Eve. It was hard to escape the house because Mum was so adamant that Christmas was family time, and various relatives were due to descend on our house and eat everything in sight. Lucky for me Mum had forgotten to buy the chipolatas to make the pigs in blankets to go with the turkey. I volunteered to get them from M&S. It had to be M&S or Waitrose – no other chipolatas would do, according to Mum. Jamie had been in bed with a severe case of man flu since he'd got back from uni so I didn't have to worry about him wanting to tag along. He called out from his sick bed in the most pathetic voice imaginable, asking me to get him some orange juice – 'the proper stuff . . . with bits in!'

So I put Kate's presents in my courier bag and legged it up the hill to Marks. It was carnage. It seemed like there was only one turkey left in the whole shop; the woman who'd bagged it was cradling it in her arms like it was her first-born child and Rumpelstiltskin was hot on her heels. I managed to get the chipolatas and the orange juice, along with an impulse-buy chocolate snowman for Kate. Then I ran up the stairs two at a time and escaped into the relative calm of Princes Street. 'Calm' wasn't exactly the word though. I swear you could see the panic in the eyes of most of the shoppers as they tried to find something (ANYTHING) to buy. People wasting their money all around me, trying to prove they loved their wives or husbands or whoever. Everyone should just hand over all their spare cash to charity and be done with it; the world would be a better place for it.

Kate was already there when I arrived at the cafe on Cockburn Street. A bunch of tourists were just leaving — they looked like they were dressed for an arctic expedition. There was a flashing red and green sign up behind the counter saying 'Erry Christ as!' due to a few blown bulbs. A massive plastic reindeer with peeling fur stood next to the fake fire. It was a pretty ropey-looking place, but the pastries were out of this world and Kate had recently developed a serious weakness for pain au chocolat.

Kate was facing away from the door so she didn't see me come in. I leaned over and brushed her hair to the side, kissing her neck. She jumped and squealed. I hadn't noticed she was wearing headphones. 'Oh my gosh, you scared the life out of me! I thought one of those Italian guys had taken a liking to me!' I loved it when she said things like 'oh my gosh' like she was straight out of an Enid Blyton book.

'They'd have had me to answer to if they had.' I sat down on the sofa next to her.

'Awwww, my little tough guy, ready to protect my honour!' She pinched my cheek. 'Can I have my present now? Please please please? The suspense is killing me!'

I laughed. 'Patience, patience. Also . . . I told you not to get your hopes up! I'm rubbish at presents.' I shrugged out of my coat but left the beanie on. The fake fire wasn't exactly giving out much heat.

'I find it very hard to believe that someone as thoughtful as you is rubbish at buying presents. Let me get you a drink and then we'll just see about that, OK?'

I asked for a tea and a pain au chocolat and Kate looked at me suspiciously. 'You're just ordering that so I can have some of yours, aren't you?'

I grinned. 'Well, *one* pain au chocolat never seems to be quite enough for you, so I figured one and half might do the trick.'

'Noooo! I need to fast before tomorrow. I don't know why Mum insists on cooking enough Christmas dinner for a small army when there's just the two of us.'

'My dad's just as bad. He likes to cook extra just in case there are unexpected guests. As if that's something that ever actually happens at Christmas.'

'I wish *I* could come to your house for Christmas dinner.' Even though I knew it was never going to happen, the thought still made me feel panicky.

'It's total chaos – you'd hate it.'

'I wouldn't.' She suddenly looked a bit melancholy, which was the last thing I wanted.

'Anyway . . . why don't I go and order and you just sit there and lower your expectations. I can't deal with all this pressure.' I smiled and kissed her quickly.

That seemed to snap Kate out of whatever she was thinking. Kate reached up to her ear and made a twisting motion with her fingers. 'OK, expectations have been dialled down. I would now officially be thrilled to bits with one of those toilet-roll holders . . . you know the ones? There's a little doll on top and you put the loo roll under her dress?'

I stood up, shaking my head and smiling. 'I have no idea what you're talking about, so I'm afraid you're all out of luck when it comes to toilet roll holders.'

'Boo! I've always wanted one.'

'Seriously?'

'No.'

I rolled my eyes and went up to the counter. The guy told me they were closing in forty-five minutes so he'd only serve us if we'd be gone by then. Not exactly brimming with Christmas spirit. You'd think he'd have been in a hurry to serve me but he did everything at snail's pace – like he was punishing me for stopping him closing up early.

I made Kate wait until we'd finished our pastries. She tried to pretend she didn't want half of mine, but she caved after thirty seconds.

'I think you should open your presents first.' She was clapping her hands in excitement. 'Oh my word, I hope you like them . . .'

'*Them*? I thought we'd agreed we'd only get each other *one* present?'

'I know, I know, but one of them didn't cost anything so I thought that didn't really count. I mean, it counts . . . because . . . well, I hope you like it. But anyway, don't be annoyed, OK?'

'I'm not annoyed.' I paused and smiled. 'Because I got you two presents as well.'

Kate beamed. 'I *knew* it! Good job we're as bad as each other, isn't it?' She handed me two parcels: a tiny one and a bigger, squishy one. The wrapping paper had snowmen on it and she'd drawn a snowpig next to a snowman on the bigger parcel. 'Open the little one first.'

I felt nervous as I struggled to open the parcel – she'd really gone to town on the Sellotape. I worried my reaction wouldn't be right. If I wasn't enthusiastic enough, Kate would think I hated the present and if I was *too* enthusiastic she'd also think I hated it and was overcompensating. It was lose/lose.

It was a USB flash drive keyring in the shape of Yoda; Kate knew I was a massive Star Wars fan. It was pretty cool. Kate was watching me closely so I smiled as genuinely as I could and told her I loved it. She started laughing so I figured I'd well and truly failed the reaction test. 'What's so funny?!'

'Your face! You do know it's not just a flash drive, right? There's something *on* the flash drive, you numpty.'

I could feel myself blushing. 'Oh. Yeah, I knew that. Of course. Um . . . what is it?'

'Yeah right, sure you did.' She rummaged in her bag to take out her phone. 'I have a copy on here. I thought we could listen to it together. It's not very good or anything. I just thought you might like it. And you said you wanted to . . .' Now Kate was the one blushing. She was right – we really were as bad as each other.

We each took an earbud and Kate fiddled with her phone. Before she hit 'play' she said, 'I really hope you like it but it's totally OK if you don't. You don't need to pretend or anything. We can just forget this ever happened and you can open your other present, because I'm almost sure you'll like that one–' I grabbed the phone from her and pressed 'play' myself. Otherwise we'd have been there all night. Or at least until old Scrooge behind the counter chucked us out.

I recognized the song straightaway, even though the version I knew kicked off with thumping drums. It was a piano arrangement of the last song Saving Serenity had played at the gig the night we met. The song we both loved, which had become 'our' song, after much debate over milkshakes one day.

I closed my eyes and listened right to the end. Then I hit play and listened again, even though I could see Kate looking at me anxiously out of the corner of my eye. It was the most beautiful thing I'd ever heard.

When I finally took out the earbud, I realized I was scarily close to blubbing. I had to clear my throat to get rid of the lump there. Kate was looking at me shyly. I forgot all about being worried about my reaction. 'Thank you.'

'Was it OK?'

I took her hand in mine. 'It was perfect.'

'Are you sure? I mean, I know you wanted to hear me play but I was way too shy to do it in person and I was going to do one of my exam pieces but then I thought that was a bit boring. And then I had a brainwave and I had this idea of how to arrange the song and it took me ages to get it right and . . . I should really shut up now because I'm probably high on chocolate or something.

Anyway . . . why don't you go ahead and open your other present?'

I shifted in my seat so I was facing her. I grabbed her other hand so she'd stop fidgeting. '*Thank* you. That was . . . well, it's the nicest thing anyone's ever done for me. I can't believe you did all that work just for me.'

'It wasn't work – it was fun!' She kissed my cheek. 'And you do know I'd do anything for you, don't you?'

I *did* know that. She didn't have to tell me. And I would have done anything for her. Anything except the one thing I should have done.

I burst out laughing when I opened my other present. It was a knitted black and white beanie hat. If you looked closely you could see the pattern was a skull and crossbones.

Kate thought I hated it, but I just handed her a parcel from my bag. She kept saying, 'What?! What's so funny?!' I told her to go ahead and open her present. She rolled her eyes but did as I asked. She unwrapped it slowly, careful not to tear the wrapping paper. She peeked inside the package and a smile crept across her face. 'No way!'

I put my new hat on and Kate did the same. Kate snorted with laughter. It was the same hat. I'd found it in a little shop on Victoria Street; it had made me smile and I thought it would make her smile too.

Once we'd stopped looking at each other and laughing, Kate said, 'What were the chances of that?! You know that's the only shop in Edinburgh that sells those hats? The woman there knits them herself.'

'That's what *she* says. I reckon she probably buys them for 50p each from some sweatshop in China.'

'Yeah, you're probably right. Now you mention it, I did think she looked a bit shifty.' Kate took off her hat and shook her head, smiling. 'I can't get over this. You do know what it means, don't you?'

I grabbed her hand and kissed it. 'That we're destined to be together forever and ever?'

'That we'll have to text before we meet up to make sure we're not both wearing the hat.'

I feigned shock. 'What?! You mean you don't want us to be one of those couples who wear the same clothes? Damn, I was thinking matching Berghaus fleeces might be a good idea too. So . . . you don't think we're destined to be together forever and ever then? Way to ruin my Christmas.' My pretend pout was nowhere near as good as Kate's – I hadn't had nearly enough practice.

Kate put her finger to my bottom lip and pushed it. 'You can put that away right now. We're obviously destined to be together forever. I just didn't want to freak you out. Astrid says you lot can be weird about that kind of thing.'

It took me a split second to realize that 'you lot' meant boys. Or men. I tried not to let the mention of Astrid spoil the moment. *Together forever.* I liked the sound of that. One part of my brain even believed it could happen, and that part of my brain was amazingly effective at shutting out the other part of my brain that saw those words for what they really were: impossible.

The man behind the counter was glaring at us so Kate had to hurry to open her other present. She even tore the wrapping paper a little. She wrapped her arms around my neck as soon as she realized what it was. 'My very own tiny unicorn horn!' It wasn't an actual tiny unicorn horn, because Diagon Alley was a bit of a trek from Edinburgh. It was a shell we'd found on the beach one day. It even had a tiny hole in it so I'd been able to string a thin piece of leather through it to make a necklace.

I hadn't wanted to get Kate some poxy expensive watch like Justin was apparently buying for Astrid, which was just as well because I was pretty skint. I'd wanted to get her something *meaningful*. From the tears shining in her eyes it looked like I'd succeeded. She turned away and swept her hair from her neck. I put the necklace on her and adjusted the length.

When she turned back round she kissed me hard. 'I can't believe you kept this!'

I looked at her as if she was mad. 'Well, duh. You don't just go round chucking tiny unicorn horns in the bin, you know. They're a pain in the arse to recycle, apparently . . . Do you really like it?' I suddenly felt shy, wondering if maybe a poxy expensive watch was exactly what she wanted – instead of some random beach detritus.

'I love it! You really do *know* me, you know? This is already the best Christmas of my entire life and it's not even Christmas Day yet.' She sighed and leaned back into the sofa. 'I'm going to miss you tomorrow.'

I leaned back too, ignoring the man who was now sighing loudly while he rolled down the blinds. 'I'll miss you too.' I'd always loved our crazy family Christmases, but the thought of spending the day without Kate was almost overwhelming.

'Will you Skype me?'

I'd been avoiding any type of video call with Kate, even though she'd been mentioning it for ages. I'd have to make sure my room was free of anything remotely girly (which wouldn't take long). Or maybe I'd call from Jamie's room when everyone was busy arguing over charades or Trivial Pursuit. Hopefully I'd be able to get away with not bandaging up my boobs or stuffing anything down my pants. That might be a bit hard to explain if Grandma Doyle wandered into my room, as she had a tendency to do these days. I'd have to be careful, but it would be worth it just to see Kate's face. I kissed her nose. 'Of course.'

After a lot of non-subtle sighing and glaring at us, Scrooge finally asked us to leave. Kate apologized and complimented him on the pain au chocolat. She asked if he baked them himself (he did) and said she'd never had better – not even in Paris. You could tell he didn't want to smile but he couldn't help himself. Kate tended to have that effect on people. He ended up wishing us a very happy Christmas and saying he was sorry he couldn't stay open longer but his son was waiting for him at home. So of course Kate asked him how old his son was, and whether he'd written a letter to Santa Claus. I had to drag her away in the end, and when we left the guy he was whistling a Christmas carol and one step away from jumping up and clicking his heels together. Scrooge had been well and truly reformed by Kate the Christmas Elf – who, incidentally, had never been to Paris.

We spent even longer than usual kissing each other goodbye. Neither of us could quite bear to tear ourselves away. I think I would have happily stayed in that moment forever. Especially if I'd have known we only had a week left. Exactly seven days.

I forgot to give her the chocolate snowman.

chapter twenty

Christmas Day was even more chaotic than usual — one of my Glasgow cousins had brought her six-month old twins because apparently they were too young to be left home alone. Everyone was obsessed with the babies, passing them round and bouncing them on knees. Everyone (even Jamie, whose man flu had somehow miraculously disappeared) put on these ridiculous baby voices when talking to them, which didn't make any sense to me. The babies obviously couldn't understand a word they were saying, so why not just talk like a normal person and *not* look like a complete idiot?

Of course one of the babies landed in my lap eventually. And of course it started crying straightaway and everyone laughed. It looked like an angry alien, face all red and scrunchy. I wasn't about to waste my breath trying to reason with it so I held it close to me and rubbed its back. The baby stopped crying and started gurgling.

'Look at that! She's a natural!' Grandma Doyle sounded delighted – and surprised. I looked up and everyone was watching me with goofy smiles on their faces.

'There's nothing more magical than a baby at Christmas . . . and we've got two!' *Oh man, Grandma's about to go off on one.* 'That's where it all started, isn't it? With a baby! It looks like Alfie's taken a liking to you, Alexandra.' That at least confirmed that it was Alfie I was holding and not . . . the other one. 'You'll have one of your own before you know it, dear.'

Not. Bloody. Likely. I couldn't even handle the responsibility of a snowpig. I smiled politely and didn't say anything. Jamie did though – the bastard. 'Oh yes, Alex wants to have *lots* of babies.' He stuck his tongue out at me when no one was looking.

'Really? Why, that's marvellous. Let me tell you something, Alexandra dear . . . there's nothing in this life as rewarding as being a mother. Of course these days women want a career too, don't they? Well that's all well and good, but they should really focus on what's important in life, and that's family. So don't you go leaving it too late, love. You find a nice boy and settle down before that biological clock stops ticking for good.'

'Grandma! I'm *sixteen*!' Something about being around my entire family never failed to bring out the whining brat lurking inside me.

Mum came to my rescue, bringing Grandma a glass of sherry even though it wasn't even eleven o'clock yet. 'Don't you go putting ideas in her head, Mother. There's plenty of time for all that. Alex is going to do great things with her life, I just know it. And if that includes children, that will be lovely. And if it doesn't . . . well, that's fine too. There's more to life than having kids. No offence, Natalie.' Natalie smiled and went back to staring into space. 'Actually, would you mind giving your dad a hand in the kitchen, Alex? Your expert potato-peeling skills would be much appreciated, I'm sure.'

I jumped at the chance to escape the spotlight. I handed Alfie over to Jamie and gave him (Jamie, not Alfie) a subtle kick in the process. I followed Mum into the kitchen to find that Dad had already peeled every single potato. He was sitting sipping a cup of coffee, flipping through the pages of the book I got him. He looked up and nodded. 'Good book, this.'

I nodded back, which was all the response Dad

required. Then I turned to Mum. 'I thought you wanted me to . . .'

Mum shrugged as she slung a tea towel over her shoulder. 'I thought you might appreciate a break from the delights of family time.'

Mum could be pretty great when she put her mind to it. I hugged her. 'What was that for?!' She sounded surprised.

'Rescuing me. Thank you. Now is there anything I can do? Apart from keeping Grandma's sherry glass topped up?'

Mum smiled at me. 'I think I've got that covered. We're all set in here, I think. If you want to hide in your room for a bit I won't tell anyone . . . I thought there might be someone you might . . . oh never mind.' She shook her head. 'Right, off you go before I change my mind.'

She didn't need to tell me twice — I scarpered. Strangely enough I didn't freak out about what she'd said — or been about to say. I had no idea how, but somehow she knew I was seeing someone. A couple of months earlier this would have felt like the biggest disaster in the world. And maybe it should have still felt like that, but for some reason it didn't. Weirdly enough I found myself feeling sort of *glad* that she knew.

Mum clearly didn't want to intrude. For one thing, she hadn't even asked me about it. And that was a big deal for her — she loved to gossip. She was always telling me about the tangled love lives of various friends and family members (Natalie had been a focus of this up till last year when she'd married her boring husband who always sat ramrod straight, as if he had a ventriloquist's hand up his arse.) So for Mum not to have said anything at all to me . . . well, that was kind of miraculous in itself.

I wondered if she knew it was a girl and that was why she hadn't said anything. I hadn't exactly reacted well to the whole I-think-you-might-be-gay chat. And she had said she'd be totally fine with me being gay and maybe she really meant it. Maybe I could tell her all about Kate and she'd be really happy for me and she'd want to hear all about her. And then she'd invite Kate round for dinner and we'd all sit around the table talking and laughing and Kate and I would hold hands under the table. I could picture it all so clearly.

But Mum would be horrified if she knew what I was doing, even if she was OK about me going out with a girl. She had very clear ideas about right and wrong, and there would be no doubt in her mind that this was as wrong as you can get. So I'd just have to hope she'd keep respecting my privacy and that her nosiness wouldn't get the better of her. And I'd have to shelve that ridiculous dream of me being with Kate and not having to hide.

I grabbed my laptop off my bed, made sure the coast was clear and ducked into Jamie's room. Kate answered the Skype call straightaway – she was on her phone. I heard her say to her mum that she'd sort out the Brussels sprouts in a minute. She flopped down on her bed and then her face appeared on my screen. She was wearing earrings in the shape of Christmas puddings. We wished each other a happy Christmas and just looked at each other for a while. It was enough just being with her, even though I wasn't really *with* her.

She showed me her Christmas presents, which she'd opened at seven in the morning, dragging her mum out of bed because she was too excited to wait any longer. She put on her skull and crossbones beanie, which made the earrings look extra ridiculous. 'Put yours on too!'

'I can't . . . it's in my . . .' Room. It was in my room. Except *this* was supposed to be my room. 'It's in Jamie's room. He nicked it last night. Can't blame him really – it is the finest hat in the entire universe.' Kate asked about my presents and I said we hadn't opened them yet. I'd actually opened almost all of them.

Telling these lies — these tiny white lies — was harder than I'd have thought. They're the kind of lies people tell each other all the time. Lies that are meaningless — harmless, even. But I had to force the words out of my mouth. I hated telling these lies. They were harder to stomach than the lie our whole relationship was based on. Like the shaky foundations of a house in an earthquake zone, it was only a matter of time before the whole structure came crashing down on top of us.

Looking at Kate — with the beanie pulled down almost to her eyebrows and her Christmas pudding earrings bobbing about as she leaned over to put some music on so her mum wouldn't overhear us — I knew she trusted me implicitly. It would never occur to her that this wasn't my bedroom. It *must* be, because I said it was. It would never occur to her that half an hour earlier I'd opened my Christmas present from Grandma Doyle to find a pink basket of heart-shaped soaps and sickly-sweet smelling things from Lush and a sparkly fake-diamond necklace from Next. No matter how many times Mum told Grandma to get me vouchers or a book token or something, every year she insisted on getting me something pink and impossibly girly. Last year it had been a fluffy pink scarf and gloves set. Jamie made a big fuss about how *fabulous* they were and made me put them on in front of the whole family. Dad laughed so hard he nearly choked on a brazil nut. Mum came into my room on Boxing Day and picked it out from my pile of presents. 'For the charity shop?' It was our little twice-yearly ritual.

Kate turned up the volume of her music and looked over her shoulder. 'So . . . I've been thinking . . .' I already didn't like the sound of that. She had a glint in her eye and as far as I was concerned that glint could only mean one thing. 'You know how we've been wanting to be . . . *alone* together? Well, I've had the best idea.' I most definitely didn't like the sound of that.

'And what might that be?' My mind was racing, trying to come up with excuses before I even knew what she was going to suggest.

'Astrid's family are going skiing in a couple of days . . . and she's going to give me her house keys so we can stay there on Hogmanay.' Kate and I had talked about spending New Year's Eve together, but I was thinking we could meet up at Arthur's Seat, maybe bring a blanket and watch the fireworks exploding all over the city. I hadn't quite worked out the details, like how to tell my parents I wouldn't be spending the evening with them like I had done every year since I was born, but I was pretty sure that I'd find a way. 'So . . . what do you think?'

'Um . . .' I couldn't say no to her. The last thing I wanted was to see that smile slip and the light go out of her eyes. Not today.

'I thought you'd be pleased!' The smile was slipping and the light was flickering.

'I *am* pleased! I was just . . . I don't know . . . is this really the best way?'

'It's the only way!' Kate leaned in closer to the phone so her face filled the whole screen. 'I need to be alone with you. I want to . . . *you know*.' Of course I knew. The subject had been coming up a lot recently. It was unavoidable, but that hadn't stopped me trying to avoid it, hoping it might magically go away and Kate would forget that the next natural step in our relationship was to get naked together.

'I do too.' Another lie, not so tiny, not so white. Actually, it wasn't exactly a lie – not anymore. I wanted to feel her skin on mine and I wanted to touch her and kiss her all over. But it could never happen, not like this.

She beamed at me. 'I've already told Mum I'm spending the night at Astrid's – she doesn't know that they're away in France and I'll just have to make sure she doesn't find out. She's not exactly Astrid's biggest fan anyway so Astrid hardly ever comes over these days.' Mrs McAllister and I agreed on one thing at least.

'Sounds like you've got it all planned out.'

'I have.' She looked proud of herself. 'Um . . . there is one thing.' Her gaze shifted so she was no longer looking at me through the screen. 'I'm not on the pill or anything. I mean, I can go to the doctor's and get it but probably not until after the holidays and obviously I don't think you have any STDs or oh gosh this is so embarrassing but I might as well say it now and then we can just pretend this conversation never happened. Could you possibly get some . . . um . . . condoms? I mean, you might have some already but—'

I slammed the laptop closed.

Too late. Jamie's head was poking round the corner of the door.

I hadn't heard the door open. I had no idea how long he'd been there.

chapter twenty-one

'I brought you a cup of tea.'

Another little ritual. Jamie insisted that no one in the house could make a cup of tea as well as I could. It had been my job to make tea for him since I was twelve years old. In return he let me read his copies of Empire magazine as soon as they arrived in the post. And I got to keep them once he'd finished with them. To sweeten the deal, Jamie had been kind enough to offer to make tea for me on one day of the year – Christmas Day. And I usually made sure to request at least ten cups, even though I would never want that much tea.

Jamie was holding out the mug – a special Christmas one he'd bought me last year for this very purpose. I could tell he was trying very hard not to look confused but Jamie's always been an open book to me – to everyone, really. He's got nothing to hide.

I had no idea how to play this. It all depended on

what he'd heard. 'Um . . . thanks.' I looked at my watch. 'This must be some kind of record. Two cups in an hour?'

Jamie shrugged as he walked over to me. 'I figured I'd get them in early so you could leave me to digest my food in peace after lunch.'

My fingers drummed on the laptop casing. 'And here I was going to go easy on you cos you've been ill.'

Silence as he handed me the mug. I took a sip of tea just for something to do. Jamie was right – I *was* better at making it. He sat down next to me on the bed. 'So I'm pretty sure this is *my* room.'

'Sorry, I was just . . .' Nope. I had nothing. Later I would think of all kinds of reasons I might have for being in his room instead of mine.

'Is everything OK?' He didn't say this in his Jamie voice. He said in a genuine, caring voice that didn't sound right on him. This was awkward for both of us.

I stood up, laptop tucked under one arm, mug of tea in my other hand. 'Yeah, everything's fine. Why wouldn't it be?' That was a mistake, asking that question. Because asking a question requires the other person to come up with an answer. Should have left it at 'fine'.

'I don't know . . . I thought maybe . . .' He sighed and shrugged – being sincere was an effort for him. 'I know we mess around all the time, and I know you're about a million times cleverer than I am and I'm probably the last person you'd ever want to talk to. But you can, you know. I know some stuff about . . . stuff.'

I wanted to thank him for not pushing the issue – for not asking why some girl on Skype was asking me to buy condoms. Because by that point in the conversation I was convinced that's exactly what he'd heard. God knows what he thought I was involved in, but he didn't seem to want to find out.

I didn't thank him. 'Yeah. Um . . . I have to . . .'

He waved me away, giving me permission to leave. He looked almost as relieved as I felt that we'd somehow managed to escape an awkward heart-to-heart. I was almost out of the door when he said, 'Happy Christmas, Sis.'

I turned to look at him, slouched on the bed, so comfortable in his own skin that it would never occur to him that other people might not be. I wanted to cry. 'Happy Christmas, Bro.'

I couldn't risk another video call with Kate. I texted to explain cutting off the call – told her my mum had come in. She wanted to talk more about the New Year's Eve plan. She wanted to cook me something nice, she wanted it all to be perfect. I told her we'd talk about it tomorrow, that I probably wouldn't be able to escape the clutches of my family for the rest of the day. I could tell that didn't go down well. She didn't reply for a full three minutes and when she did, all she said was 'OK. Have a good day.' Ouch.

I'd have to apologize – explain that our family Christmases really were insane and that full participation was expected at all times. Whether she believed me or not was up to her. I tried my best to forget about Kate for the rest of the day – or at least forget about the prospect of Hogmanay. The day did turn out to be pretty crazy – one of the babies spewed milky vomit down Grandma's best cardigan, Natalie had an argument with her boring husband in the dining room and then they both came out pretending everything was fine, not realizing that we'd heard every single word. Jamie was drinking red wine like it was Ribena and I wasn't the only one to notice that he kept looking at me. Uncle Eric, who normally doesn't pay attention to anything beyond his enormous belly, asked us if everything was OK. I replied with a defensive 'yes' but Jamie took a little longer to answer with a slightly less convincing shrug.

There was no way I could relax and enjoy myself. If I wasn't worrying about what Jamie may or may not have heard, I was worrying about Kate and how the hell I was going to deal with the whole sex thing. And if I wasn't worrying about that, I was being all wistful about an alternate universe in which I could be excited about the prospect of sleeping with Kate because she knew I was a girl and she was more than OK with it. That was even more annoying than the worrying because it was completely pointless and made me feel worse about everything.

Jamie and I usually stayed up late on Christmas Day, slouched next to each other on the sofa, him still wearing the party hat from his cracker. The past couple of years we'd watched Die Hard, because Jamie maintained it was a Christmas film. He could quote every line of dialogue and never get bored of it. I'd noticed that the DVD box was already out, next to the TV. Jamie's always been one for traditions and rituals. It was the kind of thing that would surprise people if you told them.

Grandma insisted on watching EastEnders because apparently it wasn't Christmas unless something terrible was happening to the residents of Albert Square. That was when I first mentioned feeling a bit ill. An hour and a half after that and I got up from the sofa and said I was going to get an early night. Mum thought that was a good idea – she was convinced I was coming down with Jamie's cold. I said goodnight to everyone and tried not to look in Jamie's direction. 'Are you sure I can't tempt you with one last cup of tea, Al? I'll even bring it to your room . . . how's that for service?' Jamie's eyes were boring into mine, willing me to say yes.

'No, thanks. I'll let you off for this year. I'm just gonna go straight to sleep.'

He raised an eyebrow. 'Right. Well, if you need anything, just give me a shout.'

The whole family was listening in to this little exchange; Grandma said that Jamie was 'such a kind soul' and would make someone a perfect husband one day. Uncle Eric chipped in with 'Not until he's sowed his wild oats' accompanied by a filthy laugh that turned into a hacking cough. I left the room just in time to avoid hearing Uncle Eric's reminiscing about his wild-oats sowing days. The thought of Eric's oats was enough to make me feel properly ill.

There were three texts from Kate on my phone. She was bored. She'd gone to bed early too – she'd had enough of the board games her mum insisted they play every Christmas. She didn't seem to be holding a grudge over my abruptness earlier.

The final text from Kate told me that she was lying in bed, thinking about me 'doing things' to her. She didn't elaborate on what that those 'things' might be, but I could guess easily enough. Reading that, I felt an immediate rush of heat before reality came crashing in yet again.

I texted back to say I was in bed, thinking about her. That was the truth at least. She didn't need to know exactly *what* I was thinking about her. That I was racking my brains about Hogmanay. Wondering if I could in fact 'do stuff' to her without her finding out my secret. Maybe I could come up with some reason why I couldn't get naked with her. Some horrible surgical scars or some childhood trauma that left me with a pathological fear of taking my clothes off. More lies, basically. I was layering lie upon lie upon lie, getting myself in deeper and deeper, further away from who I was. Who I am.

chapter twenty-two

I woke up on Boxing Day feeling a whole lot better about things. Sometime during the night I'd decided on a course of action. I'd go along with Kate's plan – up to a point. I'd reassure her that I was fine with going to Astrid's and that I was looking forward to spending some time alone with her. I'd tell her that she didn't have to cook for me, but if she absolutely insisted that would be very nice. And if she pushed the issue I'd even tell her that I'd bought some condoms for the occasion. We would have a lovely evening pretending that the rest of the world didn't exist and I would try to forget that we were in Astrid's house and that I was the most despicable human being on the planet. I would do my best to treat Kate the way she deserved to be treated, for a few hours at least.

We would have a perfect evening and if (when)

Kate started getting frisky I would tell her the truth. Well, not *the* truth. I would tell her that I wasn't ready to take things further. I would tell her that I didn't need to have sex with her to be able to feel close to her. And if that didn't work I would tell her that I wanted us to wait until her sixteenth birthday – which would buy me another few weeks at least. I was under no illusions – I knew Kate wasn't going to be happy about it. She was the sort of person who wouldn't give up once they'd set their mind on something. But surely she would wait – for me. Surely some part of her brain would think I was being gentlemanly and old-fashioned and respectful. And surely that would make her a little bit happy.

The role reversal would have been pretty funny if it wasn't threatening to ruin things for me. Boys do not turn down sex when it's offered to them on a plate. They just *don't*. I tried to imagine Jonni or Fitz telling their girlfriends they wanted to wait before having sex. The idea was laughable. Then again, the idea of them having girlfriends was ridiculous enough in itself.

I spent most of the day in bed, still going with the excuse that I was ill. I made it to the dinner table for Mum's special Boxing Day dinner though – basically a re-run of Christmas dinner but with cold turkey and a whole bunch of microwaved leftovers that somehow ended up tasting better than the meal the day before, much to Dad's annoyance.

Kate and I texted back and forth the whole day. I told her I wasn't feeling well. Yet another layer of lies. There was a lot of mushy stuff in those texts; I think we both needed reassurance that things were OK. I never thought I would be the kind of person who would tell someone that they meant the world to me. Or that I couldn't imagine my life without them in it. I guess I never really thought that I was the kind of person who would fall in love. It always seemed like that was something for other people to do, while I stood on the sidelines watching them – not entirely sure whether to be jealous or not.

I think being in love with Kate made me a better person. No one would ever know that having Kate in my life was making me *nicer*. I was more patient with Mum and Dad, for one thing. Sometimes I'd even talk about stuff I was doing at school at the dinner table instead of saying 'fine' when they asked how my day had been. I even made dinner a couple of times (shocker) and it was (even bigger shocker) kind of tasty. I'd never made more than pasta with a jar of sauce before but I thought that maybe it was about time I learned how to fend for myself. And yes, I had idly wondered about maybe cooking for Kate one day far, far in the future.

My family couldn't fail to notice the changes in me, but no one said anything. I think they were just glad I was slightly more pleasant to be around. I'm not saying I was helping old ladies across the street or volunteering at the local homeless shelter or anything, but I did notice that I was more considerate about other people's feelings in general. It was all down to Kate – it all came from her. I wondered if that would be her legacy when this was all over – an imprint of kindness on my brain. It was a nice thought, but I couldn't allow myself to be that hopeful.

The days between Christmas and New Year are always a bit strange, like everyone's still desperate to hang on to the festive season despite the fact that they're sick of eating and drinking and being nice to each other. I used to spend a lot of that time sitting cross-legged in front of the present pile I always stacked neatly in front of my wardrobe, gleeful because I had new things, and new things were better than old things even though the novelty would wear off and the new things would feel like old things within a matter of weeks.

This year I spent the days moping around the house, unable to concentrate on anything. Kate was in

Glasgow with her mum, staying with Mrs McAllister's best friend from school. Mags was the closest thing Kate's mum had to a sister.

I was torn about Kate being away. It was good to have a little breathing space, time to get my head together, work out how I was going to handle things at Astrid's house. But Kate had also mentioned that Mags had an eighteen-year-old son. A very good-looking eighteen-year-old son who was always joking about getting together with Kate one day. His name was Edward. Bastard. Kate had shown me a picture of him and he even *looked* like a bastard. There was a greasy quality about him that oozed out from the photo. Plus he was wearing a short-sleeved shirt that showed his bulging biceps, as if that was something people were supposed to be impressed by.

I told Kate I thought Edward looked like an untrustworthy sort of person. She laughed at me. She laughed and laughed until she was almost crying. Then she pinched my cheek and ruffled my hair. 'Awwww, is someone *jealous*?'

Yes. I was jealous. But I wasn't about to admit that to Kate. It wasn't that I thought there was any chance something would happen between them. I had absolute trust in Kate's feelings for me. She would never do anything to hurt me. But that didn't mean I wasn't jealous of Edward. He was a boy. There was no doubt about that – the muscles, the trace of shadowy stubble on his face. If he did try it on with Kate and if by some miracle she reciprocated, then he'd be able to take off his shirt, unbutton his jeans, and Kate wouldn't be disgusted. He was a real boy; I was Pinocchio. And I hated him for that – almost as much as I hated myself.

I kept in constant touch with Kate – little reminders that I was thinking about her. The only time she mentioned Edward was to say that he'd got a new girlfriend and he wouldn't shut up about it. She was only telling me that to reassure me that I had nothing to worry about. I appreciated the gesture but it did precisely nothing to reassure me. Since when has having a girlfriend ever stopped a boy from lusting after someone else? I had this crazy picture in my head of him sneaking into Kate's room after everyone had gone to bed. For some reason I kept picturing him in his underwear – tight black Calvin Kleins or something – six pack and pecs like an Abercrombie model. He would slip into the bed next to Kate, saying he wanted to talk or some such bullshit and then he would put his arms around her and hold her and she would lay her head against that broad, manly chest and then they'd have a lot of sweaty sex.

I knew it would never happen. I knew the scenario

was ridiculous, but that didn't stop it running through my head, playing out in various different ways. I was torturing myself and I knew I should stop, but I didn't – not until Kate informed me she was in the car on the way back to Edinburgh on the 29th. Just like that, smarmy Edward disappeared from my brain and was replaced by worry about New Year's Eve.

Forty-eight hours to go.

chapter twenty-three

On the morning of the 30th, Jamie informed us that he'd decided not to go back to Aberdeen until tomorrow. He said he wanted to spend at least *some* quality time with his little sister during the holidays. I didn't like the sound of that. But then he came up with this idea that we should take part in the torchlight procession *as a family*. The torchlight procession is exactly what it sounds like – a whole load of people, meandering through the streets with a whole load of torches – real ones with flames rather than the kind with batteries. It's part of Edinburgh pretending it's the best place in the world to spend Hogmanay when most people would actually rather be somewhere with temperatures *above* freezing. We used to take part in the procession every year, until one year Mum and Dad went to a drinks party instead. I guess that's how family traditions die a death. It looked like Jamie was intent on resurrecting this one with the sole intention of stressing me the hell out.

Mum and Dad thought it was a brilliant idea, until I pointed out that the vouchers you needed to get torches would definitely be sold out by now. I was quite proud of myself for coming up with that one. I'd given up the illness charade just in case Mum got all maternal on me and decided not to let me out of the house on Hogmanay. Kate would kill me if I had to bail.

Jamie smirked at me, and that was when I knew he was one step ahead. 'Nah, it's OK, Al. A mate of mine has four vouchers he said I could have.'

I had no choice. Mum was already getting excited, saying she'd make up a couple of flasks of hot chocolate for us to drink on Calton Hill while we waited for the fireworks after the procession. Dad was asking if she could put a 'wee dram' of whisky in one of those flasks.

So it was settled. Tonight was officially 'family time'. I had no idea what Jamie was up to. Maybe nothing at all – maybe he really did want to spend time with us after the invasion of extended family over Christmas. Maybe he was horribly lonely up in Aberdeen and spent his days pining for us. Somehow I didn't think so.

I texted Kate to check what she was up to. I needed to make sure there was no chance of us bumping into her or her mum. I didn't ask her if she was going to the torchlight procession, because obviously that would have led her to ask if *I* was going and that might make her ask if she could come with me. I needn't have worried – she was spending the evening with her mum. Mrs McAllister was making a steak pie, which was one of their little family traditions. They usually had it on Hogmanay but since Kate was supposedly so keen to spend the New Year with Astrid, they'd decided to celebrate a day early. Apparently her mum was *not* happy about them not seeing in the New Year together, but Kate had really laid it on thick, begging to go, making some deal about how much piano practice she'd do in January. That was what clinched the deal, of course. So I was safe to admit I was taking part in the procession and Kate was jealous about that. She made me promise that we'd go together next year. She made me *promise*.

It was bloody freezing, but there was no rain or hail or snow so Jamie's procession plan was GO. I wore my new hat pulled right down over my ears. It didn't look as good on me as it did on Kate.

The four of us walked up the hill into town; the

streets were teeming. I walked with Dad and Jamie walked with Mum, which was always the way it worked out whenever we went anywhere together. Dad was telling me about some French film he wanted to see and asking if I'd go with him. Going to see random foreign films was one of his favourite things to do. Usually he ended up going by himself, which didn't seem to bother him. He probably liked the peace and quiet – and not having Mum asking what was going on every five minutes. For an intelligent woman – and my mother really *is* an intelligent woman – she has this incredible inability to follow basic storylines. Although I reckon at least half of the time she does it so that Dad feels all clever when he's explaining things to her.

Chambers Street was heaving by the time we arrived; the queue to get our torches seemed to take forever. Just as I was starting to lose the feeling in my fingers Jamie handed me my torch. It always made me a bit nervous, carrying those torches. That was part of the fun though – wondering if some idiot would accidentally set someone else's hair on fire. Jamie always used to mess around, pretending to trip and fall – Mum hated that. There was no messing around this year though. Jamie looked solemn in the flickering firelight.

We edged our way through the crowd. I have to admit, it was still an incredible sight – thousands of torches bobbing through the darkness. It would have been cool to watch the procession from somewhere high up – a room in the Balmoral Hotel, maybe – but you'd be missing out on a fundamental part of the experience. There was something special about so many people taking over the streets like that.

It made me think about witch hunts. Add a few pitchforks into the mix and this must have been what it was like. Marching through the streets in pursuit of some poor woman who hadn't done anything wrong. Maybe she'd mixed up some herbs to cure some minor ailment or other or maybe she was just a little bit too wise or maybe she didn't have a husband. And of course that got me thinking that if I'd have been unlucky enough to be born five hundred years ago I'd probably have been near the top of the witch-hunters' shit list. I was just weighing up the options of being burned at the stake versus that stupid ducking/drowning thing they used to do (and coming to the conclusion that I didn't really fancy either option all that much) when Jamie nudged me with his elbow.

I hadn't even noticed but he'd somehow engineered it so that we were behind Mum and Dad. I asked him what he wanted but he just shook his head. Then he started slowing down, so I had to slow down to stay with him. Before I knew it, random people had moved in to fill the gap between us and our parents. I could just about still see Dad's hat if I strained my neck. 'We'd better catch up,' I said to Jamie, but he shook his head. And that was when I knew what was happening – the lion's signature move of separating the cute, helpless baby zebra from the pack. Jamie took hold of my arm and manoeuvred me towards the pavement. A few people gave us odd looks as we pushed through the crowd of onlookers on South Bridge. Someone even shouted 'Oi! You're going the wrong way!' but Jamie ignored them.

We ended up in a little close off the Royal Mile – one that was thankfully free from tramps or tourists, although it did still come complete with the usual faint aroma of piss and vomit. 'Um . . . what are you doing? Mum's gonna freak out when she realizes they've lost us.'

'I think we're a little bit too old for that whole *stranger danger* thing, don't you?' He paused and I knew he was about to say something I wouldn't like. 'Besides, I told her I'd be . . . er . . . borrowing you for a bit.' He at least had the decency to look guilty.

'And why did you tell her you wanted to do that?'

I would have crossed my arms if I hadn't been holding the bloody torch.

He shrugged. 'I said I needed to spend some time alone with my baby sis to . . . shoot the breeze.'

'Shoot the breeze?' I said, sceptically.

'What?! That's a thing, you know. It means talking.'

I rolled my eyes. 'I know full well what it means, Jamie. It's just not something you have *ever* said. Why are you being so weird?'

I knew, but I wanted him to say it.

The two of us stood facing each other in that narrow, dank alleyway, with the torchlight dancing on our faces. It would have made a pretty cool scene in a film. Except in a film we would have been co-conspirators in some kind of plot to overthrow the government or something. I had a nasty feeling Jamie wasn't in the mood to conspire with me.

'You've been avoiding me.'

This was true. 'I have *not*. I've practically been on my deathbed . . . or hadn't you noticed?'

'On your deathbed? God, Alex, I never had you down for being a drama queen. Anyway, you weren't even ill so why don't you cut the crap?'

Jamie had never talked to me like this before. Sure, he was always taking the piss out of me and he'd get annoyed at me in a very normal brotherly way. This was different – he was deadly serious, for one thing.

'So what if I *was* faking? There's only so much family togetherness I can stomach – you know that.' Some Americans walked past the entrance to the alleyway chanting 'U-S-A, U-S-A.' Every time I see them doing that on TV I try to picture us chanting 'U-K, U-K', but somehow it doesn't work – for some reason the enthusiasm doesn't really translate.

Jamie leaned back against the wall; I hoped there was some crusty old chewing gum that would stick to his expensive new jacket. 'Alex, I know something's going on with you so why don't you just spit it out so we can get back to Mum and Dad in time for the fireworks . . . I thought you might feel more comfortable talking away from home.' Jamie sort of shook his head at how nonsensical that was.

'Nothing's going on! Let's just go, OK?' I turned away from him and walked a couple of steps towards the entrance of the close.

'I heard you talking to that girl.' I stopped walking. 'I know you're . . . seeing her.' I turned around. 'It's OK, you know. There's nothing wrong with being gay. You know I don't have a problem with that – and Mum and Dad are cool with it too. You *know* that.' The torchlight emphasized the pained expression on his face. As if this was harder for him than it was for me.

'I'm not gay! Jesus! Why the fuck do people keep saying that? Look, Jamie, no offence but this is really none of your business.'

'So I suppose it's none of my business when I come back for the holidays to find half of my clothes have magically migrated from my room to yours?' He'd been snooping in my room. For some reason that felt like an unforgivable betrayal, even though I'd obviously snooped first. 'And it's none of my business when I hear you talking to some girl about buying condoms? Why the hell would you need condoms if you're . . .' My brother likes to act like he's stupid; he's not. I watched him as his brain joined the dots, creating a picture that confused him even more. 'Oh man.' He was shaking his head now.

I stepped towards him, my non-torch-bearing hand raised like I was warding off a dangerous animal. 'Jamie, it's not—'

'How is that even possible? I mean, she can't honestly think that you're . . .' I really thought he wasn't going to say it. '. . . a boy?'

The game was well and truly up – that much was obvious. Damage control was my only option. I didn't have to fake the panic on my face. 'Please don't tell

Mum! Jamie, you have to promise not to tell her, OK? This is . . . it was a mistake.'

'A mistake? How do you accidentally pretend to be a boy? That makes precisely no sense, you do realize that?'

It sounded so much worse than it was. I wasn't pretending to be anything. It was more complicated than that. Jamie needed some sort of explanation and I felt a sudden need for him to understand. I was desperate for him to tell me it wasn't that bad, that the situation was fixable. 'I . . . we met online. I didn't realize she thought I was a guy – not until we met up. And then . . . it was never the right time.'

'I can't get my head around this. Couldn't you just have . . . I dunno . . . put on a skirt or something? I'm pretty sure that would've done the trick.'

'She liked me.' Because that was what it all came down to. She liked me in a way that no one else had ever liked me before. And I liked her back. 'I'm in love with her, Jamie.'

He winced as if that was the last thing he wanted to hear. 'And what about her? What's her name anyway?'

'Kate. She's in love with me too.' It felt good to say it out loud to someone who knew the truth, as if that validated it somehow.

'She's not though, is she? She's in love with some boy who doesn't even exist.'

He didn't say it to be cruel – I knew that. But it didn't stop the words slicing through my heart like a scalpel through flesh. 'It's not like that. She *knows* me. It feels like I can be myself with her . . . Don't say it, OK? There's nothing you can say that I haven't thought of already. I hate lying to her.'

Jamie sighed. 'Then stop it. It's not too late to make things right. Maybe if you explain things to her . . . she might understand?' He didn't sound very sure about that.

'I can't lose her.' My torch was burning low. The flame looked like it might sputter out any second.

'Well you can't keep her, can you? Not like this.' He let that sink in for a moment or two. 'She wanted you to get condoms, right? I don't mean to be graphic or anything but don't you think she's gonna realize pretty quickly that you . . . um . . . don't exactly have anything to put a condom on?'

I studied Jamie's face for any hint that he was mocking me. 'I never meant for it to go this far, Jamie. She keeps on pushing me to take things further, and I want to but I . . . God, this is such a fucking mess. What am I going to do?' My voice cracked unexpectedly. I turned away from Jamie as soon as I realized there was no way to stop the tears, but he took hold of my shoulders and held me in his arms. I dropped my torch, and I think he must have dropped his at the same time.

'It'll be OK, Alex.'

I started sobbing then. Something about people being nice to me breaks my heart.

The tears dried up after a few minutes, leaving my head feeling woolly and thick. It was difficult to think straight. Jamie made a joke about me snotting all over his jacket. I breathed a shaky breath and tried to pull myself together. 'OK. OK. I'm OK.' Because if you say something three times that makes it true.

'Good.' He paused, weighing up whether I was strong enough to take what he was going to say. 'You know what you have to do then?'

I nodded.

'You promise you'll do it soon? You need to end this now before it gets more . . . complicated.'

I wasn't quite sure how it could get *more* complicated, but I was too exhausted to argue. 'I'm not sure how to explain it to her.' Not one imaginary version of that conversation ended well.

'Then maybe you don't have to . . . Maybe you could break things off quickly. Stop answering her calls. I presume she doesn't know where we live?'

'I couldn't . . .' It was a horrible thought to contemplate – doing something like that to Kate. But the alternative was even worse.

'The way I see it you have two options. Either you sit down with her and tell her the truth and try to explain how you got yourself into this whole mess . . . and that's not going to be easy . . . or you pretend to be a complete and utter bastard who's lost interest all of a sudden. It wouldn't exactly be the first time that's happened in the history of the world, would it? So it's up to you. Which do you think would hurt her less?'

That's what my decision came down to in the end. At least, that's what I told myself. I was doing the best thing for Kate; it was nothing to do with me being a coward.

chapter twenty-four

We didn't make it to Calton Hill in time for the fireworks. We stood on North Bridge and watched them before heading home. Jamie apologized and said we'd do the procession properly next year. I don't think he really believed I was bothered about the procession; I think he just wanted to say sorry for *something*.

We didn't talk much on the walk home. I wondered if things would ever be the same between us. If there was a way back to the jokey, easy relationship we'd had. I wanted him to reassure me that I'd always be his little sister, no matter how many stupid things I did. He didn't say anything though, and I didn't ask. I was still too embarrassed about crying all over him.

Jamie put the kettle on while I switched the Christmas tree lights back on. We sat in front of the TV. If I concentrated really hard I could almost feel like there was nothing wrong – that I wasn't on the verge of ruining the best thing that had ever happened to me. The audience of the sitcom we were watching was laughing way too hard over a very tall man squeezing himself into a very small car when my phone buzzed in my pocket.

I took my phone out and tried to ignore Jamie staring at me. It was a text from Kate asking me if I'd enjoyed the procession. She said she'd been able to see the fireworks from Portobello. She liked that we'd both been watching the same thing at the same time. She said it was the next best thing to being together. Kate was always sending sweet messages like that – little things that would make me smile and feel good about myself no matter what was happening around me. Those messages were like oxygen to me.

There weren't going to be any more messages like that from Kate. I was looking at the very last one. I stared at it until the words went blurry. And then I realized the words hadn't gone blurry at all – there was a film of tears in front of my eyes. I blinked hard until they went away.

Kate's message didn't make me smile and feel good about myself this time. It made me feel like I was choking. It was too much – the thought of her looking up at those fireworks, feeling happy and excited and hopeful about the future, while I'd looked up at them, knowing it was over.

I would never see her again. Not unless we passed each other in the street one day. I'd already thought of that. It was that stupid thing that Jamie had said back in the alleyway – that I should have just worn a skirt. When Kate walked down the street, she'd be scanning the faces of passing boys – cvcn if she was doing it subconsciously, she'd be half-expecting to bump into me one day. But she wouldn't be paying attention to girls. A girl wearing tights and a skirt and a silly little jacket even though it was freezing outside. So that is exactly what I would have to become. It would just be another disguise – even further away from the real me than wearing Jamie's clothes and stuffing things down my pants. Mum would probably be delighted and Jamie would probably think that I was 'fixed'.

'Alex? That's her, isn't it?'

I nodded.

'Don't answer.'

I told him about our plans for tomorrow night. There was no reason not to.

'That's perfect then. Just turn off your phone. She won't keep trying after you bail on that. Trust me. Here, give me your phone.'

I didn't, but he snatched it out of my hands. He

made a big show of pressing the 'off' button. 'There. All done. Now just forget about her. Move on.'

I looked at him as if he was a moron. Forget about her. Move on. As if either of those things were remotely possible.

'Look, I'm not saying it's easy, but it's got to be done. This is your best option, right?'

I said nothing. I was transfixed by my phone and the thought that Kate was probably lying on her bed, waiting for a reply. She'd probably assume I was busy with family stuff. How long would it be before she realized something was wrong? And what if she thought I'd been run over by a bus or something? If Kate genuinely thought something terrible had happened to me, she was hardly going to forget about it and just get on with her life. She'd find a way to track me down – at my supposed school, probably.

I told Jamie his plan wasn't going to work – not like this. He was sceptical at first, figuring I was just playing for time or trying to worm my way out of it. But then he thought about it and held out my phone. 'Fine. You're going to have to text her. Tell her it's over. Tell her you're bored of her or you've been shagging someone else or . . . it doesn't matter *what* you say as long as it's bad enough for her to stop contacting you.'

This was worse. This was actually sticking the knife into Kate and twisting it.

Jamie was still holding out the phone and waiting when there was the sound of a key rattling in the front door. I grabbed the phone from Jamie and stuffed it in my pocket. The desperate look on my face clearly wasn't difficult to translate because he said, 'Don't worry, I won't say anything.' I gave him a hard, challenging look and he added, 'I promise.'

I believed him. I didn't exactly have any choice in the matter.

The living room door opened and Mum and Dad came in, all red-faced and smiley. 'Hello, you two! Did you have a good time?' Meanwhile Dad was muttering about the fireworks being disappointing, saying it was a waste of time and money having substandard fireworks the day before the massive Hogmanay display.

I sat there and listened to my family being a family and I felt more alone than I had ever felt in my life.

One hour and six minutes after Kate's text, she sent a second: *I love you. xxx*

I replied to Kate fifty-seven minutes later: *I can't do this anymore. I'm sorry.*

Hours of thinking time and that was the best I could come up with.

Kate's reply was almost instant: *Haha, you're hilarious. So what time shall we meet at A's tomorrow? xxx*

I should have expected that. I'd probably have said the same if she'd sent me a text like that. We were so secure in how we felt about each other – so utterly sure that we were in love and nothing was going to change that. I fired back another message before I thought about it too long and chickened out: *I'm not coming. I'm serious. We need to break up.*

A couple of minutes later: *This isn't funny. You're scaring me. I'm calling you now.*

I waited. My phone rang and I let it go to voicemail. I couldn't bring myself to listen to the message.

She called three more times. I lay face down on my bed.

One more text message: *Why are you doing this to me?*

It was the hardest thing I've ever done, not texting or calling her back to tell her I was joking. I could have done that and all would have been forgiven. Instead I deleted Kate's voicemails without listening to them.

I switched off my phone and brushed my teeth and washed my face and changed into the pyjamas Mum and Dad had got me for Christmas. I got into bed and turned out the light and pulled the duvet up to my chin and stared at the darkness.

I would never, ever forgive myself for this.

I couldn't sleep. In the middle of the night I got out of bed and went over to the chair where I pile all my clothes. The beanie hat was hanging off the corner of the chair back. I took it and put it under my pillow. For some reason I couldn't stop thinking that I would never be able to wear it again. Maybe one day far in the future, when I was away at university or something, I'd technically be able to wear it. But I wouldn't. Kate probably wouldn't wear her hat again either. Maybe she'd cut it up with scissors or burn it or do whatever it was girls did when they'd been hurt by their no-good boyfriends. It made me sad to think of these two identical hats, hand-crafted with love, bought with love and worn only once or twice. It didn't seem fair on the hats somehow – that their fate was to belong to two people who couldn't bear to look at them, let alone wear them.

It wasn't long before I realized I was focusing all my energy thinking about hats because it was too hard to think about anything else. I couldn't allow myself to think about Kate, lying in her bed, crying and confused, wondering what she'd done wrong. Because that's what she would do – she'd find a way to blame herself for this. It occurred to me that it might actually be good for her to have a friend like Astrid right now – someone who'd be full of righteous indignation and 'all men are bastards' and 'you're better off without him'. But Astrid was away so Kate had no one. Maybe she'd confide in her mum. Surely mothers knew exactly the right things to say in a situation like this? Surely even Mrs McAllister had some idea of the words to say to make Kate feel a little better about things. Perhaps it would bring them together, make them feel closer to each other.

I was kidding myself. Well, I was *trying* to kid myself but doing a very poor job of it. Kate would have to deal with this by herself. At around four thirty in the morning my brain came up with this crazy idea that maybe I could dye my hair, change the way I looked so completely that I'd be able to befriend her and be there to listen to her talk about the boy who broke her heart. It was madness, of course. But I could never stop my brain when it went off on one like that. It would be *something* at least – to be her friend. Being close to her would be better than never seeing her again. And maybe one day she would look over at me and I'd see that look in her eyes and I'd know that she'd fallen in love with me all over again. And she wouldn't care that she was a girl and I was a girl, because what did it matter? Love was love.

Love *was* love. I truly believed that. And I had blown my one shot at it.

chapter twenty-five

I woke up on the last day of the year with the beanie clutched between my fingers, the wool tickling my lips. I'd fallen asleep after all. Against my better judgement I grabbed my phone from the bedside table. There were no more messages from Kate, which surprised me a little. I felt a tiny stab of disappointment, quickly followed by shame. It was a good thing, that she hadn't called or texted again. Maybe it meant that she was starting to come to terms with it. It would be best for her if she started hating me right away.

Jamie was heading back to Aberdeen straight after breakfast, so Dad had planned to make bacon and pancakes. I had to get out of bed and try to remember how to smile and laugh and talk like a normal person. It was easy enough to fool Mum and Dad, but I knew it hadn't worked with Jamie when he volunteered us to do the dishes. I washed, he dried. He asked if I was OK. I nodded.

'OK, you're clearly not, but that's alright. It'll take a bit of time, but you will be fine, Alex. I promise.'

I wanted to ask him how he could possibly promise such a thing. He'd never been in this situation. As far as I knew he'd never even been in love. He had no idea what I was going through. He didn't know Kate and he had no idea what *she* was going through. And he could never understand that I could never feel OK again as long as I knew she was hurting.

I concentrated on scrubbing every last bit of bacon grease from the plates. I wanted this conversation to be over and I wanted Jamie to be gone. He was making me feel worse.

He asked if I wanted him to stick around, go back to Aberdeen in a couple of days. He said he'd be happy to do that if I needed him, but the tone in his voice made it quite clear that he was hoping I wouldn't. I didn't blame him. He had his life to be getting back to. He didn't need to be dealing with his crazy little sister. I summoned up a smile (just a little one) and told him I'd be fine and I was feeling a bit better already. For good measure I thanked him and said I knew it was for the best. There was no hint of the lie on my face, no matter how hard Jamie looked for it.

'I'm proud of you, sis. It's what being an adult is all about – owning up to your mistakes.'

I forced out a laugh and flicked soapy water in his face. 'Since when do you have the slightest idea about being an adult? Unless I'm wrong and you've finally binned your lucky SpongeBob pants?'

Jamie retaliated by chucking the soggy tea towel over my head.

Mum came in, took one look at us and rolled her eyes. 'Will you two *ever* grow up?'

I looked at Jamie and Jamie looked at me and we burst out laughing. The laughter was real this time. I wondered how it was possible to laugh when I felt so numb inside.

Jamie left at around ten thirty, after telling me to call him if I ever needed anything and inviting me to visit him for a weekend soon. He must have known I had absolutely nothing to look forward to now.

Mum and Dad were busy getting ready for their party. Mum went to the supermarket to buy more Cava than the guests could ever drink even if they stayed until the end of January. Dad got started on the pheasant casserole. I stayed in my room, mostly. I didn't watch anything or read or listen to music. I didn't do anything other than think about Kate, wondering what she was doing now, and how long it would take her to get over me, and why hadn't she texted again?

At about four I headed into the kitchen to tell my parents there had been a change of plans and I wasn't going out after all. Dad was pleased – it meant he had me to act as sous chef for the whole evening. Mum looked at me carefully. 'Oh, that's a shame, love. I'm sorry.'

I coughed and said it was fine – I hadn't been all that bothered anyway. She squeezed my shoulder. 'I suppose it's OK for me to admit that I'm secretly quite glad we get to have you for one last Hogmanay?' She kissed me on the cheek. 'Now, would you mind helping your dad while I go and have a bath?'

I didn't mind helping out. Dad's continuous chat helped take my mind off Kate. I chopped tomatoes for the soup – the same soup every year. I'd found the original recipe last year and discovered it was actually meant to be served cold, but Dad said cold soup made him think of vomit and he had no intention of serving up cold sick for the last meal of the year.

I got changed at about six thirty – it was the one day of the year Mum insisted we all scrubbed up properly. Dad even wore a tie. I went to put on my best black jeans but something stopped me. I pulled out the only non-school skirt in my wardrobe – black denim and short. Mum had bought it for me a couple of years ago, before she lost hope that I would ever dress like a girl. I paired it with a fitted black shirt and boots and looked in the mirror. I didn't look as bad as I thought I would. I looked like me, almost. Maybe it wouldn't be too terrible to dress like this after all. I drew the line (or rather, I didn't) at make-up though.

Mum and Dad were in the living room, sipping their customary pre-party glasses of Cava and munching on cashew nuts. Some classical music was playing softly. I recognized it straightaway – Chopin. Kate had taught me well. The ache that had lurked inside my chest since yesterday turned into something much sharper. I hurried over to change the music.

Dad said, 'Oi! We were listening to that!' but neither of them really minded. I caught a look between them. I knew that look. The only time Mum used it was when she was trying to signal to Dad that she really, really wanted him to shut up, like when someone invited them to go to something she didn't want to go to and she wanted to stop him saying yes before she had a chance to think of an excuse.

Mum took a long glug of her Cava, draining the glass. 'You look nice, Alex.' That was all she said. I could tell it took a lot of restraint not to make a fuss about me wearing a skirt. I appreciated the effort. I appreciated the glass of Cava she poured for me even more.

By half past nine I'd had three glasses of Cava and half a glass of white wine even though Mum had insisted that I was only allowed two glasses max. Mum and Dad were pretty pissed, and one of the guests – Andy, a friend of Dad's from work – was completely wasted. His wife kept on shooting him filthy looks and one time she even tried to kick him under the table but she ended up kicking Dad instead. Our neighbours, Bill and Wendy, were there with their bratty daughter who was dressed like a Disney princess. Manjul, Mum's friend from her uni days, had brought his new girlfriend. She was even younger than the last one, but at least she wasn't wearing a top with her boobs spilling out. Manjul was Mum's boyfriend for two years, but it never seemed to bother Dad that the two of them were still friends. The girlfriend kept trying to engage me in conversation, probably because I was the closest one to her age in the room. She was pretty nice, actually.

Everyone enjoyed the soup and the pheasant casserole, except the bratty kid from next door who'd decided to become a vegetarian on Christmas Day.

Wendy had brought some Tupperware filled with couscous and raw vegetables and set it in front of the kid with barely disguised annoyance.

Manjul was asking me about my career plans, which seemed to be the default question for adults when faced with a teenager. At least it was better than 'How's your love life?' I was just about to say that I had no idea what I wanted to do at university, let alone for my whole life, when the doorbell went.

Mum dabbed her mouth with her napkin and looked at her watch. 'It's a bit early for first-footing, isn't it?' First-footing is this old tradition where a tall, dark-haired man has to be the first one to come into your house after midnight. For some reason he was supposed to be carrying a lump of coal, even though that seemed like a pretty crap gift to see in the new year. Manjul was always our 'first-footer' and he made the same joke every year about it being racist.

Dad made a move to get up from his chair but Mum gestured for him to stay seated. 'No, no, I'll get it. You've been up and down like a jack-in-the box.'

'Up and down like a whore's knickers, more like,' spluttered Andy. The brat from next door was the only one to laugh at that. Andy's wife hissed his name. If looks could kill.

Mum looked relieved to escape the table, even just

for a minute. For some reason this party wasn't going quite how she wanted it to. The mix of people was crucial; Dad had clearly made a fatal error inviting Andy. He hadn't known him long enough to discover that he was a disgusting pig. I felt sorry for Dad – Mum would be having words with him later.

There was an awkward silence at the table while we waited for Mum to come back and smooth things over, maybe suggest a nice friendly game of charades before pudding. Dad poured everyone some more wine – everyone apart from Andy, because his wife put her hand over the top of his glass when Dad went to refill it. The brat whispered to her mum that she really needed a wee but she wanted to do it in her own bathroom. Bill yawned so wide I could see every single one of his fillings.

We all heard Mum opening the front door.

We couldn't quite hear who it was.

We all heard Mum say, 'Alex? Yes, of course, I'll just get her . . . Actually, why don't you come in from the cold? It's nice to meet you, by the way.'

The wine had fogged up my brain. I had no idea who it could be. I didn't think for one second that . . .

Kate.

after

chapter twenty-six

Alex. Staring at me in disbelief.

There were other people at the table but I barely noticed them. Alex jumped up from his chair, knocking it over. That's when I saw the skirt.

Alex was wearing a skirt. *I'll just get her.* That was what Mrs Banks said, but I didn't think anything of it. She seemed a little unsteady on her feet; I thought she was probably drunk. After all, it was Hogmanay and most of Edinburgh seemed to be drunk too. An Australian in a novelty Guinness hat had tried to kiss me on the way to Alex's house.

My brain was trying to make sense of it all. It was trying to find a sensible explanation for Alex's mum saying 'her' and for Alex to be standing in front of me wearing a skirt, along with an expression of pure panic.

We stood there, close enough to touch, looking at

each other. Alex didn't look like Alex. The moment expanded to fill all of space and time and I began to wonder if we would be stuck inside it forever. I only snapped out of it when I felt a hand on my shoulder. 'I'm sorry, Alexandra seems to have forgotten her manners . . . Can I offer you a drink?'

Alexandra. Alexander. The words sound the same if you say them fast enough. Mrs Banks was speaking very slowly though, probably so she didn't slur her words.

'Kate?' Alex's hand was on my arm. I looked at that hand – I mean, really looked at it – and for the first time I realized how delicate it was. I mean, I'd noticed that before. I'd even commented on it a couple of times, but I'd never really given it much thought. All I knew was that my hand fit perfectly in his. It was as if all the hands in all the world had a single, perfect match and somehow I'd been lucky enough to find mine.

A man at the table said, 'She looks like she's seen a ghost! Someone get that girl a brandy!'

I took a step back, quickly followed by another. I noticed each and every person at the table now, and they were all looking at me as if I was insane. I backed out of the door, mumbling an apology.

Alex followed me out into the hall. 'Kate? Kate,

please. Can we talk about this? Let me explain . . . please?' Even the voice sounded different. Or maybe that was just my imagination.

My hands were shaking as I opened the front door. I opened my mouth to speak before realizing I had nothing to say.

Alex's hand was on my arm again, with a little more pressure this time, trying to stop me from moving. I shook it off. The last thing I heard as I hurried down the steps was Alex saying, 'Kate, I love you.'

I love you. Twenty-four hours earlier, those had been the only words I wanted to hear. When I was heartbroken and sobbing on my bedroom floor I would have given anything to hear Alex say those words again.

My life could now be neatly divided by a single point in time: *before* or *after* I found out my boyfriend was a girl.

How could you not know? How was it possible for a girl to be clueless enough to go out with a boy for months and not realize *he* was actually a *she*?

As I walked away from Alex's house, I half-expected him (HER) to come after me. But he (SHE) didn't. The streets were thronging with people on their way to the street party. Everyone was smiling, laughing, shouting, singing. I walked as fast as I could, head down to hide my tears.

There are things in life that you are so absolutely sure about that you don't have to give them any thought. The sun will rise each day. The ground is solid under your feet. Your boyfriend is a boy. And then one day you wake up and there's perpetual darkness and the ground has turned into quicksand and your boyfriend is a girl.

Alex was a girl.

I was feeling too many feelings at once; my brain didn't know which one to settle on. Shock. Disbelief. Confusion. Embarrassment. Grief. Anger. Back to shock again.

At the bus stop a woman with a baby strapped to her chest asked if I was OK and the baby made a grab for my scarf with its chubby little hands. I said I was fine, thank you. The woman smiled at me kindly before getting on her bus. What would she have done if I'd told her that I wasn't fine at all, and the reason why? Would she still have smiled at me kindly or would she have looked at me like I was the stupidest person on the planet?

The bus was almost empty – most people were heading into town, not away from it. I sat and stared up at the CCTV screen as it scrolled through the different views of the bus and its passengers. I found it hard to feel anything when I saw the girl with the red coat and purple scarf. She certainly looked normal enough. You couldn't even tell that she'd been crying. You couldn't tell that her life had been been ruined – twice in the space of twenty-four hours. You couldn't tell that she'd genuinely thought it would be a good idea to go round to her boyfriend's house to beg him to give her another chance.

Mum still thought I was staying at Astrid's – I'd been so sure I'd be able to convince Alex to take me back. I had it all planned out – this big speech about how we were meant to be together and how we could overcome any problems as long as we talked about them and that all couples go through rough patches and that wasn't a good enough reason for us to break up. I'd gone over it again and again in my mind, discarding the obvious clichés, but keeping some because clichés are clichés for a reason, aren't they? So the plan was that I'd give this big, heartfelt speech and I'd try really, really hard not to cry because I didn't want Alex to take me back just because he felt sorry for me. Then he would take me in his arms and say sorry and reassure me that nothing like this would ever happen again. He would introduce me to his parents and they would think I was charming and everything you would want your son's girlfriend to be. Then Alex and I would get the bus to Astrid's house and Alex would lead me upstairs and undress me slowly (after being all considerate and checking that this was really what I wanted) and we would have sex and it wouldn't be awkward or painful. I truly believed all these things were possible if I could only find the right words to say.

Alex texted just before I got off the bus. A single word: *Sorry*. I deleted the message.

If I hadn't gone round to Alex's I would never have found out. I would have lived every day still thinking my boyfriend had suddenly dumped me out of the blue.

I hadn't told Alex I knew where he lived, because the way I found out was a little dodgy, I suppose. I found an envelope addressed to him in his bag. It's not like I was snooping or anything – I would never do something like that. It was when we met up on Christmas Eve. He'd just arrived and gone up to the counter to order and I had this sneezing fit. I've always been embarrassed about sneezing so I always try to do it completely silently. Mum's always telling me off about it; she's probably just jealous because when she sneezes it sounds like a cross between a goose and an elephant. So I sneezed four times in a row and realized I was in desperate need of a tissue. I checked my bag but I'd run out. I didn't even think twice about looking in Alex's bag. There wasn't much inside – a pair of gloves, a copy of Empire magazine and a red envelope. There was a paper napkin right at the bottom, which I used to blow my nose. I barely even glanced at the envelope – it was clearly a Christmas card – but the address lodged itself in my brain, probably because the house number was 19 and that's always been my favourite number. And me being the idiot I am, I saw that as yet another sign that Alex and I would be together forever.

I wondered if I'd have been happier never knowing the truth. It took me about three seconds to decide that *of course* I would have been happier. Every girl gets her heart broken by a stupid, inconsiderate boy; it's a rite of passage. I'm not saying I would have got over it quickly but maybe I'd have felt better in a few months and by then maybe Astrid's boyfriend would have introduced me to one of his friends and I'd have realized that Alex wasn't The One after all. But all because I couldn't stop sneezing on Christmas Eve, things panned out very differently. This was not a rite of passage – this was a living nightmare.

The High Street was pretty deserted. I stood there shivering, trying to work out whether I should still go to Astrid's. On the one hand it would give me time to think – it might help me to process what had happened. But the thought of going back there was too much to bear. I'd been round there after dinner the night before, getting things ready. I wanted to make sure everything was perfect, so I'd gone to the supermarket and bought all the food and put it in the fridge. I'd gone through the cabinet in the dining room and found a huge silver candelabra. I'd even set the table, with crisp white napkins. I wanted everything to be ready so I wasn't stressing about it when Alex arrived. I went up to Astrid's room to see if I could see the fireworks on Calton Hill. I didn't think anything of it when Alex didn't reply to my texts. I wasn't one of those girls who expected their boyfriends to keep in constant contact. Astrid got all pouty whenever Justin took more than five minutes to reply to a text. She'd start stressing about where he was and who he was with and whether he'd found someone else, and I'd have to reassure her that everything was fine and he was probably just busy. I almost felt sorry for her; I was so smug in the certain knowledge that I didn't have to worry about *my* boyfriend because *he* was perfect in every way.

I'd been walking home from Astrid's house when I got the text. *I can't do this anymore. I'm sorry.* I actually stopped on the street and laughed out loud. *That's* how sure I was about the relationship. It was only after the next message that I started to realize that maybe things weren't OK. I had no trouble understanding the words in the message but it was hard to get my head around how they could possibly relate to me and Alex. Then when he wouldn't reply to my messages and he wouldn't answer the phone I knew something had gone terribly wrong. My mind started racing trying to work out what had happened. Maybe he hadn't liked his Christmas presents after all or I'd just been too full-on somehow? Or maybe he hadn't been joking about Edward and he didn't believe that I would never ever like someone like that in a million years. I kept on coming back to the sex issue though. There was no doubt that I'd been the one pushing for us to do it. I thought Alex was being respectful of my feelings and wanted to make sure I wasn't rushing into something I wasn't ready for. I thought I had the perfect boyfriend and all the girls at school who moaned about sex-crazed boys just hadn't found the right one yet. Either that or Alex just wasn't like other boys. I was right about that, at least.

The timing of Alex's texts had me convinced that he didn't want to sleep with me. Clearly he was so repulsed at the thought of my naked body that he'd rather break up with me than risk being exposed to it. I've never felt particularly self-conscious about my body. Astrid's always going on about her weight even though she's loads skinnier than me. Stella's the same. It's not like I think I have an amazing body, it's just that it seems to me that there are more important things to worry about. Sure, I wouldn't mind my tummy being a little flatter and my boobs being a little smaller, but there's something about seeing your so-called best friends bending over to see how much daylight they can see between the tops of their thighs that really makes it hard to care. But after Alex's messages I began to wonder if there was something horribly wrong with my body – something I hadn't noticed before or something that boys would find disgusting but no one had bothered to tell me.

I'd managed to get home from Astrid's and say goodnight to Mum and even brush my teeth before I started crying. I was proud of myself for that. I couldn't wrap my brain around the suddenness of it. One minute you have a boyfriend and you're happier than you've ever been and the world is a wonderful place to live in, and the next . . . you have nothing. It was a cruel magician's trick: now you see it . . . now you don't. Now you're happy, now you're not. There should at least be some warning signs, shouldn't there? I should have at least had some inkling that things weren't as good as I thought they were. But the last time we'd seen each other was Christmas Eve and I'd seen how much he liked the recording I'd done for him. He was genuinely touched. You can't fake that kind of thing, can you? Not unless you're a pathological liar. Or a sociopath.

I'd texted Astrid even though she'd said she probably wouldn't be using her phone in France. I got a reply straightaway; there was a lot of swearing and saying what she'd do to him if she got the chance. Of course she had to mention that she'd thought there was something dodgy about Alex, even though she'd never said anything of the sort before. She asked if I was alright. I said I thought I'd be OK, even though that was a lie. She seemed to think I needed to do some grand gesture to show Alex he hadn't won, that I shouldn't let him get away with treating me like this. She said I should go round to his house and dump all his stuff on the doorstep, preferably when it was raining or snowing. I told her I'd think about it. I'd never told Astrid that I hadn't been to Alex's house; she would have thought that was weird.

I thought I would never stop crying – that the inside of my body would start drying up and I'd end up desiccated like a coconut. I sat cross-legged on the bed with the things Alex had given me: the skull and crossbones beanie, the tiny panda from the Kinder Surprise, the shell necklace. A stranger might think they didn't amount to much, but they meant everything to me. Along with the gig ticket from when we first met and the ticket for Mary King's Close and a sachet of sugar from the day we first kissed, and lots of other little things I seem to have been collecting without even really thinking about it. Perhaps my subconscious mind knew this wasn't going to last and I should probably have some mementoes to prove to myself that it had actually happened – that it hadn't been some sort of crazy dream cooked up in the mind of a lonely girl.

Of course I wasn't going to dump those precious things on Alex's doorstep. I should have known Astrid would suggest something ridiculous like that. But it did give me the idea to go round there. I needed to see him again – for him to look me in the eye and tell me he didn't want me. And that's where the silly fantasy of him realizing the error of his ways came in. That didn't work out so well, did it?

chapter twenty-seven

I opened the front door as quietly and carefully as I could. Mum had said she wasn't going to stay up till midnight. She's never liked Hogmanay – she's allergic to all that expectation and forced merriment. But the light was on in the living room and I could hear the TV. I tried to tiptoe past the living room door but it swung open before I knew what was happening. Mum was brandishing a poker. Her glasses were askew on her head and she looked terrified.

Mum realized I wasn't a burglar/murderer and lowered her weapon. She was breathing hard. 'Oh my goodness, you nearly gave me a heart attack! What on earth are you doing here?'

I took the poker and put it back in its stand next to the fire, buying me some time to compose myself. I planned to play it exactly as I had the night before; Mum would be none the wiser and I could cry myself to sleep safe in the knowledge that she would never know how stupid her daughter is. That was the *plan*, anyway. It all went a bit wrong when Mum said, 'Actually, love, I'm just glad you're home. I was feeling . . . well, I was feeling rather lonely, I suppose.' She sat down on the sofa next to a worn copy of *Death on the Nile*; she only reads Agatha Christie when she's feeling down. There was a bottle of apple and blackcurrant cordial in an ice bucket on the coffee table, sitting next to one of Mum's best cut-crystal glasses. A bowl of pistachio nuts sat on the arm of the sofa. I don't know what it was but something about that scene made me feel sad to the core. I burst into tears.

Mum jumped up from the sofa and put her arms around me. She didn't ask me what was the matter – not right away. She stroked my hair and made soothing noises. I felt like a little girl again, running crying to mummy because I'd scraped my knee on the patio. I cried so hard I started coughing; Mum told me to sit down while she rushed to the kitchen to get me a glass of water. The crying abated a little in the few seconds Mum was out of the room, but it resumed full force as soon as she was back.

I sipped the water and the coughing stopped. My gaze drifted towards the TV; a studio with a big screen showing a countdown, interspersed with crowd scenes from London and Edinburgh.

The crying reduced to a sniffle and *then* Mum asked me what was wrong.

I had to tell *someone*. It was too much for me to deal with on my own. Astrid wasn't in the country, I barely spoke to Stella anymore and there was no one else. *Alex* was the person I confided in.

I spewed out the words before I lost my nerve. 'Alex is . . . Alex is a *girl*.'

The countdown on the TV hit zero at the exact same time. Cheering and fireworks exploding. People shouting HAPPY NEW YEAR and singing Auld Lang Syne and kissing total strangers. Mum hit the mute button on the remote control. The crowd scenes seemed a lot more sinister in silence.

'I'm sorry, I'm not quite sure what you . . . ?' Mum didn't look horrified – not yet. I might as well have said 'Alex is a robot' or 'Alex is an alien'. Either of those might have been easier for me to explain.

She didn't believe me at first. She kept saying that she didn't understand and looking at me suspiciously. I told her the whole story about how Alex and I met and that it never even occurred to me for one second that he wasn't what he seemed to be. Mum didn't seem to think it was possible; I couldn't really blame her for that. At least she didn't tell me off about meeting some stranger off the internet – that was something to be grateful for at least. She didn't even say anything about me lying about spending the night with Astrid.

After a few minutes Mum shook her head. 'I can't believe it. It doesn't make any sense! Why would someone do something like that?'

Good question. I didn't know the answer so I just shrugged. I thought I'd feel better now that I'd shared the burden, but I just felt utterly exhausted. My gaze wandered towards the TV where some old eighties band was playing a song I recognized from a car advert.

Mum put her hand on my arm so I had to look away from the TV. I recognized the look on her face straightaway. It's the one she puts on when she's about to say something she knows I'm not going to like – usually when she wants me to do an extra hour of piano practice because she once read that it takes 10,000 hours of practice to be *truly* accomplished at something.

'What?' I asked.

'Darling?' She stretched the word a little, like she was testing an elastic band to see when it will snap. And that's when I knew what she was about to say would upset or annoy me much more than the usual nagging. 'Are you . . .? Are you a . . . *lesbian?*' She half-whispered the word and winced at the same time.

I felt a rush of heat to my face and my heart started beating really fast and I felt anger like I've never felt before. How could she even *think* such a thing, let alone say it? I should have known that telling her was a really bad move. I should have known that she wouldn't understand – she's never understood me my whole life so why should this be any different? I looked down and noticed my hand was gripping the arm of the sofa so hard that my knuckles were white. I was angry with Mum for being so unbelievably stupid and totally missing the point, as always, but more than that, and much more powerful, I was angry with Alex. She put me in this situation. She did this to me.

That was the moment that it all became clear. The boy I had fallen in love with did not exist. He was a character created by some seriously messed-up girl in order to trick me into liking her. And now my mother thought I was a lesbian because she couldn't believe I was stupid enough to be fooled like that. It turned my stomach.

'*What?*' The disbelief in my voice couldn't have been more obvious, but my mother didn't seem to notice.

Her hand squeezed mine. 'It's nothing to be

ashamed of, you know . . . I even . . . I suppose you'd say "experimented" when I was in college.' She laughed awkwardly and I wanted to punch her in the face. I've never wanted to punch a person before.

I shook off her hand. 'Jesus Christ, Mum! What the hell are you talking about? I *told* you what happened. Why are you always so quick to think the worst of me?'

'Oh stop being so over-dramatic. That's not true and you know it. It's just that this is very difficult to understand. Surely you can see things from my point of view?'

Rage. That's what I was feeling, pure and simple. I jumped up from the sofa and turned on her. 'See things from *your* point of view? How about you see things from *my* point of view for a change?! I *knew* I shouldn't have told you. I must have been mad to think you'd actually support me instead of being your usual judgemental self. I can't believe you're being like this!' I was practically spitting the words at her. I took a deep, steadying breath. 'How many more times do you want me to say it before you get it into your stupid head? I. Thought. Alex. Was. A. Boy. I'm not gay and if you say it one more time I swear I'll–'

'I have no idea why you're taking this out on me. I said you should be concentrating on piano and school but you didn't listen, did you? You always think you know better.' She pursed her lips into a thin, mean line. 'Well maybe this will be a lesson to you.'

I started crying again, more out of frustration than anything else. Mum took that as a sign of victory and gestured for me to sit back down. I sat and cried. Mum put her arm around me. 'I'm sorry, love. This is all such a shock. But if you say you really didn't know about Alex then I believe you.' It didn't *sound* like she believed me. 'It's just that it's a lot to take in. I'm not quite sure what to think.'

I chewed on my bottom lip – an old habit that drove Mum crazy. I tasted blood in my mouth as I said my next words. 'She made me—'

Mum interrupted me. 'She made you *what*?!' Her eyes were boring into me.

Fall in love with her. That's what I was going to say.

'Oh my God, what are you saying, Kate? Did she . . . *assault* you?' Her hand was over her mouth as if she wasn't sure she wanted that awful word to be heard. *Assault* me? Where the hell did that come from? It was as if she was trying to misunderstand every single thing I said. She was so clueless about everything.

I clenched my fists again. 'No! That's not what I . . .' I stopped. That wasn't what I'd been going to say. It *wasn't*. But Mum was looking at me differently now – less confusion and suspicion, more concern. I wanted it to stay that way. She needed to see that *I* was the victim here. 'She did stuff . . . to me. But I didn't want to.'

chapter twenty-eight

I was expecting Mum to flip out completely. If she had I think I might have come clean there and then, but she just muttered a quiet 'oh my God' and sat very still.

Take it back. Say you didn't mean it. Do it now. 'Mum, I didn't . . .' I was physically incapable of finishing that sentence. The truth didn't want to come out of my mouth.

'What exactly did she do to you?' Her gaze stayed firmly on the TV.

I shook my head. 'I can't . . . I don't want to talk about it.' My gaze stayed firmly on the TV too.

I was sure she wouldn't leave it at that, but she did. It wasn't as if we'd ever talked about sex before. When I started asking questions a few years ago about where babies came from she changed the subject then left a book about puberty and sex on my pillow a few days later. That was the beginning and end of our birds-and-the-bees discussion.

Mum put her hand on mine and squeezed it. 'I'm sorry, love.' Then she put her arm around me and I cried some more, because what else was there to do? At around two o'clock in the morning, she sent me to bed with a mug of hot chocolate and the assurance that everything was going to be OK. I didn't believe her but I nodded anyway. There was a knock at my bedroom door a few minutes later and Mum came in and sat on the edge of my bed. She was wearing her ratty old dressing gown instead of the fancy new one she'd got from Mags for Christmas.

I hadn't even touched the hot chocolate, but Mum didn't launch into her usual spiel about 'waste not, want not'. Instead she asked how I was feeling and I answered with a shrug. I felt all hollowed out – as if someone had set about my insides with a melon baller. Every last feeling had been wrung out of my body, leaving me dazed and numb.

Mum smiled tentatively. 'I know this hasn't exactly been the best start to the New Year, Kate. But you don't have to worry anymore, OK? It's all over now. And I'm . . . well, I'm here for you if you need to talk about anything. I can't promise I'll always say the right thing, but I'm *trying*. You have to let me be here for you. I think we should . . . well, let's talk about things in the morning.' I managed to say thank you. I didn't say I had no intention of talking about things in the morning; that would just have caused another argument and I was too exhausted to think let alone fight. Mum left me, saying she'd leave her bedroom door open and I should shout if I needed anything. It was the exact same thing she said whenever I was ill.

When I was sure she was gone for good I took my phone out from under the duvet. I'd hidden it just in case Mum came up with the bright idea of confiscating it. I thought she might be worried about Alex contacting me, that she might demand to know where she lived so she could storm round and talk to her parents. But no, Mum was treating me like I was ill, because *that* was something she knew how to deal with. If she treated me like an invalid she didn't have to think about whether her daughter was a lesbian or not.

There were four more texts on my phone. One from Astrid, three from Alex. Astrid's was obviously a message she'd sent to everyone in her contacts list: *Happy New Year, bitches! xxxxx*

I wasn't surprised that she hadn't bothered to send me a personalized message, even though as far as she knew I'd been dumped by my boyfriend the night before. If she knew the truth she would probably have magically arranged to be on the next flight home just to make sure she'd be the first one to hear the juicy details. After all, gossip like this doesn't come around every day. The thought of telling Astrid filled me dread. I knew she cared about me in her own way, but Astrid's number one priority always has been, and always will be, Astrid. And her favourite thing in the world is drama. She wouldn't leave me in peace until she knew every last detail. Then she'd proceed to call everyone she knew, no doubt adding that she'd always thought there was something strange about Alex but she hadn't quite been able to put her finger on it. Astrid would never let me forget about it all; it would be unbearable.

Then it hit me. There was no reason for Astrid to know. Come to think about it, there was no reason for anyone else to know. It wouldn't even be lying – not exactly. I'd had a boyfriend, and he had broken up with me. Twenty-four hours earlier those were the facts as I knew them. No one needed to know about what had happened since. Being dumped was bad enough. There was no reason for me to be humiliated even more.

Keeping the truth from Astrid wouldn't necessarily be easy. She had an unnerving ability to sniff out things that people wanted to keep private – like the fact that Stella had started seeing a speech therapist about her lisp or that Martin Todd's dad was in prison. Still, I'd been doing enough sneaking around in the past couple of months to become quite good at it. Astrid would have no reason to suspect what had really happened – she wouldn't guess in a million years. No one would guess because it was all too bizarre. I had that going in my favour, at least.

I'd have to tell Mum that I wanted to forget all about it and swear her to secrecy. She would be fine with that; she wouldn't have to worry about people thinking her precious daughter was a lesbian.

I would do whatever it took to wipe every trace of Alex and how I felt about him (her) from my memory. Maybe one day it wouldn't hurt so much.

Alex's texts were exactly what I expected. More sorries and please can we talk about this and I can explain. More lies from this person I realized I didn't even know. I deleted each message and wondered whether I should go ahead and delete Alex's number. I was just about to do that when another text arrived: *Please. I love you.*

That was the last straw. I deleted every single message from her then deleted her number. Tomorrow

I would shut down my profile on the Saving Serenity forum and get rid of everything that Alex had given me. All those little things that had seemed so special were now meaningless. The shell necklace was no longer a unicorn horn – it was just a shell on a string. It had always been a shell on a string, of course, but things acquire a certain kind of magic when they're from someone you love.

I love you. When Alex had first said those three little words to me I thought my heart might burst with happiness. Of course, I'd said them first even though I really hadn't meant to. Astrid always said you should *never* be the first one to say it. She said it made you look weak, that it gave him (whoever he might be) the upper hand and you might as well just give him a licence to trample all over your heart. Whenever she talked like that I would roll my eyes and smile but I'd never disagree – disagreeing with Astrid was never worth the hassle. She might have been right this time though. Alex had certainly trampled all over my heart. Steamrollered it, more like.

I love you. I'd meant those words when I said them that day on Calton Hill. There had been no doubt in my mind. I'd been thinking about it for weeks, analysing every feeling from every possible angle. Asking myself if *this* was what love was. If it was thinking about someone every minute of every day or putting their happiness ahead of yours or feeling like you were unstoppable as long as they were by your side. Because that was exactly how I felt.

I had loved the boy who thought bringing a skateboard on a date would make him seem so much cooler. The boy who always walked with his head down, shoulders slightly hunched because he didn't realize (or didn't care) how good-looking he was. The boy who'd nearly cried when he listened to me playing our song. He was the kind of boyfriend every girl wants – apart from Astrid, who claimed she'd never go out with a boy without a six-pack. Which was all very well if you lived in Los Angeles or Miami but not entirely realistic if you lived in Edinburgh.

If I'd sat down and written a checklist of everything I wanted in a boyfriend, Alex would have ticked nearly every box. I couldn't have hoped for anyone better. But it had all been too good to be true; my boyfriend had never even existed.

I closed my eyes and tried to sleep but I couldn't stop thinking about that moment when I'd seen Alex, when I'd seen *her*, wearing a skirt. And it was so blindingly obvious that she was a girl. Of *course* she was a girl. Her features were too delicate, too fine. She had *breasts*. That was the one thing I really couldn't

241

get my head around. I mean, they weren't massive or anything, but they were most definitely there. And they hadn't been there before. I may be stupid and clueless but I think I'd have realized if my boyfriend had breasts. Alex's chest had been flat and hard, exactly like I'd expect a boy's chest to be. But I'd never seen him without a shirt on; I'd never touched him without a shirt on. I'd seen it in a film once where a woman wrapped bandages around her chest to flatten her boobs. Alex must have done the same thing, going to all that effort to deceive me.

I suddenly realized something, kicking myself for not thinking of it sooner. That was why she'd been so reluctant to take things further – there was no way she could allow me to see her without clothes. But was that the only reason she'd broken up with me?

She loved me. A *girl* loved me – or at least *thought* she did. She was obviously a lesbian – one of those really boyish ones who buy men's clothes and never sit with their legs crossed. Not that I knew anything about lesbians. All I knew was that the boys at school thought there was nothing hotter than two women together. But of course the women had to be blonde and skinny with huge, over-inflated boobs and loads of make-up. Astrid told me they weren't *real* lesbians. They were just actresses (if you could call them that) who did whatever they were paid to do. It made me nauseous just thinking about it.

I had liked kissing Alex. No. I had *loved* kissing Alex. I couldn't imagine that there was anyone better at kissing in the whole wide world. That was Astrid's one complaint about Justin; she said she had to teach him how to kiss the way she liked it. It was like training a dog, apparently. Astrid gave me a withering look when I told her Alex was the perfect kisser. When I'd ignored her and gone on to talk about how soft his lips were, she'd said 'Yeah, well, it's not as if you have anyone to compare him to, is it?' That had shut me up. Astrid has always been an expert at cutting people down to size; it's her special gift.

It suddenly seemed like the most important thing in the world to me: my heart had been broken and I had been lied to and betrayed in the most unimaginable way, but now I had something to focus on. A single, concrete goal. *Astrid must never, ever find out about this.*

chapter twenty-nine

It didn't go down too well, me telling Mum I just wanted to forget all about it. She'd made blueberry pancakes for breakfast; she only made them on 'special' occasions, like the morning after Dad left. It turned out she wanted to talk things over. And if I didn't want to talk to her, she thought I should talk to Someone. She said it like that — as if it had a capital letter. I had no idea who this Someone was but I was sure I didn't want to find out. I told Mum I needed some time to think — some breathing space — and she backed off, but not before telling me she just wanted to make sure she was doing the right thing by her little girl. I hadn't been her little girl for years.

I only managed to choke down half a pancake in the end — I threw the rest in the bin when Mum wasn't looking. It felt like my stomach had shrunk to the size of a golf ball overnight. Dad liked to play golf. He probably still does.

I turned off my phone after getting two more texts from Alex. It didn't matter that I'd deleted her number because I knew it off by heart. The second text asked me to tell her if I wanted her to stop bothering me, which made no sense at all. Surely the fact that I was ignoring her was enough to show that I didn't want anything more to do with her. It was like she was trying to trick me into talking to her, but it wouldn't work. I wouldn't let myself get sucked in. I pulled my desk chair over to the wardrobe, climbed on the chair, stood on tip-toes and pushed the phone out of reach. The top of the wardrobe was dusty; Mum never bothered dusting things she couldn't see.

Half an hour passed before I realized that I couldn't possibly cope without my phone; Astrid would probably text me and if I didn't reply she'd know for sure that something was up. She was due back from skiing tomorrow and no doubt she'd want to comfort me after my terrible break-up. (And by 'comfort', I mean 'be patronizing and probably gloat a bit'.) I had to use my tennis racket to coax the phone to where I could reach it and I nearly fell off the chair and broke my neck in the process. When I turned my phone on there were no texts from anybody.

Mum spent most of the day sitting at the kitchen table, tapping away on her ancient laptop. It was almost as if last night hadn't happened. But there were certain things that made it obvious something had changed. Mum didn't nag me once about piano practice *and* she suggested a walk on the beach after lunch (which I hadn't eaten). We never went for walks on the beach – not since Dad left anyway. She didn't put up much of a fight when I said I didn't feel like it. I had no idea how long it would last, Mum treating me like a human being whose opinions were valid, but I wasn't complaining. It was just a shame that something really awful had to happen in order for her to be nice to me. She made me my favourite toasted sandwich for dinner, with a tomato salad on the side. I nibbled at the crust, ate half a cherry tomato and binned the rest when Mum's back was turned.

I sat with Mum for a bit in the evening, just so she wouldn't worry. I pretended to read the book she'd got me for Christmas while she watched one of the yawnsome antiques programmes she insists on recording every single day. For some reason she seems to really care whether a couple of strangers wearing matching red fleeces make a profit on some ugly vase they've bought. She didn't seem to be enjoying it as much as usual this time though; out of the corner of

my eye I kept on catching her glancing over at me.
Usually if Mum has something to say she comes right
out and says it – she never bothers about upsetting or
offending people. These timid glances were new – and
quite irritating.

I didn't need to fake my jaw-cracking yawn before
saying I wanted an early night. I got up and leaned
down to give Mum a kiss on the forehead and she
said 'Night, night, sleep tight' which she'd said every
single night since I was little. I realized then that she'd
forgotten to say it last night.

I was just picking up my book and empty mug
when she cleared her throat and said, 'I'm sorry this
happened to you, Kate.' Her eyes hadn't left the TV
screen.

'It's OK . . . I'll be OK, you know.'

She shook her head and looked at me. 'What that
girl did to you . . . it's disgusting. I can't even imagine
how you must be feeling. She can't be allowed to do it
to anyone else.'

'I don't think she'd . . . I mean, I don't think she's
some kind of . . . predator.' I had to be careful here.

'How do you know? You don't know anything
about her, do you? For all we know you might not be
the first girl she's . . . *abused*.' Mum grimaced.

'Please can we just leave it? I really don't want

to think about it anymore. I want to forget she even exists and just get on with my life.' I found myself staring at the piano. It gave me an idea. 'You know . . . I was thinking of entering that competition this year. It would be good to have something to focus on.' I said this casually, like it was no big deal.

'Oh.' She sat up straighter. 'Now that sounds like a very good idea. Only if you want to though – no pressure.' That was a laugh. She'd only been trying to get me to enter the Young Pianist of the North competition for the last three years, ratcheting up the pressure until hardly a day went by without her mentioning it.

'No pressure,' I echoed. 'Maybe you can help me choose which pieces to play?'

She looked so hopeful, as if a pointless piano competition could really fix everything that was wrong. 'I'd like that. Now off you go to bed. And don't you worry about a thing, OK? Everything's going to be fine.' She almost sounded convinced.

The next day I woke up to a text from Edward, sent at 2.34 a.m.: *Happy New Year! A new year seems like the perfect time to dump that boyfriend of yours, don't you reckon?*

Great. Just what I needed. I couldn't say Alex and I were still together because Mum was bound to say something to Mags, even if she didn't tell her the whole truth. I replied: *As a matter of fact I have dumped him. Too busy for a boyfriend at the moment.* Hopefully that was enough to get him to leave me alone. His jokes about us getting together had become a lot less jokey recently, and the looks he gave me made me uncomfortable. I'd tried to talk to Mum about it but she said he was just teasing me – that Edward would never be interested in a schoolgirl. She had no idea.

I'd lied to Alex, saying Edward had a new girlfriend. I hadn't wanted to lie but Alex kept on asking questions about him, clearly jealous. It was a harmless lie – a white lie, definitely. It made Alex feel better and it made me feel less guilty for fancying Edward last year just because I'd had an embarrassing dream about him. That was how much I cared about Alex. I didn't want anything or anyone to make him (HER) feel bad. His happiness was my number one priority.

Edward replied straightaway even though he must have only had a couple of hours sleep: *That's the best news I've heard all year. Call me if you're feeling lonely.* I had no idea what had happened to him. He never used to be sleazy like that. Going to university had turned him into some sort of wannabe lothario and it really didn't suit him. If he really *was* expecting me to call, he'd be waiting a very long time. *I've had enough of boys for the time being.* That was what I thought when I read Edward's text. It was almost laughable that I still couldn't get it into my stupid head that I'd still had nothing whatsoever to do with *any* boys. My brain couldn't come to terms with it yet. Every time I thought about Alex, the words HE and HIM and HIS were there instead of SHE and HER and HERS. Simple pronouns were confusing to me all of a sudden. But Alex *had* been my boyfriend, even though he had technically never existed.

It would be better if Alex had died – maybe hit by a bus while skateboarding. Then I would get to be the grieving girlfriend and I'd be safe from the knowledge that it was all a lie. Astrid would feel sorry for me and the girls at school would look at me differently – they'd think I was brave and tragic and *interesting*. Mum would take care of me and probably let me off the hook about piano for a while. And maybe she would call Dad and he'd turn up on the doorstep one day and he would say sorry for being such a terrible father and he would move back to Edinburgh and I'd see him at least twice a week.

This little fantasy imploded as soon as I really thought about it. I would only know about Alex dying if it was in the papers or on the internet, and of course *they* would know she was a girl. So I would be in the same position I am now, except I'd feel conflicted about hating her, because it was wrong – not to mention pointless – to hate a dead person. The girls at school would still look at me differently, but they'd be looking at me thinking I was a total freak. So all in all it was better that Alex was alive.

There were no more texts from Alex overnight. Perhaps she'd finally given up. That would be a good thing . . . wouldn't it?

Mum was acting weird at breakfast the next morning, flitting around the kitchen like a sparrow with ADHD. I managed to eat a few cornflakes even though I still wasn't hungry. The last thing I needed was Mum jumping to the conclusion that I was developing some kind of eating disorder. She'd probably march me straight to the doctor and have me sent away to a clinic in the middle of nowhere (after she'd made sure there was a half-decent piano available for me to play).

'So!' Her voice was too loud, too bright. 'So . . . what are you up to today?'

I shrugged even though shrugging is one of her pet hates. She finally stopped flitting and sat down next to me at the table. 'When's Astrid getting back?'

At that exact moment my phone buzzed with a text from Astrid and Mum looked down and saw her name on the screen. 'Speak of the devil!' I read the message, angling the phone away from Mum. Astrid was back and she wanted me to go round to her house to keep her company while she unpacked. She didn't bother to ask how I was doing. 'If you want to get out of the house for a few hours, that's fine by me.' Mum's smile was almost convincing. She didn't like Astrid – never had. I shrugged again just to see what she would do; she didn't even flinch. She put her hand on my shoulder and said, 'I think you could do with a friend right now. It's all very well talking to me but I think you'd be more comfortable talking to Astrid, don't you think?'

'Mum! I've already told you! I don't want anyone knowing about this . . . It's . . . private.'

She held up her hands in surrender. 'I know, I know, but . . . Astrid knows that you and Alex have . . . um . . . broken things off, doesn't she? The very least she can do is provide you with a bit of tea and sympathy. She doesn't need to know the rest.'

'I don't need tea and sympathy! I need . . . God, I don't even know!' I pushed my chair back and stormed over to the sink, slammed down my cereal bowl, sloshing milk on to the clean dishes on the draining board. I grabbed my phone from the table and left the room before Mum could shout at me.

Tea and sympathy? As if that would fix anything. What I really needed was the last few months of my life not to have happened. I needed my heart to be unbroken.

I needed Alex – *my* Alex – to be real.

chapter thirty

I was sitting on Astrid's bed, watching her rummage through her suitcase for the present she'd supposedly bought me. Astrid had never bought me a present back from her holidays even though I always made sure to get her something. But sure enough she turned around brandishing a Toblerone like a sword. 'It's been scientifically proven that chocolate is, like, the official antidote to break-ups. I'm pretty sure that if you eat that all in one go you'll forget about that bastard.'

'I'm pretty sure if I eat that all in one go I'll vomit.'

'Exactly! And you're not going to be thinking about him with your head down the toilet, are you?'

I couldn't help laughing. My laughter didn't sound quite right to me though – there was something hollow about it. It was an echo of real laughter. Still, it was enough to make Astrid smile. She's beautiful when she smiles. Normally there's something pinched about her features, something you could interpret as meanness. Astrid always says that people need time to warm up to her, and she's right. If you saw her walking down the street, not smiling or laughing or anything, you'd probably come to the conclusion that she's a bitch. And she *is* a bitch a lot of the time but she can be nice too. It's just that she tends not to let people see that side of her.

Astrid made me tell her the whole break-up story in minute detail – she even wanted to see the texts Alex had sent but I told her I'd deleted them. She approved of that.

She flopped down on the bed next to me, leaving her clothes strewn across the carpet. 'God, Kate, this is all *so* weird. He seemed so *devoted* to you, you know?' I nodded dully. 'He was like a puppy, watching your every move and trying to work out what you wanted him to do.' This was not the first time Astrid had used the puppy analogy. I didn't like it any more than I had the last time. 'I mean, what kind of guy ditches his girlfriend *before* he gets laid?! This must be the first time it's happened in the whole history of the world . . . Sorry, am I being insensitive?'

Astrid often asked things like this, as if by doing so she negated anything insensitive or downright offensive she'd just said. I shook my head and she carried on. 'I *told* you there was something off about him, didn't I?'

'Congratulations, you were right. I'm very happy for you,' I deadpanned.

'Sorry! It's just that if there's one thing I know, it's people. I'm like a human weirdo detector or something. Although Justin thought there was something strange about Alex too, now that I think about it.' This was news to me. It seemed like I was the only person who hadn't had suspicions about Alex. With every excruciating minute that passed I felt more and more foolish. 'Oh God, sorry, I'm sure you don't want to hear about Justin right now. Don't worry, you can still hang out with us.'

'Thanks.' She may have been a human weirdo detector but Astrid was oddly oblivious to sarcasm.

'So let's get down to business.' Astrid propped herself up on her elbows and an evil grin spread across her face. 'What are we going to do to him?' She shook her head at my confused expression. 'Well we can't just let him get away with this, can we? No one hurts my best friend and gets away with it.'

I sighed. 'We're not going to *do* anything. You can't force someone to stay in a relationship with you.'

'Maybe not, but you can punish them when they

dump you by text the night before you're supposed to shag for the first time.'

Astrid had probably already started plotting some hugely involved, intricate plan for revenge – complete with maps and diagrams. There was only one way to stop her in her tracks, and thankfully the tears came easily. 'I just want to forget about him, Astrid – act like this whole thing never happened . . . like he doesn't even exist.'

Astrid thrives on drama but she doesn't like crying unless she's the one doing it. For some reason it makes her really uncomfortable. 'Oh don't cry! It's going to be OK, I promise. Um . . . do you want a Diet Coke or something?'

I mournfully shook my head and cried a little bit more. Astrid patted my shoulder. I sniffed. 'Sorry. It's just hard, you know? Can we maybe talk about something else for a bit?' I scrambled around in my brain for another topic of conversation. 'Have you done that assignment for English?'

The look of horror on Astrid's face was so funny that I had to smile. 'Shit! I completely forgot about it! *Shit*. What am I going to do?' She jumped up from the bed, hurried over to her desk and started rifling through a precarious pile of books and folders.

I checked the time on my phone. 4.03 p.m. We

were going back to school the next day and English was our first lesson. I'd finished the assignment the first day of the Christmas holidays. 'It's OK, you've got time. As long as you've read the book . . . you *have* read the book, haven't you?'

Of course she hadn't read the book. Astrid was usually able to charm her way around being late with her homework, but our English teacher, Ms Churchill, didn't take any crap from her – or from anyone for that matter. Ms Churchill was obsessed with preparing us for the 'real world'. She said, 'You're not children anymore and I refuse to treat you as such.' Apparently handing in your essays late was frowned upon in the real world.

Astrid started freaking out, although it was hard to tell how much of the freaking out was genuine and how much was down to her love of the dramatic. She asked if she could read my assignment 'just for an idea of what we should be doing', but she wasn't surprised when I said no.

'Look, I've got the study guide if you want to borrow it. It won't be perfect but I think you can probably get away with not reading the book.' Astrid wasn't looking convinced, so I forged on. 'If you want, you can email me your first draft tonight and I'll take a look at it.'

That clinched it. She knew I'd fix all her mistakes, even if it took me all night. It actually felt good to be helping her out; I wouldn't mind working on her essay if it took my mind off Alex for a few hours.

I said I'd run home to get the study guide but Astrid insisted on coming with me to save time. 'Every second counts!' That's when I knew she was really enjoying this. In her mind the situation had transformed into a life-or-death race against time.

I'd already decided that Astrid would wait outside while I went in to get the book, just to make sure Mum wouldn't have the opportunity to say something like 'Isn't it *awful* that Kate's boyfriend turned out not to be a boy after all?' or 'So Astrid, do *you* think Kate might be a lesbian?' I didn't actually think there was any chance of Mum saying either of those things – she knew I wanted to keep this whole thing secret – but my paranoia had reached epic levels.

We ran the whole way to my house because that's what Astrid wanted to do. She was much faster than me; I was well behind her when she turned the corner on to my road. So I was surprised to find her running back towards me, looking genuinely worried. 'Oh my God, Kate, I think something's happened!'

I had no idea what she was talking about but panic flooded my body all the same. She grabbed my arm and pulled me round the corner. I saw the police car first. It was very shiny and parked right outside my house. Then I saw a policeman with his hat wedged under his arm. He was standing at my front door, which was open. My first thought was something had happened to Mum while I'd been at Astrid's, but then I thought there probably would have been an ambulance instead of a police car. My second thought was Dad. In the few seconds it took us to get to the house I'd convinced myself that Dad was dead. A car crash or a house fire or a burglary gone wrong. But then I saw Mum standing in the doorway and she didn't look like she'd been crying. No matter how she felt about Dad now, I was sure she would cry if she found out he was dead. Mum's eyes flitted from me to Astrid and back again as we stood on the path desperately trying to get our breath back. Mum may not have been crying, but she definitely looked worried. Mags emerged from inside and put a hand on Mum's shoulder. What the hell was *she* doing here?

'Mum? What's happened?' I asked in a shaky voice. The policeman turned towards us. He was young and very good-looking; his jaw was very square, like it would sit nicely on a mantelpiece.

The policeman turned back to Mum. 'I take it this

is your daughter?' Not exactly a brilliant deduction seeing as I'd just called Mum *Mum*.

Mum nodded and looked nervously up and down the street. 'Why don't we go back inside? Um . . . Astrid, I think you'd better be getting home. Mags, could you maybe—'

'Mum? What's going on?'

The policeman straightened his shoulders and coughed. 'My name is PC Mason. I was just talking to your mother about the allegations against . . .' He winced because he had to look down at the little black notebook he was holding. 'Miss Alex Banks?'

I closed my eyes so I didn't have to see Astrid's face. *'Miss?!'*

chapter thirty-one

I barged into the house past Mum and Mags. I slammed the door to my room so hard my panda calendar fell on the floor.

There was no end to this nightmare. Astrid *knew*. By tomorrow lunchtime everyone at school would know and I would be a laughing stock. I wanted to die. I bet Astrid was already planning who to tell: Justin first, then Stella. She'd probably want to tell everyone else in person so she could see the looks on their faces. As I lay on my bed I kept expecting a knock at the door and for Astrid to come in and start grilling me, or at least ask for the study notes. But then I realized all thoughts of doing the assignment would have disappeared from her head immediately. Knowing Astrid she'd probably tell Ms Churchill she'd been unable to complete the essay because she'd been so *traumatized* by my situation.

Astrid was all I could think about, even when I heard voices coming from the hallway. Mum and Mags. I had to keep thinking about Astrid because if I stopped thinking about Astrid I would be thinking about why my mother had called the police and what on earth I was going to say to them.

The voices outside my door were muffled so I crept over to the door.

'I practically had to barricade the door to keep that Astrid girl out. Anyway, I sent her off home and she swore she wouldn't tell a soul.' Mags had never met Astrid before so she had no idea how unlikely that was. 'You did the right thing, Belinda. You didn't have a choice.'

'But did you see the look she gave me? She hates me!' Mum sounded like she was crying.

'She's a *teenager*! Hating parents is part of the job description. But seriously, she'll thank you for this one day. Sometimes we have to be the ones to make the tough decisions.'

I couldn't hear what Mum said next no matter how hard I pressed my ear to the door. Then I heard Mags saying she'd better be heading off or she'd miss her train. Mum thanked her, saying she wouldn't have been able to handle this alone. Then I heard the front door open and close and she was gone. Presumably the policeman was still lurking around somewhere but I couldn't hear him.

I lay back down on the bed, pulling the duvet on top of me as if it could shield me from this mess. I hadn't meant for this to happen. I hadn't meant to lie – Mum had just got the wrong end of the stick. I should have put her right, but I was so desperate for her to stop questioning my sexuality. And I was angry with Alex – of course I was. But if I'd thought that Mum would do something insane like calling the police I'd never have let her go on thinking Alex had forced me into anything. I genuinely thought she'd want to forget all about it – how could I have been so unbelievably naïve? I should have known she'd talk to Mags – those two told each other everything. Mum was always going to her for advice. She treated Mags like some kind of Yoda figure for some bizarre reason. *Of course* she'd tell her. And of course Mags would say she should call the police. I should have seen this coming.

There was a knock at the door and Mum didn't wait for an answer before coming into the room. She said nothing for a minute or two, so I was forced to come out from under the duvet to see what she was up to. Mum didn't look like she'd been crying, but it was always difficult to tell with her. 'Look, before you say anything . . . I know you're not happy about this but it's the right thing to do. It *is*. We can't let that . . . *girl* . . . get away with this.' I started to speak but Mum held up her hand to silence me. '*No*. You have to listen to me. What if she targets someone else, just because you did nothing? How would you feel then?' She sounded so sure about it all – forceful almost. The uncertainty that had been in her voice when she'd talked to Mags was nowhere to be found.

There was so much I wanted to say but what was the point? I had no one to blame but myself. I'd set this in motion and there was nothing I could do about it now. Mum sat down next to me on the bed and brushed my hair from my face. Her face was softer all of a sudden. 'You don't want this hanging over you for the rest of your life. It'll haunt you, Kate . . . trust me.'

Trust me. I couldn't let myself think about what she meant by that. So I let my mother lead me by the hand from my bedroom. I knew I should just tell her the truth, let her explain everything to the policeman and make him go away so he could catch some real criminals. I *knew* that was what I should do, yet I couldn't bring myself to do it. I was a coward.

There were three empty mugs on the coffee table in the living room. PC Mason, Mum and Mags had clearly been having a good old chat before I arrived.

PC Mason was examining a photo on the shelf above the TV. I think he was looking for clues. His hat was still wedged under his arm and I wondered if it was against the rules to put it down in case anyone stole it. He turned and smiled when he realized Mum had managed to wrangle me from my room. I think the smile was supposed to be reassuring, but it was anything but.

Mum asked him if he'd like another cup of tea and you could tell he wanted to say yes but there was probably some rule about that too. Mum didn't bother asking if *I* wanted a cup of tea. We sat on the sofa and she clamped her hand on to my knee. PC Mason made to put down the photo but it fell over and dislodged one of Mum's favourite ornaments. He moved lightning fast to catch it but dropped his hat in the process. He stuttered and apologized and two little red patches appeared on his cheeks, making him look about twelve years old. He replaced the ornament and the photo frame and stuttered an apology. He picked up his hat and brushed off some invisible dust, probably offending Mum in the process.

Finally he was sitting across from us and asking whether it was OK if he could ask me some questions. I nodded and Mum gave my knee a squeeze of approval. 'Good girl,' she whispered.

'Right, this shouldn't take too long. I'm just going to need a few more details – hear it from the horse's mouth, as it were.' He looked vaguely embarrassed saying this. 'OK. Can you tell me the suspect's full name, age and address?'

The suspect. Alex was now a suspect. I guess that meant that I was now a victim. I told him Alex's name, age and address and apologized for not knowing the postcode, as if he was going to send her a greetings card (*Congratulations! You've been accused of a crime you didn't commit!*).

PC Mason asked me to briefly describe the nature of the offence. He said he appreciated this might be difficult, then he looked at Mum. She gave my knee another squeeze. 'Go ahead, sweetheart.'

This was the moment I would tell them it had all been a terrible mistake. Mum had got her wires crossed and Alex hadn't actually done anything to me and I was dreadfully sorry for wasting his time. I glanced at Mum and she smiled encouragingly. I took a deep, shaky breath and opened my mouth and lied.

I said that we'd been kissing one day and Alex had forced her hand inside my underwear and touched me and kept touching me even though I kept saying 'no'. And I tried to push her off me but she was stronger than me. PC Mason blushed again when he asked if she had penetrated me with her fingers and I must have blushed too when I nodded. He wrote everything down in an illegible scrawl.

He asked me where the 'alleged offence' had happened and the question threw me slightly, even though it was an obvious one. Every crime needs a crime scene. My bedroom. I said it had happened in my bedroom when Mum had been out. I said I couldn't remember the date and I could tell that didn't go down well. I didn't want to risk picking a random date and having Mum say she hadn't left the house that day. Just my luck to have a mother who writes everything down on the kitchen calendar. I said it was sometime in late November or early December. A Saturday or a Sunday. PC Mason pushed me to try and remember but I just shrugged and looked as apologetic as I could.

'OK, well I think that's about all we need for now.' He read through his notes and said, 'Just one more thing? Your mother mentioned that you were not . . . um . . . aware that Miss Banks was female?'

I nodded. He looked like he wanted to ask more, perhaps to ask how that was even possible, but he just shook his head. Mum chipped in, 'That makes it worse, doesn't it? What she did. It's fraud, isn't it?'

PC Mason shook his head. 'There *is* an offence of obtaining sexual intimacy by fraud, but it looks like what we're dealing with here is sexual assault.' He winced. 'I mean, it *would* be, if the allegations–'

'You are going to arrest the girl, aren't you? She took advantage of my daughter. Kate's not even sixteen yet!'

PC Mason stood. 'I'm fully aware of that, Mrs McAllister. I'm sure the ages of both Kate and Miss Banks will be taken into consideration. From the looks of things, we certainly have grounds to talk to Miss Banks. One of my colleagues will be in touch to keep you up to speed and someone will be along to take a full statement from Kate.'

'Alex is going to be arrested?' I asked before I could stop myself. I hadn't thought about the age difference between Alex and me. Surely it wasn't relevant?

PC Mason turned towards me. 'You *do* want to press charges, don't you? You need to think about this very carefully. If there's something you're not telling me, now would be a good time to mention it.'

'Of course she wants to press charges! And even if she doesn't, *I* do.' Mum stopped and narrowed her eyes. 'And what's that supposed to mean anyway? *Something you're not telling me.* Kate told you exactly what happened.'

'I wasn't implying anything, I just want you both to be aware that these are very serious allegations.

In all likelihood Miss Banks will be arrested in the morning.'

Another chance to tell the truth. It wasn't too late, even then.

This is wrong and you know it. This is not the kind of person you want to be.

My mind snapped back to the scene at her house on Hogmanay. The horror and confusion and betrayal. Those feelings hadn't gone away. If anything they were amplifying, getting uglier and uglier as they festered away inside me.

What that girl did to me was unforgivable, even if it wasn't exactly what Mum and the police *thought* she'd done to me. It didn't matter; Alex deserved to be punished for what she did. Maybe it was lucky that Mum had misunderstood what I was trying to say that night. And maybe I should be glad that Mags had talked her into calling the police. There was no other way Alex was going to get what was coming to her. It was her word against mine now. And I planned to make sure that my word was very, very convincing.

chapter thirty-two

Mum wouldn't let me stay home from school the next day. It was a Friday though, so at least I only had one day to endure before the weekend. Astrid was waiting for me, sitting on the wall next to the school gates, even though it was freezing cold. She'd tried to call me several times the night before but my phone had been switched off. She hugged me then grabbed my arm and marched me off round the corner so we could talk in private.

'I've been worried sick! I thought you'd been, like, arrested or something! Why didn't you answer my calls?!'

'Mum took my phone. Sorry.' The lie came easily.

'God, Kate . . . I can't believe it! Why didn't you tell me about Alex?!' As if that was the most important issue here – Astrid being kept up to date at all times.

'I'm sorry. I didn't know until . . .' I dissolved into

tears. They were real tears – they just happened to be extraordinarily well-timed. Astrid patted my back and muttered apologies and words of comfort. By the time I stopped crying the bell had gone and we had to go our separate ways for registration. Before she left I asked her if she'd told anyone.

'No! What do you take me for?! Give me *some* credit!' She turned away and then back again. 'I mean obviously I told Justin, but I tell him *everything*. And he'd *never* say anything, so there's nothing to stress about. Listen, let's go to the park at lunch. No one else will be there in this weather.' She gave me another quick hug. 'I'm here for you, Kate. And I really want you to know that I don't think any less of you or anything.'

She left me leaning against the wall, wondering what possible reason she could have for thinking less of me. I wasn't remotely reassured by what she'd said. As far as I knew the news had spread round Justin's school by now; it would only be a matter of time before the same thing happened here.

Astrid and I didn't sit together in English; Ms Churchill had devised a seating plan to make sure no one sat next to their actual friends. God knows how she managed to procure that information. I saw Astrid talking to Ms Churchill at the start of the lesson, obviously trying to explain why she hadn't done the assignment. I watched as Churchill's face changed from sceptical to neutral to downright sympathetic, but not once did she look over at me. I took that to mean that Astrid hadn't used me as her excuse after all. That was something to be grateful for.

I had Maths with Stella after break. I hadn't seen her at all over the holidays and had barely spent any time with her since going out with Alex. She was always better friends with Astrid than she was with me; Astrid was the pinnacle of our bizarre little isosceles triangle of a friendship.

Here was the real test of Astrid's loyalty. I hugged Stella and sat down next to her. I asked about her Christmas, and thanked her for the card she'd sent to my house. I hadn't bothered with cards this year, and even if I had they'd have been tiny cheapo ones handed round at school, rather than the huge fancy embossed ones with first-class Christmas stamps on the envelope that Stella had sent. Stella talked a bit about her Christmas and the fact that her sister had flown back in the middle of her gap year in Guatemala to spend it with her family. I think that was when I knew. Stella's not really one for elaborating – at least not with me. The best I can usually get out of her when

I ask about her weekend or something is 'fine thanks, how was yours?' but this time she said at least seven consecutive sentences. When it was her turn to ask about my holidays, she couldn't quite meet my eye. I could tell she was trying really hard but the closest her gaze got was somewhere above my left shoulder, as if there was a parrot perched there. Astrid had told her. The lying bitch.

I didn't let on to Stella that I knew she knew – I didn't want Astrid knowing that I was on to her. I *knew* she wouldn't be able to keep her mouth shut. For the rest of the lesson I was acutely aware of Stella stealing glimpses when she thought I wasn't looking. I wondered what kind of spin Astrid had put on the story. Was I the poor, pathetic, innocent victim or had she sown a seed of doubt in Stella's mind? *'She must have known . . . surely.'* Maybe she'd dropped in a little comment about that time she'd supposedly caught me staring in the H&M changing rooms. Whatever Astrid had said, Stella couldn't escape fast enough after Maths, muttering something about having to take books back to the library. In all the time I'd known Stella she had never once borrowed a book from the school library. It was a little bit tragic that she couldn't come up with a better excuse for abandoning me.

*

I waited outside the classroom and watched carefully as everyone rushed to the canteen or to get their coats for the lunchtime dash to Greggs. Every time someone looked in my direction I examined their face for signs that they knew. It definitely seemed like more people were looking at me. I could usually walk the corridors without anyone paying me any attention; it was a simple matter of staying close to the wall and keeping your head down. It was the exact opposite of Astrid's method. She walked the halls like she was on a catwalk. It didn't matter to her in the slightest that people thought she looked ridiculous and sometimes even laughed in her face. She was so secure in who she was that she didn't need any outside validation. You had to admire that.

Rachael Meadows walked past with a girl whose name I didn't know and I could have sworn Rachael said something like 'That's her' or 'Did you see her?' Her eyes swept over me as if I wasn't even there, but that could have been down to her being a lot more subtle than Stella. I couldn't tell if the other girl was looking at me, because her fringe hung too far down over her eyes. I bet she was though.

Astrid must have told more people. It was far more likely that she'd been the one to spread it around rather than Stella. I caught a boy from the year below looking at me and smiling. I wanted to storm up to him and ask him what was so funny or tell him to wipe that smile off his face. That was what people did on TV. It's a lot easier to be brave when you're fictional.

I'd 'forgotten' to bring my lunch with me. The salad that Mum had carefully prepared that morning was still in the fridge at home. I'd only had half a piece of toast for breakfast but I wasn't hungry. Astrid had finished eating her sandwich by the time we got to the park. She offered me a bite when she'd eaten all but the last corner; I said no. I let her witter on and on about the fact that she was sure her Maths teacher had had a boob job over the Christmas holidays and did I think Suzanne Perkins had put on weight.

I've always liked the park next to school, but I only like it when it's quiet. I like to look at the trees and the ducks and the swans and the ripples across the pond. I don't mind the old ladies or the dog-walkers or the little kids on their scooters – they *belong*. But I hate it when other kids from school are there – they ruin it somehow. That freezing cold day in January the park was practically deserted. There was a bald man walking a poodle wearing a camouflage coat (the poodle, not the man) and a woman sitting on a bench. She was sitting up straight, feet neatly together, handbag on her lap. She was staring at the pond, which was half-frozen. All the birds were clustered in the unfrozen patch of water right in the middle.

Astrid and I stopped at the huge tree stump next to the pond, where there was at least some shelter from the wind. She hopped up on the felled tree next to the stump and sat there looking at me expectantly.

'What?'

'Are we going to talk about this or are you just going to let me talk *at* you for an hour?' She was infuriating.

I was considering the best response other than pushing her from her perch when my phone buzzed in my bag. There was a missed call from Mum; she'd left a message. It wasn't a long message. Her voice was very matter of fact. Straight to the point, she didn't ask how I was getting on or say that she appreciated how hard it must be for me being back at school. I stared at Astrid as I listened to the message and then listened to it again, as if I hadn't quite understood the first time. She was on her phone, probably texting Justin to say she was just about to get the lowdown and she'd tell him *everything* later.

My phone slipped out of my hand on to the frozen mud. I didn't drop it out of shock or anything dramatic like that, it just slipped from my fingers because of the cold. I picked it up and promptly dropped it again. My hands had somehow lost the capacity to grip.

'Kate? Are you OK? You look really weird.'

I swallowed, with difficulty. 'Alex has been arrested.'

chapter thirty-three

Arrested. By the police. Like a criminal. When I pictured the scene, Alex was *my* Alex. A boy wearing jeans and a shirt and the hat I'd got him for Christmas. His hands were behind his back because he had been handcuffed. A faceless policeman (not PC Mason, for some reason) was pushing down on Alex's head to make sure he didn't bang his head when he was bundled into the car. Not because he cared whether Alex hit his head or not, but so that there couldn't be any accusations of police brutality. The car door would slam and Alex would flinch. He'd look out of the window at his mother. She would be standing on the stone steps in front of their flat, sobbing. A single tear would trickle down Alex's face and he wouldn't be able to wipe it away because of the handcuffs.

Or maybe it had happened at school – wherever that might be. I'd already realized that he'd (she'd) lied about going to Fettes – which explained why he (she) had been clueless about the head boy when Justin asked in the café.

'Arrested? Seriously? That's, like, serious.' Astrid frowned and wrinkled her nose. 'But what have they arrested him – sorry, her – for? That Mags woman wouldn't say, even though I'm your best friend and I said you'd tell me anyway. Is it fraud or something? For pretending to be a guy? Kate? Hellooooo?'

I pictured Alex (*my* Alex) in a prison cell. I'd never seen a prison cell in real life but the one in my head was dark and smelly, with a filthy yellowing mattress in the corner. Alex was sitting on the floor with his back against the wall, hugging his knees.

I knew the pictures in my head were over-dramatic to the point of being ridiculous but that didn't stop my brain coming up with them. And it didn't stop me feeling like I was going to throw up. Alex had been arrested. What had I *done*? The boy who cried 'Wolf' had nothing on me.

Astrid was waving her hand in front of my face now; she couldn't stand being ignored.

'Sorry . . . I was . . . It's just a bit upsetting, that's all.'

'Upsetting? It's fucking brilliant. I mean, talk about the ultimate revenge! Don't mess with Kate

McAllister – she will take you *down*. Anyway, it's not as if that freak's going to go to prison for pretending to be a boy, is it? It'll teach her a lesson though. What the hell was she thinking, doing something like that? It's all very well being a lesbian or whatever but just go and find yourself another lesbian to harass, rather than preying on some random straight girl on the internet . . . You *are* straight, aren't you? It's totally cool if you're not, you know. I really couldn't care less. I mean, *obviously* I care. I just mean that I'm not anti-gay or anything. You know that, right?'

'Alex was arrested for sexual assault.' There was no point lying – everyone would know soon enough.

'*Sexual assault?* But you two didn't even *do* . . .'

'Why did you tell Stella?' Attack is always the best form of defence.

'I didn't!'

'Liar!' That shocked her. No one ever called Astrid out like that.

She got down from the tree trunk and strode towards me. '*What* did you say?'

'You heard me. I can't believe I trusted you! I should have known better – it's not like you've ever been there for me before. Why should this be any different?' I'd only called her a liar to distract her; I couldn't have her asking questions about the charges against Alex. But what I'd said was true, and I realized I *was* angry. I was angry at Astrid for being a terrible friend and angry at Mum for calling the police and angry at the police for arresting Alex and angry at Alex for ruining my life.

'I'm your best friend!' Astrid looked genuinely upset, which was surprising.

'Oh give me a break! You don't know the *meaning* of friendship. Your idea of a friend is someone who agrees with you all the time and doesn't mind being treated like garbage. Do you even know how messed up that is?' I had no idea where this was coming from, but it was all true. I'd thought these thoughts before but I never would have dreamed of saying them. Until now.

Astrid said nothing, and when Astrid goes quiet that's when you should really start to worry. It usually means she's about so say something so exceptionally awful that your hand will fly to your mouth and your eyes will go as wide as they possibly can and you'll say 'ASTRID!' in a shocked voice, and then you'll laugh because you can't help yourself because after all, it *was* funny. But this time was different. Astrid narrowed her eyes. 'Why have you stayed friends with me then? If I'm so terrible?'

I shrugged. 'I didn't exactly have any better options, did I?'

She blinked and for a second I was sure Astrid was going to cry. I knew I should apologize, tell her I didn't mean it. There were lots of reasons why I stayed friends with Astrid despite hating her on a regular basis. She could make me laugh like no one else on earth and she could be unexpectedly kind and generous. It was complicated, just like most things in life.

I started to speak, started to say that I appeared to have temporarily lost my mind but Astrid jumped in and stopped me. 'I think you've said enough, don't you?' Any hint of tears had disappeared, which made me think that they probably hadn't been real in the first place. 'Look, I was willing to be your friend and stick by you through this . . . whatever *this* even is . . . but from the sounds of it you don't need me after all. I don't need to stand here and take this shit, you know? I've got better things to do.' She turned away, nearly flicking her hair into my face. I exhaled. I'd got away quite lightly, all things considered.

I watched Astrid strut away from me and decided not to go after her. I'd catch up with her later and grovel like I'd never grovelled before. She was right: I *did* need her. There was no one else I could talk to.

Astrid stopped when she was maybe ten steps away from me. She didn't turn round straightaway and that's what made me tense up. After what seemed like an age – it was probably only a second or so – she did turn to face me. There was a hint of a smile playing on her lips, but it did nothing to reassure me. 'Do you want to know a secret?' I had no choice but to nod; Astrid's smile spread wider. 'You may think I'm a bad friend . . . but that's nothing compared to having me as an enemy.'

She was clearly delighted with this little show of theatrics. I thought she was going to add something else, but I think she must have forgotten her next line so she turned around again, flicking her hair even more vigorously. She couldn't strut away as fast as she'd have liked because a couple of child-minders with giant buggies had taken up the whole path.

I knew straightaway that I'd made a terrible mistake – I just wasn't exactly sure why yet.

chapter thirty-four

Astrid texted me straight after school: *Reckon we should talk? Call me.*

That was as close as Astrid would ever get to trying to smooth things over. When we'd had minor disagreements in the past, I was always the first one to crack – the first one to text or call. I didn't answer; Astrid couldn't bear being ignored. She needed attention like most people need oxygen.

I dreamed about Alex that night. Everything was normal and good and my boyfriend was a boy just like he was supposed to be. We held hands and we kissed and he touched me and I liked it. I woke up feeling good; the feeling lasting approximately three seconds before I remembered. Then I was disgusted with myself. My brain was betraying me, trying to trick me into feeling sorry for Alex, but I wouldn't let it. The shock I'd felt about Alex's arrest had faded. I'd talked to Mum about it when I got home from school the previous day and she reassured me I'd done the right thing and that Alex needed to be held accountable for her actions. Weirdly enough, the reassurance worked even though I knew full well she'd never say such things if she knew the truth. It was just nice to hear soothing words and to know that she was on my side even if she didn't really *get* it. When she hugged me I could almost imagine everything was going to be OK and this mess would magically sort itself out.

It was only when I checked my phone a few minutes after waking up that I realized just how big a mistake I'd made getting angry with Astrid and, even worse, ignoring her peace offering. I hadn't really been on Facebook much since I'd got together with Alex. He didn't even have a profile. I'd thought that made him cool and interesting, because everyone I knew was on Facebook (even Mum, who had an annoying habit of 'liking' all of my statuses even though I'd asked her not to). At the beginning of the relationship I'd posted one or two status updates that could have been interpreted as smug – talking about how happy I was and what a good day I'd had, but I never mentioned Alex by name (mostly because of Mum's habit of stalking my profile). As soon as things started getting serious with Alex I hardly ever went on there. I'd somehow lost interest in seeing what people were up to and what music they were listening to, and I didn't want to see yet another photo Astrid had taken of herself pouting into the mirror or Stella quoting obscure song lyrics to make herself look deep and clever. Over the past few days I'd been back on Facebook, not posting anything, just watching people's lives happening. There were more photos of Astrid, and more song lyrics from Stella. My life had been turned upside down and inside out but nothing had changed on there. I couldn't decide if that made me hopeful or not.

Astrid's status jumped out at me right away, mostly because of the number of comments and likes it had. The status had been posted at 9.37 p.m. the previous night. There was no photo attached to this one:

Have you heard the joke about the girl who found out her boyfriend was actually a GIRL and then had him/her/it ARRESTED?! Oh wait, turns out it's NOT a joke. Truth is stranger than fiction, people.

Forty-eight people had liked the status and there were sixty-two comments. There was a lot of NO WAY?! and WTF?! and SPILL! and combinations of the three. Suggestions of names were being thrown around and promptly disputed by the girls in question. There were filthy jokes and bad spelling and the usual outpouring of glee at someone else's misfortune. The penultimate comment was from some boy Astrid used to fancy: *U comin out of da closet, Astrid?* Followed by not one but three winky faces.

Astrid hadn't added anything to the conversation up until that comment. She'd clearly been content to sit back and enjoy the chaos she'd caused. She had to reply to this one though, because her little plan would backfire spectacularly if people thought this was about her: *LOL very funny. I don't think Justin Maitland will be too happy to see you calling him a girl. My boyf is ALL man.* Stella had 'liked' that comment – her only contribution to the proceedings.

I didn't cry, not even when I refreshed Astrid's feed and a new comment appeared in front of my eyes. Rachael Meadows: *If no one else is gonna have the balls to come out and say it . . . KATE MCALLISTER.*

I watched as the responses racked up (the very first one being *Who????*). It seemed like everyone from school was on Facebook that morning, like they'd been waiting for this to happen. I imagined Rachael Meadows sitting at a table, eating a bowl of cornflakes – spoon in one hand, phone in the other. I imagined Stella trying to pretend she wasn't enjoying this, looking around guiltily in case someone saw her smiling. I imagined Astrid lying in bed (she never got up before midday on Saturday), but I couldn't quite picture her face. Part of me was sure she must be feeling bad, regretting what she'd done. But part of me knew Astrid would be loving every second, basking in the attention she craved so badly.

I didn't cry when someone said: *Bollocks! How can you not notice your boyf doesn't have a cock?!!!?!*

Justin was the next person to comment: *Or bollocks, for that matter.* That comment got the most likes over the next half hour or so.

Eventually I forced myself to switch off my phone. I felt strangely calm, considering that almost everyone I knew was laughing at me and gossiping about me – not to mention all the people I *didn't* know. A few months ago this sort of thing would have ruined me. But the worst thing that could happen had already happened to me; I was already ruined. At school the day before, I'd been panicking about people finding out, not realizing that it didn't make any difference – not really. Astrid would be disappointed if she ever found out that she hadn't managed to hurt me. She wouldn't find out, though, because I couldn't imagine ever talking to her again. And knowing that felt suspiciously like relief.

Maybe Astrid had done me a favour, telling everyone like this. They'd have found out as soon as the court case started anyway. It would be all over the papers, for one thing – even if they weren't allowed to name any names because I was still a minor. I'd seen it on some TV programme – the police had to be especially careful not to name victims of sexual assault. I wondered why Astrid hadn't mentioned the sexual assault thing; perhaps she was just biding her time until she dropped that little nugget of information into the mix to spice things up when interest was waning. The weird thing was, I was almost certain she knew – or at least strongly suspected – that I'd lied to the police.

Astrid knew that I'd lied, and she'd already shown that she was perfectly willing to hurt me. I should have been freaking out – doing everything in my power to make sure she kept quiet. And the fact that I wasn't freaking out baffled me almost as much as the fact that I'd decided not to go back on Facebook and not to bother investigating Astrid's Twitter feed to check if she was attacking me on ALL the social networks.

I was getting out of the shower when I realized that Mum might see something on Facebook. Not that she was friends with any of my friends – that would have been a step too far even for her – but she might see if someone posted on my wall. I wrapped my towel around me and hurried back to my room and adjusted the privacy settings on my account. I was still antsy about it though – she would blow things out of all proportion if she found out what Astrid had done – so I unfriended Mum, just to be on the safe side. If and when she noticed I'd tell her it must have been a glitch on the site. With a little bit of luck she wouldn't even notice and I could go back to being a normal person who *wasn't* friends with their mum on Facebook.

It occurred to me that nobody would think I was 'normal' anymore; that should have made me happy. Hadn't that been the very thing I'd hated about my life last year? That people thought I was boring. No one had ever said it to my face (apart from Astrid that one time I wouldn't try vodka at her sleepover), but I knew that's what people thought when they saw me. They looked at me and thought they had the measure of me. A piano-playing geek who'd never done anything remotely interesting in her whole life. Wasn't that why I started listening to different music and buying new clothes? And wasn't *that* why I'd joined the Saving Serenity forum and started talking to Alex in the first place? It all came back to that creeping fear that had taken hold in my mind – the one that convinced me I was missing out on something. It felt like I was missing out on *life*. If only I didn't spend every spare moment playing the piano, if only I could break free from Astrid's shadow. If only *I* could believe I was someone interesting and worthwhile – someone people didn't ignore.

Be careful what you wish for. No one would be ignoring me for a very long time. Lucky me.

Mum was vacuuming the living room when I went through. She'd vacuumed two days ago so I was immediately suspicious – it's always been her least favourite household chore, mostly because she refused to buy a decent vacuum cleaner, leaving us stuck with one that seemed to spew out as much dust and rubbish as it sucked in. I tapped her on the shoulder, making her jump.

'Morning,' I shouted, because she didn't bother turning off the vacuum.

'Morning!' she shouted back. *Then* she turned it off. 'Did you sleep OK? The phone didn't wake you this morning?'

I said no, I hadn't really slept OK, thanks very much for asking, but I hadn't heard the phone either. The two facts were not mutually exclusive, after all. I asked who'd been on the phone, which had clearly been the point of her asking if I'd been woken up. My mother was infuriating a lot of the time – often taking the long, scenic route instead of getting straight to the point. She plumped up some cushions, turning them so that they were at an angle on the sofa and swapping them so that the identical ones weren't next to each other. The world would probably end if the identical ones stayed next to each other. 'Oh, yes. It was the police.'

'PC Mason? Is it Alex? What's happened?' From nowhere I had the clearest picture in my mind of Alex, her limp body dangling from a pipe on the ceiling, a belt around her neck. It was stupid – a hangover from too many films and TV shows. Alex would never do something like that, no matter how bad things got. I knew that. It definitely felt like something I *knew*, even though I was well aware that I didn't know very much about Alex at all. Still, maybe it was possible that I knew something of the person she really was, deep down. I must have seen something real in all that time we spent together.

'No, it wasn't PC Mason, actually. It was a woman, more senior, I think . . . She was ever so polite . . .'

'Mum!' My exasperation seemed to surprise her.

'Someone got out of bed the wrong side this morning, didn't they? Anyway, as I was saying – if you'd just let me finish – they're coming round this morning to interview you. I just want to make sure the place is looking a bit better than when PC Mason came round. I wouldn't want them getting the wrong idea about this family. You always have to think about these things, you know, when you're a single mother.' Mum didn't like to think of herself as a single mother – she hardly ever used the term – so I wasn't sure why she was mentioning it now.

'I don't understand why they have to interview me again. I told them what happened.' I tried to keep the panic from my voice. I'd known this was coming but that didn't make the prospect any more appealing.

Mum shrugged. 'I know, love, but that was just a preliminary interview. They have to take down an official statement, I think. The woman explained it all on the phone and I'm sure she'll be happy to explain it again if you ask. It's nothing to worry about, love. I know it's not easy for you to talk about, but I'll be there with you.'

There was nothing remotely reassuring about that. Mum being there just meant having another person to listen to my lies. I asked what time the police were coming and Mum looked at her watch. 'Half an hour, love. Would you mind making me a cup of green tea? I'm gasping after all this.'

I retreated to the kitchen and put the kettle on. I took a deep breath to try to calm down but it just made me feel even more light-headed. I should eat something – I knew that. I'd barely eaten over the past few days – just enough to keep me going. I poured some cereal and splashed some milk into a bowl. I managed four or five bites, which was better than nothing. My heart was trampolining with anxiety. I hadn't thought this through. I hadn't allowed myself to think about anything beyond PC Mason's interview, which was why the arrest had come as such a shock even though he'd said it was going to happen.

There was a whisper in my ear in a voice that sounded like mine telling me that I should see this as an opportunity – another chance to put things right. *Tell the truth*, the voice said. What's the worst that can happen? A slap on the wrist for wasting police time? Mum would be furious but she'd get over it in time. A mother should be happy to find out her daughter *hadn't* been assaulted. This whole situation had snowballed out of control. I never meant for this to happen. *I* hadn't been the one to get the police involved. That was what I kept telling myself, because as long as I remembered that then none of this was my fault – not really.

I poured boiling hot water into Mum's favourite mug and on to my hand. Not on purpose. Not really. 'FUCK!' I screamed. Mum came running, remote control in one hand, damp cloth in the other. 'What is it? What's happened?' She saw me clutching my hand

and hurried me over to the sink. 'Oh, you silly thing! You need to be more careful, don't you? It'll be fine, just keep your hand under that tap for five minutes. Shhh, it's OK, there's no need to cry.' I wasn't crying – I wasn't even close to crying – but as soon as she said that, I started.

The pain was white hot and deep and showed no signs of abating. I was grateful for it; it washed all other thoughts from my brain. All I had to do was concentrate on keeping my hand under the stream of cold water. An endurance test. The tears stopped. Everything stopped, apart from the water streaming on to my hand, which had now turned red – either from the boiling water or the freezing water. There was no way to tell where the pain and redness was coming from anymore. Hot and cold felt exactly the same. Like right and wrong.

chapter thirty-five

She was a sergeant. A Special Something or Other Officer, trained to deal with cases involving sexual offences. Sergeant Tanaka's hair was scraped back in a severe bun – not a strand out of place. She made me uneasy for some reason. I think it was the way she paused before speaking, as if she was measuring her words, planning out what to say instead of just *saying* it. She also seemed to be very keen on eye contact, which is something I tend to avoid with people I don't know.

PC Mason had come along for the ride too, and I was strangely glad to see a familiar face. He didn't say much this time and he seemed a lot less nervous. He didn't drop his hat once. Sergeant Tanaka asked what had happened to my hand; Mum had bandaged it up even though there was really no need. She used to do that when I was little too. One time I fell on my wrist in the three-legged race on sports day (Astrid's fault entirely) and Mum made me a sling from a tea towel. I always liked that she took my injuries seriously, no matter how small they were. I told Sergeant Tanaka what had happened and she paused before saying that making tea could be a very dangerous business. Mum laughed nervously and said, 'On that note, how about I risk my life to make us a brew?' Polite laugher all round and the police officers accepted the offer. Builder's tea for Sergeant Tanaka and Earl Grey for PC Mason. I didn't want anything apart from a glass of water. My throat was so dry I had to keep clearing it, and every time I did that Sergeant Tanaka turned to look at me. I think she thought I was trying to catch her attention.

While Mum made the tea, the three of us settled into our seats in the lounge. PC Mason sat in the same seat as last time, but Sergeant Tanaka sat next to me on the sofa. That meant that Mum would have to sit in the uncomfortable chair by the window – the antique one that looked more like an instrument of torture than anything else. She wouldn't be able to hold my hand this time. The sergeant explained why they were here and that she would be recording the interview 'if I didn't mind'. I got the distinct impression that it didn't matter whether I minded or not. She explained that she would be my main point of contact 'going forward' and that she hoped I'd feel free to ask her about anything I wasn't sure about or any worries I might have.

I glanced towards the half-open door before turning back to her. 'I was . . . wondering about Alex. How is she . . . ? I mean, have you *seen* . . . ?'

Another pause from her before she nodded. 'I have seen her. But I think it's best if we focus on you for the time being.' Then she launched into the spiel about appreciating that this was difficult for me but she had to take my statement. She needed to hear what had happened 'in my own words', as if there was any chance I'd be able to borrow someone else's for the occasion. Mum came back carrying a tray. She'd filled the mugs too full and tea had sloshed on to the tray so she had to rush back to get some kitchen roll to mop it up. I could tell she was annoyed about not getting to sit next to me but she couldn't exactly do anything about it. Throughout the entire interview I could see her out of the corner of my eye, fidgeting and shifting in her seat.

Sergeant Tanaka took out a tiny grey recording device and placed it on the coffee table in front of us. She put it on a coaster. Maybe she was worried the words I was about to pour into it would overflow and stain the table. They wouldn't just stain it though – they would corrode it like acid. The lies would drip through and fizz on to the carpet below. They were so vicious and powerful they would go through the floorboards and reach the stone foundations of the house.

While I'd been imagining my lies, Sergeant Tanaka had been speaking into the recording device, telling it the date and who was present etc. The voice she used was different from before – more clipped, slightly posher. She asked me to say (in my own words) what had happened between me and Alexandra Banks, then she sat back and looked at me expectantly. PC Mason was doing the opposite – sitting on the edge of his chair, pen poised above his notebook. I didn't see the point of him taking notes, unless he was supposed to write down things that wouldn't appear on the recording – my body language, perhaps. Of course, as soon as I thought about body language I became horribly aware of my posture (hunched) and my limbs (arms crossed in front of my chest). So I reached over to get my glass of water, took a sip, then made very sure to put my hands back in my lap. I straightened my spine a little too; I had nothing to be ashamed of. Then I ruined it all by giggling nervously. 'Um . . . I'm not really sure where to start.'

Sergeant Tanaka smiled kindly. 'Why don't you

start at the beginning? Describe how you came to meet Miss Banks?' I wished they would stop calling Alex 'Miss'. It felt like they were reminding me of my stupidity.

I was incredibly thirsty all of a sudden, even though I'd taken a sip of water a few seconds ago. My lips felt dry and chapped and my throat was scratchy. I wouldn't allow myself to drink more water though – not for a couple of minutes at least. Surely there was a direct correlation between thirstiness and lying? If there wasn't, there should be.

After one last anxious glance over at Mum, I started talking. I got distracted every time PC Mason scratched away at his notepad. I'd never know if he was writing a detailed analysis of my speech patterns and body language or a shopping list of things to pick up at Asda on the way home. Sergeant Tanaka nodded occasionally, kept me on track when I veered off on to a tangent (which happened a lot – it's hard to tell a story in a straight line sometimes). She asked questions, which were always 'just to clarify', even though it seemed to me that some of them were 'just to be intrusive'. The sergeant seemed particularly interested in finding out who had suggested meeting up at the gig, and precisely why I'd thought Alex was a boy.

I felt myself start to blush. 'It was just obvious . . . from the way he talked about things, and from his profile picture. He was a boy. I mean, obviously it wasn't obvious, because I was wrong, wasn't I? But anyone else would have made the same mistake.'

'And you definitely had no suspicions to the contrary?'

'*No.*'

That seemed like a satisfactory answer. Sometimes it was best to keep it short and sweet; there was less chance of tying yourself up in knots and getting confused. It made me uneasy that it sort of looked like I was the one who pursued Alex, but there was nothing I could do about that because it was true. Anyway, it was hardly as if I'd been some kind of sexual predator. They would never think that, surely?

I skipped over the bit about our first kiss, but Sergeant Tanaka pulled me up again. She asked who'd made the first move. Seeing my discomfort, she apologized and said that it was really important for them to get a clear timeline of the 'events'. I glanced over at Mum and she nodded and gestured with her hand for me to continue. She probably didn't want to hear this any more than I wanted to say it. I admitted that I'd been the one to make the first move, cringing with embarrassment as I told them.

Sergeant Tanaka nodded and paused for even longer than usual. 'Would you say that was normal behaviour for you? Being . . . forward with boys?'

'What? No! No. Not at all. I've never even . . . Alex was my first boyf . . . relationship.'

'I'd have thought an attractive girl like you would have boys flocking around you.'

That made me laugh out loud, but the laughter echoed round the room and by the time it came back to me it sounded bitter and angry. And I didn't want the police to think I was bitter and angry, even though I had every right to be. Sergeant Tanaka and PC Mason were both waiting for me to elaborate. Apparently laughter doesn't constitute a proper answer in this situation. Mum came to the rescue. 'Kate has always been very busy with her piano playing. This . . . interest in the opposite sex – oh well, you know what I mean – is a fairly recent development.'

'Thank you, Mrs McAllister, but could I ask you to remain silent while the interview is in progress? We really need to hear Kate's side of the story.' While she was saying this, Sergeant Tanaka gave a shrug and rolled her eyes at Mum, as if to say 'What can you do? I don't make the rules.' Mum nodded and mouthed 'Sorry!' All eyes were back on me.

'Um . . . boys have never really noticed me before,

I suppose. And I haven't been all that bothered. Like Mum said, piano practice keeps me really busy.' I sounded like a pathetic loser.

'But all that changed when you met Alex?' I wasn't sure if she was trying to imply something.

'I suppose so. He was different.' I almost expected one of them to laugh, but that wouldn't exactly have been professional. No one corrected me on using the wrong pronoun either. Perhaps they found it as hard as I did to remember that Alex was a girl.

Sergeant Tanaka asked a lot of questions about where Alex and I used to spend time together, and whether I'd introduced him (her) to any of my friends. I told her about Astrid even though I didn't see how it could possibly be relevant. I had to give her last name and address too. I just had to hope they weren't going to talk to her. I couldn't see why they'd need to – it wasn't as if she was there when the sexual assault happened (didn't happen).

Finally, after I'd talked and talked and talked, the sergeant asked about the physical side of our relationship, specifically the day I'd been assaulted. I said our relationship didn't have a physical side, other than kissing. I thought I detected a hint of scepticism in Tanaka's eyes, which was sort of funny because I was actually telling the truth.

'Have you had any previous sexual relationships?' she asked.

I shook my head, confused. 'No, I told you. There was nothing before Alex. No one.'

'I'm sorry, I know it must seem like we're going over a lot of the same ground, but you have to understand that this is exactly what would happen in court.' Would. She said *would*. Then she hurried on, 'So, prior to meeting Alex Banks you had never been intimate with anyone else. Is that correct?'

I nodded; she pointed at the recorder. 'Yes,' I said.

'Can you tell me the date the alleged offence took place? I believe you weren't sure when you talked to PC Mason?' PC Mason nodded. *He* was allowed to nod. *Alleged* offence. She had to talk like that, I thought; Alex was innocent until proven guilty.

I was ready for this question; I'd had time to think about it. Mum always kept last year's calendar for at least six months, just in case she needed to refer to it. I've never seen her refer to it once, but I was glad to find it hanging behind the new one in the kitchen. I flicked through to November and tried to decipher Mum's coded writing. She has a habit of writing things in shorthand, as if it's just too much effort to write whole words. Pickings were slim for that month – Mum's social life was almost as dire as mine. There was one Sunday afternoon towards the end of the month where she'd written 'Aft Tea w/M', which translated as 'Afternoon tea with Mags'. Mags and Mum have embarked on this neverending, lifelong quest to find the perfect afternoon tea. Every couple of months Mum gets the train over to Glasgow or Mags gets the train here and they try a new place. Mags has even created a ratings system — that's how seriously she takes her afternoon tea.

I remembered this particular Sunday; Alex and I had gone to the cinema. I'd actually tried to convince him to come over to my house, knowing that Mum was going to be gone for hours, but he'd said he really wanted to see this film and it was one of the last showings. We'd held hands and eaten a mammoth tub of popcorn and shared a blue slushy drink that came with two straws. Our tongues turned blue. The film wasn't very good and Alex apologized for dragging me along to see it. I didn't mind though, because I was happy as long as he was happy.

I did have a slight worry that Alex might be able to prove we'd been at the cinema that afternoon, but we hadn't seen anyone we knew and it wasn't as if we'd done anything to draw attention to ourselves. I didn't think Alex would have kept the ticket (even though I'd kept mine). Anyway, it wasn't like I had much choice in the matter – it was the only weekend day I could be sure Mum hadn't been at home. It was the best I could do in a bad situation, but it was far from perfect.

I told Sergeant Tanaka the date and she raised her eyebrows. 'And now you're absolutely sure of that?'

'Yes, I checked because I knew it would be important.' I explained about the calendar and how I'd invited Alex round because Mum would be out. I avoided looking over at Mum because she wasn't exactly going to be happy about that.

Sergeant Tanaka leaned forward in her seat. 'Why were you so keen to invite Alex round when your mother wasn't going to be home?'

I was about to say something like 'It's obvious, isn't it?' which would have been disastrous. I'd have to be more careful with my choice of words without looking like I was weighing things up before I said them. 'Um . . . I wanted us to spend some time together.'

'And you couldn't have done that with your mum here?' Tanaka's eyes were wide and bright and she asked the question in an innocent enough way, but I knew what she was doing. Mum did too because she said, 'I'm sorry, I know I'm not supposed to be saying anything, but I'm not sure what you're trying to imply here.'

'I'm not trying to imply anything, Mrs McAllister.

I'm merely trying to establish the facts, and make sure Kate is prepared for a potential court case. I'm afraid there are always difficult questions to be asked in these situations. It's never easy.' She looked like she felt bad about this, she really did. PC Mason was busy writing in his notebook. I was now almost certain he *was* writing a shopping list.

Mum didn't look convinced but she nodded and said it was fine for the interview to continue. A trace of a smile appeared and promptly disappeared on Sergeant Tanaka's face. Mum was the only one in the room who didn't seem to realize that it wasn't up to her whether this interview continued or not.

I tried again. 'I wanted Alex and I to spend some time *alone* together. We always met up in town. I thought it would be nice to chill at home for a change.' I'm almost certain that was the first time I'd ever said 'chill' in this context. 'And . . . um . . . people don't tend to want their mothers around in situations like that. It's not exactly romantic.'

'So you were hoping to have a romantic afternoon together? Would you say that's fair?'

I frowned, a little confused. 'I suppose so.'

Tanaka asked me to talk her through the afternoon. She seemed particularly interested in whose idea it had been to spend time in my bedroom. I said it had been

Alex's idea, and that I'd wanted to stay in the living room. 'Why?' asked Tanaka.

'I didn't want him . . . getting the wrong idea.'

'Had Alex done anything to give you that impression? Had he been asking you to take things further . . . in your physical relationship?'

I shrugged, wishing I'd thought this through better. I didn't want to overplay it – subtlety was the key (I hoped). 'Not really. I mean, maybe he'd been hinting sometimes. About wanting to go further. But I just pretended I didn't notice. I was happy just being with him. I certainly wasn't in any rush to . . . you know.' A quick look over at Mum confirmed the approving nod I'd expected to see.

Sergeant Tanaka nodded. 'Could you describe what happened after you went into the bedroom?' Her voice was softer now, coaxing almost.

I took a deep, wavering sort of breath. Then I told her a story.

chapter thirty-six

We were sitting on the bed watching a film on my laptop. Alex had closed the curtains and turned off the light – to keep the glare off the screen, he said. It was just like being in the cinema, he said. After a few minutes he started stroking my arm, kissing my neck. He closed the laptop and suggested we lie down for a bit. I didn't really want to but I went along with it anyway. We kissed and it was nice. I didn't think there was anything to worry about – not then. After a while, Alex suggested I take my top off. I said no, obviously, but he kept on about it, saying he just wanted to *see* me. I said he wasn't going to be able to see anything – the room was pitch-black because of my blackout blinds. He said he wasn't going to do anything so eventually I let him take my top off. I kept my bra on though. That was non-negotiable. I let him touch my breasts on top of my bra. That seemed to be enough for him for a little while. Then his hand started going lower and lower and each time it did I took it and moved it back up again. I think it was some kind of game to him. 'Let me touch you,' he said. 'I just want to make you feel good.' I said no. More than once. He behaved for a minute or two but then the hand was back, rubbing my crotch through my jeans. And I . . . I let him continue – just for a few seconds. I know I shouldn't have but I did and I regret it. I didn't really notice him unbuttoning my jeans but he must have done because before I knew what was happening his hand was inside my underwear. I said 'No' again, more forcefully, but he didn't listen. I tried to move his hand but he was stronger than I was, and he was on top of me and suddenly the weight of him made it hard for me to breathe. I struggled and tried to push him off me, but he took my hands and pinned them above my head. He was strong. 'Please! I don't want to. Please. Stop it. Stop it!'

'Shhh. It's OK . . . Don't worry about it. It's OK. Just relax and enjoy it.'

'No . . . please. I don't want to . . .'

Then he put his fingers inside me and it really hurt. He seemed to be in a hurry all of a sudden and he was ramming his fingers in and out and I was crying but he said it would stop hurting in a minute, I just needed to get used to it but I didn't get used to it and it hurt so much and I just kept saying no no no, begging him to stop but he didn't. He kept kissing my neck, murmuring words that were meant to reassure me but didn't.

Then he stopped and rolled off me. I was still crying. I covered myself with my T-shirt but didn't put it on.

'Oh my God, I'm so sorry. I'm sorry I'm sorry oh God I didn't mean to . . .' He started to cry. I turned on the light. He sat on the edge of the bed with his back to me, his shoulders heaving as he sobbed. I stopped crying. I don't know how long we stayed like that before he turned to look at me. He reached out and touched my hand. 'Kate . . . I'm so sorry. I can't even begin to . . . I don't know what I was thinking. Kate? Say something, please?' I said nothing; it was hard to even look at him.

He kept crying and apologizing over and over again. And after a while I started to listen. He looked so devastated by what had happened. He apologized some more and after a little while more I started to believe him. Even later on I started to feel sorry for him. I let him hold me and we lay on the bed. 'Can you ever forgive me? I'll understand if you can't. Just tell me to leave and I'll never contact you again, I promise.'

I didn't answer straightaway. What had happened was already starting to seem unreal somehow. Alex wasn't like that — I *knew* Alex. He was sorry. It wouldn't happen again. He was really really sorry. 'Can you forgive me?' he asked again. He sounded so vulnerable and I knew that it would break him if I told him to leave.

'I forgive you.'

No one spoke for a few seconds after I finished talking. I could hear Mum crying but I couldn't allow myself to look at her. I felt guilty — *of course* I felt guilty. I knew it was wrong — the worst thing I had ever done, by a long way. But I would make it up to Mum by being the best daughter I could possibly be. I would start being serious about piano again and I'd stop whining about it. I would enter that stupid competition. I would cook at least three times a week and go to the shops to buy milk whenever she asked. I would mow the lawn and do all the vacuuming. I would study Music at university even though I wasn't sure I wanted to and I would invite Mum to the end-of-term concert and she would be *so* proud. And maybe she would look back on this terrible thing that had happened (not happened) to her daughter and she would see it as a turning point — when her annoying, ungrateful daughter turned into a grown-up. She would never know that her annoying, ungrateful daughter had only turned into a grown-up to try to make up for an unforgivable lie.

I didn't really think about Alex, which is really strange when you think about it. Alex had turned into a not-real person in my head. It was made easier by the fact that I didn't know who Alex was anymore. As I was telling my story, I could almost see it in my head. I could almost believe that this thing had happened to me. That scared me. I wasn't sure who *I* was anymore.

Sergeant Tanaka asked more questions. Every time I thought there was nothing else she could possibly need to know she would ask another question. She wanted to know why I hadn't gone to the police at the time. My answer wasn't particularly great: 'I loved him.' She wanted to know what happened afterwards, whether our relationship had gone back to normal, whether anything like that had ever happened again. 'Nothing.' 'Yes.' 'No.' I was all talked out. I'd finished my glass of water over an hour ago but I didn't feel like I could ask for another. PC Mason's stomach made a loud gurgling noise and Tanaka shot him an annoyed look. By the time she asked about the end of our relationship I was stupefied from tiredness. Telling lies is a lot more exhausting that telling the truth. Finally here was something else I could be honest about – mostly. I had to omit the part about me being desperate to lose my virginity, but I told the bit about going round to Alex's house on New Year's Eve exactly as it happened.

'And how did you feel, when you found out that Alex was a girl?' I thought I could detect a hint of tiredness in Sergeant Tanaka's voice too. We all wanted this to be over.

'Upset.'

'*Upset?*'

I'd been trying to be succinct. Clearly that wasn't going to be good enough. 'Shocked. Angry. It was . . . I couldn't believe it.'

'And up until that moment you had absolutely no idea? Even when you were . . . intimate.'

'We weren't intimate! She *assaulted* me.' Tanaka held her hand up and nodded, which I suppose was meant to count as an apology. 'How many times do I have to tell you? I didn't know she was a girl! If I'd known that I wouldn't have gone anywhere near her. I wanted a *boy*friend.'

Tanaka fiddled with the cuffs of her shirt. 'Would it be fair to say you felt betrayed when you found out the truth?'

Betrayal. That word pretty much summed

everything up – the anger and hurt and confusion. It was a word that could have been invented for a time like this – if this was a normal thing that happened to normal people. But I had to be careful here. Betrayal is one side of a razor-sharp blade; on the other side is revenge. People who are betrayed often want revenge and I could not be seen as someone wanting revenge. I shrugged as if I hadn't really thought about it. 'I don't know . . . I suppose so, but mostly I was just really, really upset.'

Tanaka nodded slowly – sympathetically, almost. 'I imagine it must have been very hard for you.'

This was not a question. I'd got used to her asking questions, so this had me stumped. I said nothing. The silence went on a little too long; I stared at the recording device and wondered what it would be like to listen to this conversation. Awkward, probably.

Tanaka cleared her throat and asked about what happened when I left Alex's house. I was back on safe ground again and I could feel my shoulders relax slightly – hopefully not enough for anyone else to notice. It was nearly over.

'Am I right in thinking that it was not your idea to inform us about the assault?' No 'alleged' there. I wasn't sure whether that meant anything or whether

I was just driving myself up the wall trying to analyse her every word.

'It hadn't crossed my mind. Mum called you guys without me knowing.'

'How did you feel when she found out that she'd done that?'

I looked over at Mum and she gave me a sad little smile. She knew this was an ordeal. 'I was angry. I'd told her those things in confidence, and I never thought for a minute that it was a police matter.'

Tanaka's eyebrows shot up. 'You didn't think sexual assault was a police matter?'

'I wasn't thinking of it like that – I wasn't thinking much at all. And that thing with Alex had happened months ago so I suppose I didn't realize that you could still . . . do something about it. It's not like there's any evidence, is there?' I thought it definitely went in my favour, that I hadn't been the one to call the police. I hadn't asked for this to happen.

'Plenty of sexual assault cases have been successfully prosecuted months, even years, after the event. Physical evidence isn't always necessary to secure a conviction.' Was I happy about that? Worried? I genuinely had no idea. 'You *are* happy for this to go to court, aren't you? You want Miss Banks to be prosecuted for this offence? In cases like these, the victim's feelings are usually taken into account. Of course, you are a minor so we also ask your legal guardian . . .'

Mum snorted. 'Of course she wants to prosecute! We both do. What that girl did was disgusting and she shouldn't be allowed to get away with it.' I nodded vaguely and said a very quiet 'yes'. What Alex had done *had* been disgusting and she really shouldn't be allowed to get away with it.

Tanaka leaned towards the recording device and said, 'Right. I think that just about wraps things up here. Kate, is there anything else you'd like to add? Anything at all?'

Tanaka looked at me. PC Mason looked at me. Mum looked at me. I couldn't stand it; I had to close my eyes, just for a second. I could do it now, couldn't I? I'm sorry. I made the whole thing up. It was an accident, honestly. I never expected Mum to call the police. I was scared. I didn't want to get in trouble for wasting anyone's time. And yes, maybe I did want to punish Alex for hurting me, but it's all been blown out of proportion. I'm so sorry. I don't want to go to prison for perjury or whatever it is so please, please can we just forget all about this? I've never done anything like this before and I never will again and I . . .

I opened my eyes; they were still looking. 'Sorry.

Dizzy spell. There's nothing more I'd like to say. I just want this to be over with as soon as possible.'

A phone buzzed and both the officers checked their pockets. It was PC Mason's. He apologized and left the room. Sergeant Tanaka turned off the recording device and I felt like I could breathe for the first time in hours. We sat in silence. Mason's voice was hushed so I wondered if it was his girlfriend calling to add something to that shopping list of his. Then he stuck his head round the door and gestured for Sergeant Tanaka to join him. She closed the door behind her. They must have been whispering because I couldn't hear a thing. 'Are you OK, love? Want me to get you some water?' Mum whispered. I shook my head, answering both questions in one go.

Sergeant Tanaka came back into the room first. PC Mason hovered in front of the radiator next to the door. Their faces were expressionless. 'Well, it looks like you might have got your wish for this to be over soon.' I looked at her and waited. 'That was one of my colleagues down at the station. Apparently Miss Banks has confessed.'

I stopped breathing. Total incomprehension. Which must have shown on my face before I shut it down. 'Oh,' I said. Tanaka was watching me closely and I knew – for the first time that morning I really *knew* – that she wasn't sure I was telling the truth. I wasn't sure why or how, but she suspected me of lying. But now Alex had confessed and she probably wasn't sure what to think anymore.

Alex had confessed. Why would she do that?

'That's good news, isn't it?' Mum didn't sound entirely sure. Most of her legal expertise came from watching those two-hour dramas on ITV.

'It means things will move much more quickly. The first hearing is already scheduled for Monday. Alex pleading guilty, coupled with Kate's statement, should mean it's fairly straightforward. Otherwise we would have been talking months before the case came to trial.'

'She will go to prison, won't she?'

Tanaka paused and looked at me before answering Mum's question. 'It's not my place to say, Mrs McAllister, but it's more than likely that Miss Banks will be sentenced to serve time in a Young Offenders Institution, yes.'

Alex was going to prison. Because of me.

chapter thirty-seven

Mum and I didn't talk about it for the rest of the day. She'd tried to, briefly, as soon as the police left, but she saw that I was in a daze. 'Take as much time as you need. I know this must be hard for you, but remember, you did the right thing.' I shook my head but she continued, 'It's not just about punishment, you know. Maybe Alex will get the help she needs – there's clearly something not right with her.' She hugged me and stroked my hair and suggested I go for a lie down in my room and she would bring me a sandwich in a little while.

I hadn't imagined the searching look Sergeant Tanaka had given me as she was leaving. She handed me her card and told me to call her if I remembered anything else that might be useful to the investigation. Anytime, day or night, she said. I wasn't sure why she didn't come right out and accuse me of lying – but I thought maybe the police had to be really careful in these situations. You can't risk accusing a victim of sexual assault like that. Another layer of guilt wrapped around me when I thought about what would happen if anyone found out the truth. I would just be another example rolled out by those idiots who think that date rape doesn't exist and that women lie about being raped when they regret having sex with someone.

A week ago my life had been perfect. But that had been a lie too. My relationship with Alex had been one of those movie facades that make you think you're looking at a street in somewhere glamorous like New York or Paris, but if you take a closer look or see it from a different angle, you know you've been tricked. And then you look at it and can't believe you didn't see it straightaway. Everything was too perfect – the buildings were free from graffiti and there were no overflowing bins on the pavement.

What was Alex thinking, confessing to something she hadn't done? I couldn't think of a single possible reason for doing something like that. It was pure insanity. I should have been glad – it would mean I wouldn't have to testify in court. I wouldn't have to see her ever again. It meant that Sergeant Tanaka would have to forget about her suspicions; if the accuser and the accused said the same thing, why would anyone else have any reason to question it?

I wondered exactly what Alex had said to the police, because she had no way of knowing what I'd said. Unless they asked the questions in a certain way, giving her the information she needed to be able to lie convincingly. I didn't think the police were allowed to do that though – ask leading questions, but maybe that was something I'd got from TV as well. Whatever she'd said, she'd somehow got them to believe her. I supposed the police were predisposed to thinking people were guilty anyway. No smoke without fire or something like that.

Alex must have been feeling guilty for lying to me – that was the only explanation I came up with after lying on my bed for over an hour. But if you're feeling guilty about hurting someone you buy them flowers or a box of chocolates, you don't lie to the police. You don't risk going to prison just to show how sorry you are. No one in their right mind would ever do that. It made me wonder. Ever since that night Alex had been some sort of Disney villain in my head – someone whose sole purpose in life was to humiliate and destroy me. My love had turned to hate in an instant. The feelings I'd had for Alex, the ones that had built up message after message, day after day, kiss after kiss, had been hit by a wrecking ball the size of Jupiter. But what if she thought her feelings for me were real? And what if they hadn't gone away? Would *love* be enough reason to lie?

Stella texted me late on Saturday night: *'You should check Facebook.'* I don't think I'd ever had a text from her that was emoji-free. I ignored the message at first. I could easily imagine the things people were saying – there was no point in looking. I didn't need anything to make me feel worse than I already did. But when I was in bed an hour or so later, curiosity (inevitably) got the better of me.

It was worse than I thought. Astrid had somehow managed to find Alex on Facebook. Alex had obviously lied about not having a profile. I should have known. What kind of person *isn't* on Facebook? I'd done a search for him (her) even before we met up – trawling through every single Alex Banks on there to no avail. Of course *I* hadn't been looking for Alexandra Banks. Astrid must have been paying attention when we'd come home to find PC Banks on the doorstep, because I was almost certain I'd never told her Alex's surname.

Astrid had posted the link to Alex's profile page. You couldn't see any information about her but you *could* see her photo. The same photo she had on the

Saving Serenity forum – not quite looking at the camera, hair in front of her eyes. I'd stared at that photo for hours, until I could picture it in my head whenever I wanted to. I thought I could tell what kind of person Alex was, just from looking at that picture. He was kind and gentle. He was quiet and soulful and probably liked to read. He was exactly the kind of boy I would want as a boyfriend. And then we started chatting on the forum and every one of my hunches was proved correct and then reinforced when we met up in person. I'd only been wrong about one crucial detail.

Above the link, Astrid had written: *Boy or girl? YOU decide!*

She'd only posted it a couple of hours ago but there were already lots of comments. People were saying horrible, awful things about Alex. The cruelty was hard to comprehend. More than one person had suggested that Alex was intersex (these comments had more 'likes' than the rest of them combined). A few boys from school had written vile sexual things that made me feel sick. No one had stepped in to defend Alex, to suggest that maybe it was wrong to attack a stranger like this. Stella hadn't commented; I wondered if she'd texted me out of kindness. There was no way of knowing without texting her back, and

I wasn't going to do that. She'd only report straight back to Astrid. I knew it would be killing Astrid, not getting a response out of me. It's not very rewarding torturing someone who isn't even paying attention. It wasn't much but it was the only power I had and I wasn't willing to give it up. The most likely scenario was that Astrid had *told* Stella to text me, just to make sure I'd see what she was up to. I wouldn't give her the satisfaction of knowing.

I looked at Alex's photo again. *Really* looked. Was it obvious that she was a girl? If someone had shown me this picture and asked the question Astrid was asking, what would my answer have been?

Boy.

Girl.

Definitely a boy. A boy with features that were slightly more delicate than you might expect. There was a softness there – a certain fragility that you didn't usually see on a boy's face.

Definitely a girl. An androgynous girl, but a girl nonetheless. Her features weren't in any way masculine, but there was something in the hunch of the shoulders, as well as a sense of not quite fitting in your own skin, that was reminiscent of the boys at school.

Was it possible that Alex was as confused as me?

Maybe she wished she was a boy. Maybe she thought she'd been born in the wrong body. Or maybe she'd just realized that I'd assumed she was a boy and was too embarrassed to correct me. And perhaps it snowballed out of control too fast for her to do anything about it. Just like me with the police. But I had no way of knowing and there was nothing I could do about it now. We had both played our parts in this little drama and now there was nothing to do but wait and see how it was going to end.

I tried to hold on to the one thing I knew for sure. Alex *had* betrayed me. She had let me fall in love with her. *Him*. I'd fallen in love with him. A boy. Not a girl. If anything, it was getting harder rather than easier to keep that straight in my head.

My Facebook wall didn't make for pleasant reading. You'd think these people had never heard that you could get prosecuted for online bullying. Not that I was going to tell the police or do anything about it. I'd wait until the fuss had died down before deleting my profile. I would go back to school on Monday and hold my head up high and let the looks and gossip wash over me, but I wouldn't let them stick.

In a weird way, I felt sort of strong. These people meant nothing to me. If I had to walk to school by myself and have lunch myself and spend every minute of the school day by myself, that would be fine by me. I would come home straight after school and practise piano until my fingers ached. School friends were overrated anyway. The only thing I had in common with these people was that we happened to be born in the same year, so we were legally bound to spend five days a week in each other's company until we were old enough to escape. I would be fine on my own. Absolutely fine.

chapter thirty-eight

The nights were the hardest. If I wasn't lying awake and panicking about the situation I'd found myself in, I was dreaming about Alex. The worst dreams were the happy ones – the ones where we were walking on the beach or lying on my bed and doing all the things couples do. The happiness of those dreams, the absolute joy and the fullness of my heart, made it unbearably painful to wake up and remember. And the unhappy dreams were just unhappy. Asleep or awake, I couldn't win.

Mum tried to talk to me over breakfast on Sunday. I sipped tea while she ate homemade granola. 'I know you haven't been eating. I'm not as daft as I look, you know.'

I shrugged, not in the mood for a lecture about eating disorders. I didn't have an eating disorder, I just didn't feel like eating. It was strange because whenever

I'd been upset in the past, I'd always turned to food. Crisps, mostly. Chocolate too. But now food was the last thing on my mind. I could eat it – and did when Mum was watching me – but I didn't really want to. 'Mum, it's fine. I am eating. It's just . . . hard.' My voice wavered and I gulped down the lump in my throat, wondering if that counted as one of my five a day.

Mum scooted her chair over and put her arms around me. 'Oh love, I can't even imagine what you must be going through. I wish you'd come to me sooner . . . I feel like the worst mother in the world, sometimes. It breaks my heart that you didn't come to me as soon as . . . you . . . it . . . happened. What kind of mother doesn't even know when her daughter's hurting like that?'

I held her tight as the tears started to slip down my face. 'You've done nothing wrong, Mum. Nothing, OK? I don't want you thinking like that. I . . . I'm sorry. I'm sorry for everything. This should never have happened.'

She pulled away and looked at me, then brushed away my tears with her finger. Her eyes were glistening too, but she'd managed to hold it together so far. 'Well there's no use crying over spilled milk, is there? And no one's better than us McAllister women at making the best out of a bad situation. We'll get through this, Kate. I'll be with you every step of the way.' We hugged again and I didn't want to let go. It felt good to have her on my side, even under false pretences.

Mum let me get away without eating breakfast, but she said she would make anything I wanted for dinner that night – I could choose anything in the whole world (provided it was something she knew how to cook). 'Macaroni cheese?' I said, without thinking. And my mouth started watering at the thought of it – the crispy, golden breadcrumbs on top of gooey, cheesy pasta. Obviously my brain had been lying about me not wanting food. 'Deal,' Mum said. 'Double helpings for both of us, I think.'

I smiled. 'I think I might do some piano practice later too.' This was the one thing guaranteed to make Mum's day. She loved to listen to me play. She would prop some cushions behind her head and lie on the sofa with her eyes closed. She said it was the only time she felt truly relaxed. She adored music – that's why she was always on my back about it – and she really did think I had a chance at a professional career. I wasn't so sure, and I don't think my teacher was all that convinced, but if I doubled the amount of practice I'd been doing there was at least a chance I could do well in the competition. I'd missed playing, I realized.

It soothed me too, as long as I only played pieces I was actually good at. Otherwise it was the most frustrating thing in the world. I resolved to play some of Mum's favourites that afternoon. It would be good to get back to normal in at least one area of my life – an area I could control.

Mum's eyes lit up, just like I expected them to. 'I would *love* to listen to you play. I've really missed it. Now why don't I pour you another cup of tea? And there are some biscuits in the jar if you fancy . . . they're your favourites.' My mother could be crafty when it suited her.

My stomach was crying out for food, I realized. How had I not noticed before? I took a few chocolate digestives from the jar (to Mum's obvious delight), got a fresh cup of tea and headed back to my room. I took a bite of biscuit and accidentally moaned at how amazing it tasted. I jammed three biscuits in my mouth then licked the chocolate from my fingers.

I was brushing some crumbs from the corner of my mouth, feeling guilty for being a disgusting pig, when my phone buzzed. It was lying face down on my pillow. I expected it to be Stella, or maybe even Astrid. I didn't recognize the number. I had to read the message a few times before I understood.

'You don't know me, but I know all about you.

Alex Banks is my sister. I need to talk to you – urgently. Can we meet up today? DON'T ignore this message. Jamie.'

Another message arrived as I was re-reading the first one. 'I'm not a psycho or anything. And I'm not one for blackmail . . . but I STRONGLY suggest you meet up with me. Alex doesn't know I'm doing this.'

My stomach churned and the biscuits very nearly made a reappearance. I had to sit down on the edge of the bed as I was overwhelmed by dizziness and nausea. Alex's brother, the famous Jamie.

I didn't know what to do. I wondered if I should tell Mum, but she'd probably call the police. I was sure there was some kind of law about this – Alex or anyone in her family shouldn't be allowed to contact me. Wasn't it witness intimidation or something like that?

And what kind of person says they're not one for blackmail? You'd only mention blackmail if you were intending to blackmail someone, right? There was nothing he could use against me though – there was nothing left of my life for anyone to ruin.

I wondered how he reacted when he found out that his little sister had been dressing up as a boy. He couldn't possibly think that that was OK, could he? No one would ever think that was a normal thing to do. But surely the only reason he'd be contacting me would be to get me to drop the charges against Alex. Either he believed she was innocent, or he thought she might be guilty but wanted me to drop the charges anyway. I shouldn't meet up with him. What if he wanted to hurt me? From what Alex had told me about Jamie he didn't sound like a violent sort of person, but you never really know what someone is capable of until they're pushed, do you?

It would be crazy for me to see Jamie. I should ignore his texts and wait and see what happened at the hearing the next day. Yes, that was exactly what I should do. I read his messages again and then switched off my phone.

Twelve minutes later I turned my phone on again and texted him back. *'Meet me on Portobello Beach at 4 p.m. By the pub at the end of Bath Street.'*

His response was almost instant: *'OK.'*

There are some things you do in life even though you know you shouldn't. They are the things which make us human. I hadn't done many things like this – up until last year, at least. Eating six bags of crisps in one day was about as risky as my life got. Meeting up with Alex at the gig had been my first proper risk. There was a chance he would turn out to be some old geezer pretending to be a teenage boy to lure girls off the internet. (It had never occurred to me that there was a chance of him not actually being male.) Going to the gig felt like a good risk to be taking; it was exciting. For the first time in my life I had no idea what was going to happen, and when I finally laid eyes on Alex I knew all the angst and nerves and changing my outfit four times had been worth it.

This could not have been more different. This was a risk without any possible positive outcome. It was stupid. Sergeant Tanaka would definitely not approve, and Mum would kill me if she found out. There was a chance it could jeopardize the court case – there might be some obscure legal loophole no one had told me about. But I had to meet up with Jamie. I needed to hear what he had to say.

In the back of my mind I knew the real reason I had to meet up with him, but I tried my best to block it out. The truth was, I wanted to know more about Alex. I wanted to *understand*.

chapter thirty-nine

It was bitterly cold outside and the wind was vicious. That was partly why I'd chosen the beach – it would probably be quiet. Jamie and I would be able to talk without being overheard, but there would hopefully be a couple of people around if something went wrong (even though I wasn't exactly sure what that 'something' could be).

I told Mum I needed to go for a walk to clear my head. I thought she was going to say I couldn't go, but she just nodded and said, 'I think some fresh air will do you good – blow those cobwebs away.'

I kissed her on the cheek and told her I'd play the piano after dinner. Then I thanked her, which took her by surprise. 'Thanks for what, love?'

I shrugged. 'Everything, I suppose.'

Mum smiled a pretty smile and it made me wish she'd do it more often. 'We're going to have a lovely evening, just the two of us. Maybe we can watch a film later – take your mind off . . .'

I said that would be nice and then I left the house to go and meet the brother of the girl I had accused of sexual assault.

A couple of men were standing outside the pub on the promenade. One of them was having difficulty lighting his cigarette in the wind. Neither of them was wearing a jacket; the one who wasn't smoking had both his hands jammed into his armpits for warmth. The pub looked busy, with lots of big groups having leisurely Sunday lunches – grandparents and parents and kids and babies. Everybody looked like they were having a good time, all cosy and warm and *together*.

A runner wearing black leggings with fluorescent yellow shorts on top was sprinting along the shoreline. A man was walking along the promenade with two out-of-control Dalmatians; he kept hissing at them to 'heel' while trying to look like he was totally in control. There was an old couple sitting on a bench, huddled together against the cold. The woman poured something from a red flask into red cups and the man smiled at her lovingly. It was probably their little Sunday ritual – a walk on the beach after lunch, no matter the weather. I wondered if the flask had alcohol in it.

'Kate?' My first thought was: Alex. The voice was almost the same, maybe ever so slightly deeper. I turned and it was hard for me to think clearly for a second or two. The boy in front of me looked so much like Alex that I couldn't help but stare. Then I started to see the little differences, then the differences became more obvious and after a full five seconds there was just your standard family resemblance. But those eyes . . . I kept on coming back to those eyes. They were so much like Alex's it was incredible. Except the softness was missing; Jamie's eyes were narrowed and not particularly friendly.

'Hi,' I stuck out my hand for him to shake and he stared at it before eventually grasping it for a millisecond. I hadn't meant to do that, obviously.

'Thanks for coming.' His ears were red from the cold. I was grateful for my woolly hat. He wasn't wearing a hat or gloves, but he had a thin grey scarf wrapped round his neck several times. He was wearing a jacket I recognized; Alex had worn it once. It fitted Jamie a bit better – he was taller and broader.

'You didn't exactly leave me with much choice, did you?'

He winced and said, 'Sorry about that. I didn't think you'd come otherwise. Sorry.'

His apology surprised me. I'd half expected him

to arrive all guns blazing, maybe pin me up against a wall and threaten me. 'Um . . . it's OK.'

'Shall we walk?' He nodded down the promenade and we started walking. The old man on the bench said 'Good afternoon' to us and Jamie said the same back, then added something about the terrible weather which made the man and the woman laugh. I could feel them watching us after we passed them. They probably thought we were just like them – a couple in love, out for a Sunday stroll. Although maybe the fact that you could have ridden a bike through the gap between Jamie and me was a bit of a giveaway.

Jamie didn't say anything for a couple of minutes, but his eyes kept flicking towards me and then back towards the sea. My eyes started watering from the cold and I swiped away the tears with my gloved hand, hoping Jamie didn't think I was crying.

We were halfway to the end of the Promenade when he spoke. 'The last time I was here was with Alex.' I said nothing. 'The weather was almost as bad too.' This time he looked at me so I felt an obligation to nod. 'Why are you doing this?' He stopped walking; I stopped too.

'Doing what?' He just stared at me, waiting me out. 'I don't know what you want me to say. We really shouldn't be talking about this anyway. If the police knew I was here . . .'

'Fuck the police! This is my little sister we're talking about. This is her *life*. Why are you doing this to her?'

'She *assaulted* me.' The words sounded strong and true. Jamie just stared at me some more, forcing me to continue. 'I'm the victim here.' These words sounded timid and unsure.

'My sister would never hurt anyone.'

Anger flared. 'I suppose you thought your sister would never dress up like a boy to trick some girl she'd met on the internet. Your *sister* hurt me. She ruined my life!' The tears that appeared now had nothing to do with the driving wind. I turned away from Jamie, wiping away my tears.

When I turned back to Jamie he was staring out to sea. A huge tanker was making its way up the Firth of Forth. 'She'll go to prison, you know – Young Offenders. How do you think she'll cope in a place like that?'

I had enough sense not to shrug. 'I don't know.'

Jamie sighed and ran his fingers through his hair. 'You're really going to sit back and let this happen?'

'She's the one who confessed.' I was sounding more and more like a child.

'Yeah, that took everyone by surprise. Mum and Dad couldn't believe it. They had a hard enough time wrapping their heads around the idea that she's been borrowing my clothes, but they didn't believe she'd ever be capable of hurting anyone. Not until she spoke to the police yesterday. Then all of a sudden they're wondering where they went wrong, how they could have raised a daughter who would *abuse* someone. They believe Alex, because why would she lie about something like that?'

'Why *would* she lie about something like that?' I was on dangerous ground but I really wanted to hear his answer.

Jamie's gaze was steady. 'Love.'

'*Love?*' Never has the best word in the world sounded so wrong.

'She loves you.' I shook my head, but he ignored it. 'She loves you so much that she's willing to go to prison in some screwed-up attempt to make things right.'

'And I suppose she told you this, did she?'

'She's not that stupid. She knows that I'd tell anyone who'd listen – that I'd do whatever it takes to get her out of this mess. But I know how her mind works, and I know how she feels about you. Because she told me that much, at least. Before . . .'

'What did she say?'

So Jamie told me how he'd confronted Alex and forced her to tell the truth about what she was doing. It turned out that he'd been the one who'd made her break up with me. She'd told him that we were supposed to have sex on Hogmanay. He *knew* we hadn't gone any further than kissing. His belief in his sister was unshakeable. He was a good brother. It must be nice to have someone like him in your life – someone to defend you even when you make terrible mistakes.

He moved a little closer to me, his eyes imploring. 'Don't do this, Kate. Please don't do this to her. I'm not condoning what she did, deceiving you like that. I can't even begin to imagine what that must have been like for you. I'm pretty sure I would completely lose my shit if something like that ever happened to me. But she really cares about you, and I think deep down you *know* that. My sister is a good person – the best person in my life, probably. She's just . . . confused, I suppose. She doesn't know how to be the person she wants to be.'

'That's hardly my fault, is it?' I crossed my arms against the cold, but he probably thought it was defensiveness.

'I'm not saying it is, you just have to know that she

would do anything for you. She broke her own heart to try and make sure you never found out the truth about her. She knew you'd never be able to understand, and she didn't expect you to. She never wanted to hurt you.'

'Well she *did*.' Nothing Jamie could say would make me forget that.

'So now you're going to pay her back by making sure she goes to prison for something she hasn't even done? She'll have a criminal record, you know. Even if she gets away with a short sentence, that will follow her around forever. For the rest of her life.' He paused and looked away. His shoulders were tensed up and his jaw was tight. 'Please don't do this to my sister. I'm begging you.'

There was no point in trying to convince him that my accusations were true. He knew Alex wasn't guilty. There are some things you just know about the people you love. If a stranger suddenly accused Mum of committing a crime, I would know they were lying (unless it was illegal parking, because she's always doing that). It didn't matter though; Jamie couldn't do anything about it as long as Alex was insisting she was guilty. It was strange to think of the two of us working together in this – the only two people in the world who knew the truth.

'How is she?' I hadn't meant to ask. Jamie seemed as surprised as I was at the question.

For a second I thought he was going to tell me I had no right to ask such a thing. But maybe he thought it would help change my mind. 'She's shut down completely. Won't talk to Mum and Dad. She's been pretty much holed up in her room since I got back.'

'But I thought she'd be in . . . ?' I stopped and thought about it. All this time I'd been picturing Alex in a grimy prison cell, but she'd been at home. It was obvious, when you thought about it. They weren't going to put a sixteen-year-old girl in with the hardened criminals; it wasn't like she was a danger to society. I felt stupid for letting my imagination run away with itself, but most of all – and much more powerful – I felt relief. My legs felt weird so I propped myself up against the low wall separating the promenade from the beach.

Jamie leaned next to me. 'She always looked up to me, you know. Even when I did things I wasn't necessarily proud of. When we were little she'd always copy everything I did and want to hang out with me and my friends. Sometimes it was annoying – my mates didn't really appreciate always having a girl follow us around – but mostly it was kind of sweet.' He stopped talking and I realized he was trying not to cry. He blinked hard and shook his head, managing to control himself. 'It's weird, cos Mum and Dad are busy blaming themselves for what they think Alex has done, and Alex's blaming herself for hurting you, and all the time I'm wondering if there's something *I* did. Or didn't do. Maybe if I'd been there for her more, she'd have felt like she could have come and talked to me about things instead of being all secretive. I might have been able to stop this whole thing from happening.'

People always blame themelves, don't they? Even when there's no possible way they could be held accountable, people always find a way. I think it's because we like to think that we *matter* – that everything we do has an effect on other people. I didn't believe for a second that Alex pretended to be a boy just because she looked up to her older brother. The only person who knew the real reason she'd done it was her, and I'd never even given her the chance to explain.

'You can't blame yourself.' If the situation had been different I might have hugged him, or at least patted his arm.

Jamie turned to look at me. We were standing closer to each other now. I found myself thinking that he was really very attractive. What would have happened if he'd been the one on the forum instead of Alex? Nothing, in all probability. He was three years older than me and from what Alex said he was very popular with girls. He would never have any reason to look once at me, let alone twice. Even now, in this horrible situation, I could tell he had that confidence that was so appealing to girls. Not to me though. I preferred boys who didn't think they were God's gift. Boys like Alex. Ones who don't exist in real life. Astrid, on the other hand, would be all over Jamie like cheese on nachos.

Jamie was staring at me and I wondered if he was trying to work out what Alex had seen in me. Maybe he was thinking that I wasn't pretty enough or special enough for her to have gone to all that effort. Maybe he was going to apologize for sort of threatening to blackmail me. Then his blank expression turned dark. 'I don't blame myself. I blame you.'

He turned and walked away.

chapter forty

At first I thought he expected me to follow him, but he didn't look back to check on me. I watched as he walked back down the Promenade, shoulders hunched against the wind. I could almost imagine it was Alex walking away from me but in that little scenario she would be going to buy some takeaway hot chocolate so we could sit on a bench like that old couple. She would hurry back and we would snuggle close to keep warm.

The movie in my head came to an abrupt halt.

She. The Alex in my daydream had been a *she*. Not my Alex, the boy I'd fallen in love with.

I sat on the bench recently vacated by the old couple. They'd probably gone home to watch Midsomer Murders and have a slice of lemon drizzle cake.

I stared out to sea as the sun went down. It got colder and colder. I took off my hat and gloves and let the coldness nip at my ears and fingers. Before long

I was completely alone, apart from the occasional cyclist hurtling along the Promenade. I thought about Alex and Jamie and Astrid and Sergeant Tanaka and back to Alex. It always came back to Alex.

My phone rang and my numb fingers struggled to get it out of my pocket. It was Mum, wondering where I'd got to. Worrying, as usual. I said I was on my way home, and she really didn't have anything to worry about. I was a big girl and could take care of myself. The silence on the other end of the line told me exactly what Mum thought of that. 'Do you feel a bit better though?'

'Yes, I think I do.' And strangely enough, that was true.

I felt better now I had a plan.

After an evening of carb overload and rusty piano-playing, sneaking out of the house was surprisingly easy. Mum could sleep through the zombie apocalypse so I didn't have to worry about creaking stairs or anything (mostly because we lived in a bungalow). I'd gone to the trouble of arranging some pillows under my duvet to look like a sleeping me, just in case she got up to check on me later. I think I only did that because that's what people do on TV; there was no way my mother would ever be fooled.

The only other person on the top deck of the bus was a snoring middle-aged man in a black suit and black tie, with a black overcoat on the seat next to him. I sat four seats behind him and watched his head loll from side to side and occasionally jerk upright before lolling again. He'd been at a funeral, that was my guess. No one in his immediate family, but someone close enough to make him want to drink far too much at the wake. Maybe an unrequited love from years ago. He'd probably been meaning to drive home but some sensible person had confiscated his car keys and packed him on to the bus.

I got off the bus on Princes Street. The white lights on the trees were still sparkling and the castle looked like something out of a film set. Everything was closed and there were only a few people around. I walked fast to try and keep warm but by the time I got there my teeth were chattering. There was a light on in the front room – the living room.

I keyed in the number and sent a text message: *I'm outside.*

I didn't have to wait long for a reply: *You shouldn't be here. I'm not allowed to talk to you.*

I texted back: *This won't take long.*

No reply. I waited underneath a lamp post, thinking about Mr Tumnus and lions and witches and wardrobes. I jumped up and down a few times to try to get some feeling back into my legs. I checked the time on my phone. 12.31.

At 12.37 I resigned myself to the fact that this had been a waste of time. At least I'd tried. I started trudging back up the hill towards town and I was about to cross the road when I heard her calling my name in that quiet half-shout people do when they don't want to draw attention to themselves.

I walked towards her. Her arms were crossed and her hair was damp and slicked back like she'd just got out of the shower. She looked so different to my Alex with her hair like that. You could really see her face. She was wearing a big coat that looked like it might belong to her dad. Underneath that there were a pair of striped pyjama bottoms and hi-top Converse with the laces trailing on the ground.

I wasn't prepared for the shock of being face-to-face with her. To see those features that I knew so well, those eyes I'd spent hours gazing into, that mouth I'd kissed. The pain was almost too much to bear. But there was something else, lurking behind the pain . . . Was it relief?

'Hi,' I said. I stared at her shoes. Our matching Converse. We'd sat on a bench in Princes Street Gardens one Saturday and I'd taken a picture of our feet. I'd texted it to Alex that night, saying we were 'solemates'. I'd thought I was so clever.

'Hi,' she said, eyes on the pavement. She waited for me to say something then shook her head when the silence went on for too long. 'Listen, whatever it is you have to say you'd better be quick. Mum and Dad would freak if they knew you were here.'

'Same here. Well, I mean, my mum would freak. My dad wouldn't even . . . Um . . . How are you?' Our breath formed icy clouds as we spoke. We weren't standing close enough for the clouds to mingle.

Finally she looked me in the eyes. 'I've got court in the morning.' That didn't answer my question but told me everything I needed to know. 'Why are you here?'

'I wanted to ask you something.' She waited. 'I . . . Oh God, it seems stupid now. I'm sorry, I shouldn't have come. I'm just going to go. Forget I was here, OK?'

She sighed. 'You're here now so you might as well just spit it out.' Her voice was softer, but still impatient.

'I . . . wanted to know why you did it.'

'Did what?' But I could tell from the look in her eyes that she knew what I was talking about.

'Why you let me think you were a boy. You

knew I liked you, didn't you? Before we even met, I mean.'

Alex sighed again and for a second I thought she wasn't going to answer. She looked up at the sky before her gaze locked on to mine. 'I didn't think it was possible that someone like you would like someone like me. And I didn't think it was possible for me to like you either.'

'Why?'

'Because you're a girl.' She said this so quietly I wondered if I'd misheard.

This made no sense whatsoever. 'So you're not . . .?'

'*Gay?* It's OK, you know. You can say the word. It's not going to infect you or anything.' She didn't say this with spite or venom – more a sort of weary sadness. 'I don't know what I am. And I honestly don't even care anymore. Straight or gay or bi or whatever, people can think what they want. What does it matter, anyway? People are people.' This sounded rehearsed, like something she'd been telling herself over and over again.

Alex was right: people *are* people. And people deserve to be told the truth about what they were getting themselves into. 'You could have told me though. That you weren't a boy.'

'Yeah, cos that's really easy to slip into the

conversation. Not awkward at all.' And there it was, a tiniest hint of the smile I'd loved.

'You should have told me.' The tiny smile was gone.

'I know.' Very matter of fact.

'I can't believe you went to all that effort. It must have been stressful.' Such a banal thing to say.

Alex shrugged. 'It's amazing the things you'll do when you're . . .' She looked down and some of her hair fell in front of her eyes. And just like that *my* Alex was standing in front of me.

'When you're what?' My throat felt like it was closing up, trying to stop me from asking the question.

Alex's eyes met mine and I couldn't look away. I didn't want to. 'When you're in love.'

I'd known, I suppose. Of course I'd known. Love makes people do crazy things. Once you've found it you'll do anything in your power to keep it. I knew because I'd felt the same way. I blinked hard in an effort not to cry.

Alex coughed awkwardly. 'Is that all? I'd better get back inside. Got to get my beauty sleep for tomorrow.' She didn't sound bitter or angry, and I couldn't understand why.

The full force of it all hit me at that moment. What had I been thinking? How had I let this happen?

Somewhere along the line I'd managed to forget that this was real life and it's messy and difficult and people will hurt you but that doesn't give you a licence to destroy them.

I panicked. 'You have to tell them you didn't do it!'

'Didn't do what?' She was going to make me say the words out loud, to admit what I was accusing her of.

'You know . . . assault me. You have to take back your confession. They'll send you to prison!'

'I thought that was what you wanted.'

'No! I . . . I made a mistake, OK?' My voice cracked and the tears began to flow. 'It's not what you think! I said something to Mum and she got the wrong idea and then she called the police. I swear I didn't know she was going to do that. But when the police came to interview me I felt . . . I don't know . . . I hated you for lying to me and I was too scared to tell the truth. I'm sorry! You have to tell them you didn't do it. They'll believe you. I'm sure the police thought I was lying anyway, but then you confessed and I suppose they thought you'd never confess to something you hadn't done . . .' The words eventually lost their battle against the rising sobs. My shoulders shook and I was so ashamed for crying – so ashamed for everything – that I didn't know what to do. Was I expecting Alex to comfort me? To hug me and hold me and stroke my hair and say everything was going to be OK? That was never going to happen. She would never touch me again.

Alex shook her head. 'It's too late. No one will believe me. They'll just think I got cold feet about pleading guilty.'

'But you didn't do anything!' I shouted and the noise seemed to echo off the darkened windows looking down on us.

Alex took a step towards me. 'I hurt you,' she said quietly. 'Even if I didn't do what they think I did, I still hurt you.' Her gaze was steady on mine. 'I'll never be able to forgive myself for that. I don't care what happens tomorrow. None of it matters anymore.'

'But you're going to go to prison! This is your *life* we're talking about, Alex!' I wanted to shake her, make her realize how crazy this was.

'I don't care. I've seen what they're saying about me online, you know. Maybe after a year or two in a Young Offenders place the heat will die down and I'll be able to get on with things. Maybe it's best for both of us if I disappear for a bit.' Who was she trying to convince?

'No! Alex!'

She took another step towards me. 'I want you to know that I understand why you did it. Why you said that to the police. I hurt you so you hurt me back. I *get* that.'

How could she be so calm when I was in the process of destroying her life? 'I'm sorry! This is all . . . how did it all go so wrong?! It was so . . . I thought you were the best thing that ever happened to me.' No, that wasn't exactly what I wanted to say. 'You *were* the best thing that ever happened to me.'

Alex smiled wistfully and started backing away from me. 'It could have been good, you know. In another lifetime, maybe.'

'It *was* good. Please, Alex, you have to tell them you lied. They'll find you not guilty, I'm sure of it.' I tried to sound less hysterical, desperate to make her see my point of view. A scattering of snowflakes started to fall and the scene might have been romantic. In another lifetime, maybe.

'They won't listen to me. There's only one person they'll listen to.' Her voice was gentle; she knew this wasn't what I wanted to hear.

I started to speak and then stopped. I couldn't. I just couldn't. Mum would never forgive me. If Alex changed her plea to not guilty, they'd find her innocent (they *would*, wouldn't they?) but no one would have to know I'd lied. They'd just think there wasn't enough evidence for a conviction or something. And even if everyone else did think I'd lied about what happened to me, Mum would still believe me. And maybe one day . . .

'Alex, I *can't*.'

She backed away another couple of steps, still holding my eyes with hers. 'I know.'

Her hand was reaching out to open the front door.

Say something.

She was opening the door.

Stop her.

'Goodbye, Kate.'

She was gone.

I was lost.

chapter forty-one

I didn't move. The snow turned into icy rain. The light in the front room went out. Before long I was shivering uncontrollably. I watched the door even though I didn't expect it to open again. I wondered how long I could stay out in this cold before I would die. If I curled up into a little ball on Alex's front doorstep would I be dead by morning? Would Alex come outside, all dressed up for court, and find me frozen to death, a fine layer of ice blanketing my body? No one would be able to hate me if I was dead.

Eventually I started walking back up the hill. It was hard to walk at first – my joints were Tin-Man stiff. I should never have come. Seeing Alex again hadn't solved anything; there was no closure. There was just a heaviness in my heart that wouldn't go away, and the picture in my head of her backing away from me. I'd never forget the way she looked at me – the sadness and the understanding and the love. The love was definitely still there; I wasn't imagining it. How could she still love me after what I'd done?

I had to wait twenty-five minutes for a night bus. There was a couple in the bus shelter. They looked like students. He was sitting on the bench and she was standing between his legs. They did a lot of kissing. I moved down to the other end of the bench, stealing glances at them every once in a while. *Life must be so easy for them. She's a girl and he's a boy and that's that.* No one would ever give *them* weird looks for kissing or holding hands in public.

It was after two o'clock by the time I put my key in the front door. I was cold and exhausted and full to the brim with self-loathing. I changed into a hoodie and tracksuit bottoms and my thickest, warmest pair of socks and got into bed. I checked my phone before turning out the light. No new messages.

I didn't sleep.

I got up an hour before Mum's alarm went off, took a long shower and was sitting at the breakfast table sipping a cup of tea by the time she came through.

'Morning, love. How are you feeling? Did you sleep OK?'

'Fine, thanks.'

She put some bread in the toaster and went to get the jam out of the fridge. 'I hope you're not too worried about today. Sergeant Tanaka said she'd keep us informed so I'll text you as soon as there's news. We should hear something this morning.'

'OK.'

Mum stopped what she was doing and looked at me. 'Oh, Kate. It will all be over soon, I promise. That girl will be sent away and you'll never have to worry about her again.'

I nodded.

'You know, there aren't many girls your age who'd have had the courage to speak out about something like this.' Like I'd had any choice in the matter. She sat down next to me and squeezed my hand, which was clammy and warm from holding the mug of tea. 'It makes me think I must have done something right, at least. I'm proud of you.'

She was *proud* of me.

When she carried on preparing her breakfast I sent a lightning-fast text. The reply arrived before Mum had even sat down.

I nodded and smiled my way through breakfast then I told Mum I wanted to get to school early to finish off some homework. Normally she'd have given me a lecture about leaving my homework to the last minute but today she told me to give myself a break, that I shouldn't be worrying about schoolwork at a time like this. She even said she'd have a word with my teachers if I wanted her to.

I didn't hug her or kiss her goodbye because that would have made her suspicious.

A bus arrived almost as soon as I got to the stop, which never happens when you're in a hurry and actually want to get to where you're going. On the way into town it seemed like every traffic light went in our favour and all the cars of Edinburgh had stayed home just to make sure I didn't arrive too late.

The sky was grey and unforgiving; everything and everyone looked miserable. Even the castle looked less majestic than usual – just an old building on a rock. I tried to clear my mind and focus on putting one foot in front of the other on the icy pavement. If I stopped to think about things I'd turn around and get on the first bus home. It helped that I hadn't actually worked out exactly what I was going to do. There was no grand plan. I just knew I had to be there.

I wasn't sure what I was expecting outside the courtroom. Photographers? A TV van or two? A baying mob with hand-made placards? It was nothing like that at all. A few people were milling around near the door – smokers, mostly. One man had a tattoo on his neck, with orange and red flames creeping up from his shirt collar. I assumed he was a criminal and then instantly told myself off for judging him. Maybe he was a lawyer. Or a judge.

A couple of tourists were taking photos of the statue right outside the courtroom. Someone had put a traffic cone on its head. They asked me to take a picture of them together in front of the statue; I said yes but angled the camera so you couldn't see the traffic cone.

I checked my phone; I was half an hour early. I couldn't make myself take the last few steps inside. My legs were rebelling against my brain, and my brain was starting to whisper that I should get back on the bus and go to school. No one would ever have to know I was here.

'Shit!' A woman was standing behind the statue, struggling with an enormous orange leather bag, a Starbucks cup and what looked to be a half-eaten bacon roll. She started hopping around on one foot trying to get a look at the bottom of her shoe. Eventually she gave up and looked around helplessly. Her eyes met mine.

'Sorry, could you possibly . . . ?

'Do you want me to hold those for you?'

'Oh, you're a life saver!' She started unloading things on to me and I put the bag over my shoulder and ended up holding the cup and the roll. Bright orange yolk started oozing out of the roll on to the napkin and I had to hold it upright to stop it dripping on the ground. The woman took off her shoe and scraped it on the base of the statue. The sight of that coupled with the oozing egg made my mouth flood with saliva – I was sure I was going to vomit there and then. I tried to breathe slowly, through my mouth.

Eventually, the woman turned to me, satisfied that her shiny purple shoe was now clean. She was younger than I'd first thought – maybe twenty-four or twenty-five? Curly red hair and a slash of bright red lipstick. I could see lipstick smeared on her teeth when she smiled as she thanked me. She carefully manoeuvred the handles of the bag off my shoulder and over the cup in my left hand and nodded at me to give her the cup and the roll. 'Thanks for that. I'm all over the shop this morning. Not enough sleep. I *knew* I should have had an early night. What kind of moron stays out till two the night before starting a new job?' I could have sworn she was talking to herself rather than to me, but she looked at me when she finished talking so some kind of response was required. I shrugged but she seemed to expect more so I asked if she was a lawyer. 'God, no! You couldn't pay me enough. I'm a reporter.' She said this around a mouthful of food and I felt bile rise in my throat again.

My heart slam-dunked. 'A journalist?'

She smiled like she was talking to a simpleton. 'Yeah, first day covering the courts. Last week it was ladies of Morningside sewing a giant quilt, this week it's all about the hardened criminals. Bit of a promotion, I suppose.' She finished the roll in three bites and wiped her mouth on the napkin. Then she gulped down some coffee and winced. 'Ghastly stuff! Would you mind chucking these in that bin over there?' For some reason this woman thought I was her personal slave. I did as she asked.

When I returned she was looking at the mirrored surface on the back of her phone. She rubbed her teeth with her index finger and I wondered if any of the dog shit had touched that finger.

'*Kate?* What are you doing here?' I turned towards the voice I vaguely recognized. Sergeant Tanaka. PC Mason was right behind her. Both of them looked unimpressed to see me.

I stepped away from the reporter, who was now looking at me – *properly* looking at me. Her eyes flickered down to take in my school uniform and that's the moment when it must have all clicked into place. As soon as her eyes lit up I knew which case she'd been assigned to cover that morning. 'Wait! Hold on a second . . . are you Kate McAllister?!' Her hand was rummaging blindly in her bag because she wouldn't take her eyes off me. It emerged from the bag grasping a recording device identical to the one Tanaka had used.

Sergeant Tanaka put herself between me and the reporter. She was eyeing the recording device as if it was a lethal weapon. 'Look, you know you're dealing with minors here, don't you? You're not allowed to publish any names. Kate, please come with me. We can talk inside. George, you stay here and deal with Ms . . .?' PC Mason's name was George? He really didn't look like a George.

'Brookmyre. Lara Brookmyre,' the reporter supplied. 'And *you* are?' Brookmyre's chin jutted out defiantly.

'*Sergeant* Tanaka. You're new, aren't you? Well, how about you have a little chat with my colleague here and I'll see you inside.'

Brookmyre tried to manoeuvre herself round Sergeant Tanaka but PC Mason (*George?*) stepped in and stood right in her way. Brookmyre wasn't giving up so easily though. '*Kate?* Is there anything you'd like to say? Off the record, of course.'

I shouldn't have come. What little courage I'd had disappeared as soon as the police turned up. I shouldn't be here.

'*Kate!* Let me just . . . Don't touch me, OK? That's police brutality right there.' There was a scuffle as Brookmyre tried to squeeze between the wall and PC Mason. 'Ow! You're hurting me!'

PC Mason stepped back with his hands up. 'I didn't touch her!'

Tanaka rolled her eyes. 'She knows full well you didn't touch her! She's just trying her luck.' She stepped in between the reporter and me for a second time. 'OK, I'm going to have to insist you leave Miss McAllister alone. She has nothing to say to you. Why don't you go inside and we'll stay out here for the time being?' You could tell Tanaka was trying so very hard not to lose it. People were already stopping to watch us. The man with the fire tattoo was leaning against the wall, munching on a chocolate bar and smiling.

Brookmyre's face now matched her hair and lipstick. She was saying something about knowing her rights and not letting anyone push her around. She was breathing hard, eyes shifting left and right, trying to figure out her next move. Tanaka had her back to me, but I could see her shoulders were tensed up; she was ready to move fast if she had to. PC Mason's attention was elsewhere – he was staring across the street. Everyone seemed to have forgotten about me. Apart from Tattoo Man – he was still watching, grinning.

'Um . . . Sergeant?' PC Mason's voice was quiet. Tanaka was busy trying to reason with Brookmyre so she didn't hear until he said it louder, more urgently. '*Sergeant!*'

Sergeant Tanaka turned to him, clearly annoyed, but then she followed his gaze and swore under her breath. I looked too and the world stopped turning.

Jamie Banks was getting out of a taxi on the other side of the road, followed by Mr and Mrs Banks. Alex was already standing on the pavement. She was staring up at the court building, taking in the grandeur and seriousness of it. And then she was staring at me.

She looked like she was dressed for a funeral – all sombre and black. It seemed appropriate somehow. She was wearing a skirt – the same one she'd worn on New Year's Eve, it looked like. And that seemed right too, or rather it didn't seem wrong. It was just a fact.

My eyes locked on to hers and I swear the space between us – the road and the cyclists and the people rushing to work – compressed into nothing and she was right in front of me and if I wanted to I could reach out and touch her. I could whisper in her ear and no one else would hear.

'Kate? *Kate?* We've got to get you inside. You really shouldn't be here. You're not supposed to see her.' Tanaka's hand was gripping my shoulder, trying to steer me towards the door, but I wasn't going anywhere. I was immovable. I was a statue.

Brookmyre realized who Alex was straightaway – reporter's instinct, perhaps. Alex and her family hadn't even made it safely across the road before she started hurling questions at them. Mr and Mrs Banks spotted me and tried to hurry Alex inside. She was in between them, Jamie a couple of paces behind. He wasn't surprised to see me – after all, he'd been the one who'd told me where to be and when.

I reached in between Tanaka and Mason and grabbed Brookmyre's arm. 'I do have something to say . . . *on* the record.' I spoke quietly but for some reason everyone stopped what they were doing and looked at me.

'Yes?' Brookmyre asked eagerly, sticking the recording device right under my nose. Her eyes were wide with excitement.

Alex was only a few feet away from me now, being swept along by her parents, their faces grim with determination.

I looked at Alex and Alex looked at me and everything that had seemed so confusing before suddenly seemed simple and obvious. I smiled and something changed in Alex's eyes. She knew what I was about to do. 'Kate, don't!' She shook off her mum's arm but her dad held firm.

I took a deep breath.

Brookmyre looked ready to interrupt with a question so I cleared my throat and began to speak. 'I'd like to state, on the record that—'

'Kate! Please don't do this!' Alex was really close now, her eyes pleading with me. Other voices were added into the mix. Alex's parents, Tanaka, Mason all talking over each other, but I took another deep breath and blocked everything out – everything but *her*.

'I would like to state, on the record, that Alex Banks is innocent. She did not assault me. I lied.'

Alex's shoulders slumped. Mrs Banks looked triumphant (*'I knew it!'*). Mr Banks looked confused. Jamie looked relieved. The reporter was trying hard not to smile – trying so hard to be serious and professional and remember what she'd been taught in journalism school or wherever it was she'd learned to be so annoying. Tanaka realized there was nothing she could do. This was going to play out whether she liked it or not.

'Are you going to go inside and testify to that effect?' Brookmyre asked.

I looked at Sergeant Tanaka for an answer but she just shook her head. 'I . . . I'm not sure. I'll do whatever it takes to make this right.'

'Even if it means facing charges yourself?'

I hadn't really considered that possibility, but I nodded.

Alex had tears in her eyes; she was close enough to touch.

The reporter asked two more questions. 'Why did you lie about the assault? And what prompted you to come forward today?'

I looked up to the sky to see the sun starting to peek through the clouds. I closed my eyes. There was warmth there, if you concentrated hard enough.

I opened my eyes and reached out my hand.

'Because I love her.'

Her hand met mine halfway; her fingers intertwined with mine.

She didn't let go. She *never* let go.

Acknowledgements

As always, thanks to the wonderful team at Quercus: Roisin Heycock, Niamh Mulvey, Alice Hill, Talya Baker. Huge thanks to Sarah Lambert for her enthusiasm and help in the early stages of this book.

Thank you to my agent, Julia Churchill, who is utterly brilliant in every way *and* posts ridiculously cute pictures of donkeys on Twitter.

Thanks to Sarah Stewart for telling me to write this book.

Thank you to Lauren James, for creating the epic playlist I listened to while writing this book.

Thanks to the Sisters: Keris Stainton; Susie Day; Luisa Plaja; Keren David; Tamsyn Murray; and Sophia Bennett.

Thank you to Cate James, Lara Williamson, Nova Ren Suma, James Dawson, Ciara Daly and Tanya Byrne.

Thanks to the awesome UKYA bloggers, whose passion and enthusiasm never fail to amaze me.

Thank you to Rob Clarke.

And finally, merci beaucoup to my wee family for keeping me sane: Caro, Jem, Scout, Griffin and Ruby.

*Read all the books
by the brilliant, bestselling*

CAT CLARKE

'Undoubtedly one of
the most exciting and
talented YA writers
in the UK'

Library Mice

How
you
the

CA

'Incredibl

A secret too horrific to tell,
too terrible to keep...

torn
CAT CLARKE
BESTSELLING AUTHOR OF ENTANGLED

CAT CLARKE
entangled

FROM THE BESTSELLING AUTHOR
OF TORN AND ENTANGLED

CLARKE

simple' Writing from the Tub

From the bestselling author of
TORN and ENTANGLED

a kiss
in the
dark

Can love survive the biggest lie of all?

CAT CLARKE

For special offers,
chapter samplers,
competitions
and more,
visit . . .

www.quercusbooks.co.uk
🐦 @quercuskids